Christmas
in Cupid Falls

Christmas in Cupid Falls

HOLLY JACOBS

Montlake
Romance

Text copyright © 2014 Holly Jacobs

Published by Montlake Romance, Seattle

www.apub.com

Amazon, the Amazon logo, and Montlake are trademarks of Amazon.com, Inc., or its affiliates.

ISBN-13: 9781477825037
ISBN-10: 1477825037

Cover design by Mumtaz Mustafa

Library of Congress Control Number: 2014905948

Printed in the United States of America

To Jessica: This one's for you!

PROLOGUE

The Legend of Cupid Falls, Pennsylvania

To the south of Erie, Pennsylvania—south of the Great Lake that shares a name with the city—is Falls Creek. It is bigger than most creeks, but not quite large enough to be considered a river. It runs through field and forest to a ridge, carved millennia ago by a glacier. There, it plunges over the edge, falling to a hollowed-out swimming hole before becoming a creek again and meandering on its way.

Local legend has it that when George Washington visited the nearby town of Waterford in 1753, one of his retinue was touring the area. The locals took him to the falls, and there he met a farmer's daughter. He married her later that same year and they settled near the creek. Years later, their daughter went to the falls with a group of friends and noticed that one of the boys in the group might be more than a friend. They married later that same year. And so it went, year after year, decade after decade, couple after couple, until the small waterfall, which in actuality was little more than a creek tumbling over a small cliff, became known as Cupid's Falls.

When a town grew up a few miles away, the residents named it Cupid Falls as an homage to their waterfall.

And to this day, it is said that when two people meet at the falls and declare their love, they are destined for a long, happy romance . . .

Even if that's not what they went to the falls looking for.

CHAPTER ONE

"Arf, arf," Clarence Harding barked as he entered Kennedy Anderson's shop minutes after she'd opened for the day. He pulled off his thick knit cap and exposed an ice-grey head of hair. "Mornin', Mayor."

"Good morning, Clarence. And it's Cupid's *Bow*quet. Bo—long *O*. Bow, like bow and arrow—Cupid's bow and arrow. It's not bow, short *O*, like bowwow."

For more than three decades, Kennedy's aunt had owned the flower shop and it had been Betty's Flowers. But Aunt Betty had been gone three years. This was Kennedy's shop now, and she thought it was a great marketing strategy to play off the town's name. Last year she'd realized that when you lived in Cupid Falls, Pennsylvania, Cupid's *Bow*quet was a perfect name for a flower shop.

"It's a dumb name, Mayor, if you don't mind me saying."

Kennedy did mind, but she was enough of a businesswoman not to say so. "What brings you in today, Clarence?"

"Seems I'll be needing to send the old ball and chain some flowers. I got in late and ran over her new frog."

Joan Harding collected frogs. Lots of frogs. They were everywhere inside and outside of her house. She even had some plastic bullfrogs she'd nailed into her giant maple tree and proudly told everyone they were tree frogs.

Clarence pulled off his gloves and stuffed them in his heavy winter coat's pocket. "Course, I don't know how she could tell I ran one over. I hid the pieces and there must be about a million frogs around now. Plus we've got all this snow . . ." He shrugged, as if figuring out the mystery of his wife was too much for him.

Clarence was a regular. It seemed he was always doing one thing or another to annoy Joan, but crushing a frog called for more than just some flowers. "It just so happens I might have something to get you out of the doghouse."

"*Frog*house is how I put it," he grumbled. "And I seem to be in it more than any man should be."

Despite his less-than-endearing endearment *ball and chain*, Kennedy had seen Clarence and Joan together. She knew they fit. They worked. Clarence might get in trouble for running over frogs, but the Hardings were one of those couples that no one could imagine not being together.

She liked to think her small flower shop helped to keep them that way . . . together.

"One of the vendors I order from had these, and I thought of you when I ordered it." Kennedy reached under the counter and pulled out a small box and slid it across the counter toward the elderly gentleman.

Clarence opened the lid and pulled out a frog planter. "Now, this is just the ticket. The perfect thing to get me out of trouble. You'll stick some plant or something in it for her?"

"Definitely," Kennedy assured him. Clarence was the kind of customer she liked to think of as job security. "Do you have anything in mind?"

He handed her the planter. "Whatever you want, Mayor. Bill me, okay?"

"Sure thing, Clarence. I'll deliver it this afternoon."

"Maybe I'll be out of the froghouse before dinner then. See ya later, Mayor."

The bell rang merrily as he left.

That was easy. Maybe she'd be lucky and the rest of the day would go that smoothly. Kennedy really, really needed an easy day.

She was in the back workroom transplanting a spider plant into the frog planter when the bell out front rang again. "Coming," she called as she pulled off her gloves.

Kennedy didn't groan when she saw May Williams scowling in her direction. She knew without a doubt that this wasn't about flowers. May visited even more frequently than Clarence, but to the best of Kennedy's knowledge, May had never ordered anything. No, flowers weren't May's reason for visiting. She was here to complain about something. May came in at least once a week to complain about something.

There was an actual mayor's office at the Town Hall, the small brick building farther down Main Street—Cupid Falls' small business district. Town Hall also housed the one-man police department, the one-man streets crew, and the volunteer fire department. It also had a big meeting room where the town council met on a monthly basis. But Kennedy did 90 percent of the town's business from right here in the shop. Being mayor of a small town had some advantages, and working from the flower shop was one of them.

She forced her best business smile. "Good morning, May. How are you today?"

"I'm lucky to be alive, Kennedy, and that's the God's honest truth of it. Jay Peterson hasn't shoveled since yesterday's snow, and his sidewalk is a hazard. I'm seventy-one years old, and when I walk in Cupid Falls, I don't think it's too much to expect a clear sidewalk."

Kennedy didn't think it was wise to point out that Jay Peterson was well past eighty himself. "You're right, May, it's not. I'll give Jay a shout. I know he has someone who normally shovels for him. I'll see if he can call them over now."

"I'm heading down to the drugstore and I'll expect it cleared before I walk home. Good day, Kennedy." And with that, May flounced out of the store.

Kennedy called down to Jay's, but no one answered his phone. She knew she could call the town's street crew, which was a fancy name for Lamar. He took care of everything from patching roadways to plowing the streets in the winter. She didn't call, though, because he was probably still out removing the last of the snow from Cupid Falls' residential streets.

Jay's house was one block over, so Kennedy, who'd campaigned with the slogan *The buck stops here*, put on her own oversize parka and gloves, flipped the sign on the front door to "Back in a minute," and took her shovel down the street. Five minutes later, Jay's sidewalk was clear. She was unlocking the front door of the store when she heard a car pull up behind her at the curb.

She turned, ready to call out a greeting to whomever it was. Cupid Falls was small enough that she knew everyone except the occasional out-of-towner.

The smile on her face evaporated as Malcolm Carter IV got out of his black Pilot.

"Hi, Kennedy," he called as if he'd seen her only last week. "Pap said you wanted to see me as soon as I got in town."

"Wanted? That is not quite how I'd put it," she clarified. "*Needed* to see you is closer." She opened the door to the flower shop and said, "You might as well come in."

Kennedy had known this particular conversation was inevitable, but that didn't mean she was looking forward to it. As Malcolm came in, he seemed to fill the doorway. He was a big man. Almost six feet tall. But it wasn't his height that made him stand out. He was simply dark-haired, chiseled-bone-structure, designer-suit-wearing perfection.

Well, not perfection.

No. She wouldn't allow herself to think of Malcolm as perfect. She wouldn't even allow herself to think of him as Mal anymore.

Mal was the boy next door.

Mal was the high school football hero.

Mal was the kid who she'd had a slight crush on once upon a time.

Malcolm was a self-assured, successful attorney. That was the man she had to deal with.

Like May—some people needed to be handled.

So Kennedy put on her best professional front and simply faced the problem head-on.

She didn't flip the sign on the door back to "Open" because she didn't want any customers or constituents interrupting this particular talk.

"Why don't you come in the back?" She didn't wait for his reply. She simply turned and walked into the back room, which served as her office slash workroom. "Have a seat." She pointed to one of the chairs in front of her desk.

Malcolm slipped off his coat before he sat down. "So?"

Kennedy didn't know how to say the words even though she'd known she was going to have to tell him sooner or later. She'd actually thought it was going to be sooner. Much sooner. Malcolm was supposed to come into town months ago. But his visit with Pap kept getting pushed back.

And now she didn't know what to say, how to tell him.

Well, she didn't really need words.

She simply unzipped her parka and then slid it off. She watched Malcolm's expression move from curiosity to shock.

"You're going to be a father soon" was all she said as she rested her hand on her ever-expanding baby bump.

~

Malcolm stared at Kennedy, and suddenly all of Pap's pestering made sense. His grandfather had never nagged him before, but last week he went beyond asking and instead practically ordered Mal to come home. Mal lived in Pittsburgh, which was only a couple of hours away. He tried to come home as often as possible. He'd fully intended to be here sooner, but as an attorney, his schedule was not always his own. He practiced corporate law, and some of his biggest clients had recently had major acquisitions and projects. He had to put their needs first.

And right now, thinking about his clients seemed far easier than thinking about the implications of Kennedy's announcement.

"How long until the baby?" he asked, more as a stalling tactic than anything. Because he knew exactly what night this child was conceived. April first. This was the ultimate April Fool's joke.

"Less than two months," she said gently. "Around Christmas."

"And you were going to tell me . . . ?" He let the question hang there.

Gone was the gentle Kennedy Anderson, and in her place was a spitfire whose blue-grey eyes snapped with annoyance. Her strawberry-blonde hair looked redder under the heat of that look. "Obviously, I was going to tell you as soon as you came home. I was going to tell you back in July, when you were supposed to come in town for the fireworks. Then a few weeks after that and . . ."

He'd had at least half a dozen aborted visits scheduled since April. He wouldn't be here now if his grandfather hadn't called him to say he was re-retiring. Malcolm was the actual owner of the Cupid Falls Community Center even though Pap ran it. If his grandfather retired, Malcolm didn't have any choice but to come deal with the business.

But now, Malcolm realized, it wasn't the Center Pap wanted him to deal with. It was Kennedy. Kennedy and her baby.

Kennedy and his baby.

Their baby.

He'd obviously been silent for too long, because she finally said, "I didn't think this was the kind of news to share over the phone, or in an e-mail."

"You could have come to Pittsburgh," he pointed out. "It's only a couple hours."

"I'm the mayor of a small town and the sole proprietor of the shop. Two hours down, two hours back. It's easier said than done. You could have come to see Pap sooner. It's only been a little over half a year since he lost your mom, his only daughter. He's been lonely. He's needed family around him. He's needed you."

Mal gripped the arm of the chair and studied her. "You're scolding me?"

Kennedy finally sank into the chair next to his. "Yes, I guess I was. Your grandfather has always been there for you and your mother. Losing her . . . well, he still hasn't recovered from that. I can't imagine the pain of losing a child. He needed you. But you took off and went back to your life in Pittsburgh without a backwards glance. You left him to deal with his pain on his own."

"My schedule—"

Kennedy held up her hand. "I get it. *We all get it*, Malcolm. The entire town gets it. You're an important, big-city lawyer. How you handle your grandfather is on you and I have no right to interfere. I wanted you to know about the baby. I also wanted to tell you that I don't want or expect anything from you. But you deserved to hear it from me before you heard it on the streets. Cupid Falls has been all abuzz that their unmarried mayor's pregnant. You wouldn't have made it far before someone said something, and since you can do basic math, it wouldn't take you much longer than that to know that the baby is yours."

"So what are we going to do?"

Kennedy looked surprised. She leaned backward in the chair and twisted a strand of hair around her finger. It was back to looking more blonde than red. She twisted and stared at him with her oddly colored eyes.

Those eyes.

They'd intrigued him since he first met Kennedy in high school. They weren't blue. They weren't grey. They were a sort of combination and on any given day looked more one color than the other. Today they were a biting blue.

She stopped twirling her hair and leaned forward. "*We* won't be doing anything. *I* will be having a baby in a few weeks and then I'll come back to work."

"We—" He cut off his retort as he remembered the snow shovel that Kennedy had been carrying when he arrived.

"You were shoveling snow," he accused.

Kennedy Anderson was pregnant with his child and she was shoveling snow. He might not be a doctor or an expert on pregnancy, but he knew that there was no way that she should be out in the snow, shoveling.

"Yes, I was. And if you're looking for a list of my day's activities, before that I was transplanting a spider plant into a frog, and before that—"

"You are carrying my baby. There's no way you should be—"

She went to jump up from her chair, but her swollen stomach made anything more than struggling out of her seat impossible. Still she managed it and placed her hands on her hips . . . or where her hips would be if she weren't so swollen.

She scowled at him and said, "Stop right there, Malcolm. Not one more word from you while I explain a few things. I am pregnant. I am not an invalid. I shoveled a couple inches of snow from a sidewalk. Seriously, have you lived in Pittsburgh so long that you've forgotten what real snow looks like? This was only a dusting. Not one of those heavy, wet snows we get. It was well within my capabilities. I lift boxes all the time that weigh more than that snow did. And I only shoveled one very small section of sidewalk—not that I owe you even that much of an explanation."

"You shouldn't be lifting boxes, either," he grumbled.

"Malcolm, I understand that you're a junior partner in your father's firm and you're accustomed to growling orders at your staff and having them jump to attention. But I am not your staff. We're two old friends, and I'm using the word *friend* in its broadest sense. You're a guy I went to school with. You were a neighbor. You are the son of a woman whose friendship I treasured." Her voice broke as she mentioned his mother, but she recovered and went on. "And finally you are the grandson of a man whose friendship I still value. Please note that not one of those definitions of our relationship gives you the right to tell me what I can and cannot do. You don't get to growl orders at me."

"You forgot a definition. The most important one." He paused a moment and uttered for the first time, "I am the father of your child."

"Yes, there is that." Kennedy sank back into the other chair. "You are biologically responsible for half of my child's DNA."

"Our child," he maintained. The way she referred to the baby as *hers* rather than *theirs* grated on him and he wasn't sure why.

"Malcolm, no one in town knows this is your baby. Not even Pap, though I'm sure he suspects. You live in Pittsburgh and I live in Cupid Falls. The baby will live in Cupid Falls. There's no reason for anyone to know you're his or her father."

Malcolm needed to say something. He knew he had legal rights to this child.

His child.

He was going to be a father.

The idea of being a father couldn't seem to find a foothold in his head. He could think the words, but he couldn't get a firm handle on the concept.

Father.

He wasn't sure what to do.

Mal had always prided himself on doing what was right. And he knew that starting to spout legalities to the mother of your child wasn't right.

He knew that fact better than most.

So instead he said the first thing that came to mind. "We can get married."

Mal was proud of his ability to read people. But Kennedy Anderson had always been an enigma. She was generally smiling and pleasant. The few times he'd seen evidence of a temper, it had been like today, there for a flash, then gone. Those flashes made him think that Kennedy had hidden depths, but it was tough to tell what she was actually thinking most of the time.

This was not one of those times.

Shock.

She was shocked at his offer of marriage.

Well, her shock had nothing on his own shock upon hearing he was going to be a father.

Malcolm liked to plan every word he uttered with great care. When he went into a courtroom, he had everything he wanted to say carefully crafted and well thought out. He was not prone to blurting without analyzing.

Yet that's what he'd done.

But even if he hadn't planned to propose, as he said the words he knew they were right.

Kennedy was going to have his child.

It might be old-fashioned, but in his opinion they needed to be married. Immediately.

His child should have his name.

He waited for her shock to fade and for her to agree that their marriage was the proper thing to do.

"Malcolm . . ." She paused.

He was sure she was trying to think of an appropriate way to thank him.

". . . not if you were the last man on earth."

That was not what Mal expected to hear. "Why?" he blurted again.

"I refuse to call my baby a mistake, but it wasn't planned for. It wasn't that we were in love and created this baby out of that love. You'd lost your mother and I'd lost her, too. Your mom and grandfather . . . well, after you went away to school and then went to work in Pittsburgh, we all got close. And I was reeling from losing her, too. That night . . ."

He remembered every moment of that night.

"We were two people in need of comfort. But I never deluded myself into thinking it was anything more than that. We were simply trying to find some sort of equilibrium after a profound loss, and for that one night we found some comfort with each other."

"But—"

"And I'll always appreciate the fact you asked. It was very . . ." She paused as if searching for a word. "Honorable. Yes. It was honorable of you. But Malcolm, I'm not some damsel who needs rescuing. No one's stitched a scarlet letter to my chest. I didn't plan on this baby, but I've had time to not only get used to the idea of being someone's mother—I'm excited. I'm not rich by any stretch of the imagination, but I make a comfortable living. I'm financially and emotionally able to care for this child. I'm not asking for anything from you. I simply thought it was only right you knew."

"But—"

"So you take some time and process the idea, and we'll talk again before you leave to go home to Pittsburgh. But right now, I've got a couple orders to fill so they can be delivered, and I've got a lunch meeting today."

"Kennedy." Mal was at a complete and utter loss for words. He didn't know what to say. How to react.

She reached up and patted his cheek as if he were a small child. "It's okay, Malcolm. I've got everything under control. I don't need or expect anything from you. We'll talk later."

She led him toward the door. "Oh, and Pap told me that he's retiring from running The Community Center and he was leaving town as soon as you got here. Since the Center belongs to you and you live in Pittsburgh, you'll probably be looking for someone to manage it. I'd like to talk to you about that when you have the time. I have a proposition for you."

Those were the last words she said to him before he found himself on the sidewalk in front of the flower store. Cupid's Bowquet.

She'd changed the name. No more Betty's Flowers.

Kennedy Anderson had taken the store and made it her own.

Kennedy Anderson had a business proposition for him.

Kennedy Anderson was going to have his child.

Kennedy Anderson had it all figured out.

She'd had months to figure it all out.

He'd had minutes.

But one thing Malcolm knew for sure—things weren't going to go exactly the way Kennedy Anderson had planned.

CHAPTER TWO

After Malcolm left, Kennedy sat for a long time in the office. Her knees were literally too weak to support her.

Their meeting hadn't gone the way she'd expected. Not that she was sure exactly what she'd expected, but a marriage proposal? That wasn't anywhere on her list of possible scenarios.

She corrected herself—an *obligatory* marriage proposal.

Well, she was pretty sure she had let Malcolm Carter IV know how she felt about that.

He was flabbergasted by her response.

That went to show how conceited Cupid Falls' golden boy was. He'd expected her to be grateful. To thank him for *saving* her. Well, she didn't need saving. She'd meant what she said. She'd thought about the implications of having a baby on her own, and she knew she could handle it.

She also knew that if she ever married, it would be for love. Aunt Betty had taken her in out of a sense of obligation. She'd given Kennedy someplace to live, but she'd never given her love.

She wrapped her arms around her stomach. This child would know what it was like to have a home . . . to have a place where they belonged, where they were loved.

She took a deep breath and felt better. She went out front and flipped the sign on the door back to "Open," then continued to work on Clarence's frog planter.

There was something so soothing about putting her hand in the soft, rich potting soil. Some people settled their souls by watching a sunset or listening to music, but she'd always found a sense of solace in a garden, and later in her aunt's shop with the plants and flowers.

She gently put a small spider plant into the planter. It looked perfect. She'd known the minute she'd seen the planter that it was meant for Joan.

Kennedy tucked a small yellow tea rose in the planter. It wouldn't live as long as the plant, but yellow roses meant *forgive and forget* in the language of flowers. That seemed appropriate.

She took out a box and was about to wrap the planter when she heard the front door open.

Kennedy resisted a sigh. She didn't want to see anyone else today because so far everyone who'd walked through her front door had either barked at her, complained to her, or offered her a compulsory marriage proposal.

Most days she loved when people came to her with their problems. It made her feel like she was needed. But today she could handle being a little less needed. She didn't want to think about what problem the next person would bring.

Knowing she couldn't hide in the back all day, she looked out into the front room and immediately changed her mind about not wanting to see anyone else. Jenny Murray had come in with her youngest, Ivy. Ivy looked like a mini-Jenny. Both had caramel-colored skin, straight brown hair that bordered on black, and vivid blue eyes.

Ivy flew in as if someone had launched her from a catapult. "Hi, Ms. Mayor. Whatcha doin'? Did ya know Pap's leaving town? He's got his suitcase packed and everything. He said he'll come tell you good-bye, but he's going. But I ain't going nowhere. I'm here to see you."

Kennedy was charmed, and for the first time that day she simply felt happy to see someone. "I'm glad you did."

Ivy grinned. "Yeah, I know. I'm a bright light on a dark day. That's what Pap says." Something caught Ivy's eye and she launched herself toward the back of the store.

"Ivy Murray, don't you run in the mayor's shop," Jenny called out, but it was too late.

Ivy bumped against a stand, sending the half dozen bud vases on it falling to the floor. Thankfully, they were empty, but there was glass everywhere.

"I'm sorry," Ivy cried out, then sank to the floor and started to cry in earnest.

"Oh, Kennedy, I'm so sorry—" Jenny started.

Both mother and daughter wore the same distraught expression, which only made them look even more alike.

"Jenny, Ivy, stop. Accidents happen." Kennedy knelt with difficulty and looked at Ivy. "Do you know what my aunt used to say about accidents?"

Ivy shook her head.

"'Say you're sorry and help clean it up.'" Aunt Betty had been a straightforward sort of woman. Kennedy couldn't help but wonder what she'd have said about the baby. Probably the same thing. And basically, that's what Kennedy had done. She'd told Malcolm she was sorry and she was handling it.

"Pap always says you can't cry over spilled milk," Jenny added to her daughter.

"I didn't spill no milk," Ivy informed her mother. "I broke Ms. Mayor's stuff."

"Well, you said you were sorry, so all that's left is helping me clean it up," Kennedy told the little girl with a smile.

"I'm real sorry, Miss Mayor. Mama says, 'Ivy, don't you run inside, that's for outside,' but sometimes I forget. I can pick up the pieces."

If Ivy and a table were trouble, Kennedy couldn't even imagine what Ivy and glass shards would be, so she shook her head. "It's glass, so that's a grown-up job. I'll do that part. But," she hastily added when Ivy looked as if she were going to complain, "you can go in the back and get the broom and dustpan for me. Then you can hold the dustpan while I sweep."

The little girl brightened immediately. "I can do that." She ran into the back room.

"Walk." Jenny sank onto a stool. "Thanks, Mayor. I'll pay for the damage."

"It's nothing. I had Georgie Miller working here last summer, and next to all his accidents? Really, this is nothing. Now, what can I do for you today?"

"Missy's sick today. I wondered if you could send her a little something? I don't have much money, but if you could do something inexpensive but nice, I'd appreciate it."

She knew that Missy babysat for Jenny's kids when she worked. "I can do that. I'll take it over."

"Great."

Ivy came back with the dustpan in one hand and dragging the broom in the other. "I'm gonna spend the afternoon with Mama 'cause Miss Missy is sick," Ivy said. "Mama says we'll have ta eat macaroni and cheese all week 'cause she's losin' a day at work, but that's okay, 'cause I like smacks and cheese."

Kennedy knew that times were tight for Jenny. Her good-for-nothing ex had left her with three kids and a mortgage. The young mother worked at The Cupboard, the local restaurant. She worked days, which meant she didn't get premium tips like she would at night, but it was better for her kids' schedules, she said.

"You know, Jenny, I take back what I said earlier. When someone does damage to someone else's property, they should have to pay for it." Jenny started to look nervous, so Kennedy smiled and hastily added, "And since the person who broke my vases is here, why doesn't she stay this afternoon and help me at the shop in order to work off her debt? I have a lunch meeting at The Cupboard, so she can come in and visit at lunch, then come back with me and help me put together Missy's arrangement."

Jenny shook her head. "Kennedy, you don't have to—"

Kennedy interrupted. "I don't *have* to do anything, but I'd like to, if you'll let me."

For a moment, she thought Jenny was still going to decline, but finally the frazzled young mother nodded and said, "It would help me out so much. I hate to impose."

"It's not an imposition. Frankly, I could use some training. I'll be in your position soon enough. And us single moms need to stick together, right?" Kennedy patted her baby bump—which recently felt more like a baby boulder. It made her remember that Malcolm was back in town. Hopefully he was packing up now and heading back to Pittsburgh.

"You're right," Jenny said. "We do need to stick together. So I'll say yes, if you promise to let me help out when the baby comes."

"Yeah," Ivy agreed, "and I'll help, Miss Mayor. I know all kinds of things about babies."

"You do?" Kennedy asked the little girl.

Ivy gave her a look that basically said *duh*. "Sure I do. I used to be one."

Kennedy valiantly held back a smile as she nodded solemnly. "Well, that does make you an expert. So how about you and I put together a few orders? We can go to lunch, then deliver them, and you can tell me everything I need to know about having a baby."

Ivy's head bobbled up and down so hard and fast it was a wonder it stayed mounted on her neck.

"Oh, yeah, Miss Mayor, I'll do that. It'll take a long time to tell you everything, 'cause I know lots of stuff. Like did you know that a baby poops"—she dropped her voice to a stage whisper—"in his pants? And you can't yell, 'cause they still do it. And it smells."

"Why, no, I don't think I did," Kennedy assured the little girl, then she turned to Jenny. "Thank you so much for leaving Ivy with me. I obviously have a lot to learn."

"Thank you," Jenny said again. She leaned down and looked at Ivy. "Be good."

"I can help Miss Mayor real good, Mom. You don't need to worry about her."

Kennedy knew that wasn't exactly what Jenny had meant, but she couldn't help but chuckle.

Jenny smiled at her daughter, then past her at Kennedy. "I know you can. You remember your manners, and if the mayor gets a customer, you be quiet while she waits on them."

Ivy bobbled her head again. "Okay, I will."

Jenny looked up from her daughter. "Kennedy, really, thank you."

"Scoot," Kennedy said. "Go home and get ready for work. I'm sure Gus and Tavi will be thrilled you're coming in."

"Yeah, Tavi wasn't pleased when I called and said I couldn't make it."

Kennedy could almost imagine the feisty waitress's response. "I've seen Tavi when she's annoyed. I'm glad I saved you from that. We'll see you at lunch."

Jenny flew from the shop, and Kennedy looked at her new assistant. Her hand strayed to her stomach, and as if it knew she was thinking about it, the baby kicked. She looked down at Ivy and said, "Take your coat off and let's get started."

"And did you know that babies burp so hard that sometimes they puke? My friend Ronny puked at school and everyone said *ew* and then the janitor came and . . ."

~

Mal looked at his grandfather, who was packing another suitcase. Frankly, he'd packed so much that Mal was starting to wonder if he was ever coming home.

"I can't believe you didn't tell me," he said for the umpteenth time.

"It wasn't my place." Pap was a big man, and though time had changed his hair color to grey, he still carried himself with the ease of a man much younger.

"But you knew the baby was mine," Mal insisted.

"I didn't know anything of the sort. I knew that I missed you. And I knew you needed to come home and take care of your responsibilities." He zipped the suitcase.

"That's what I mean. If you'd told me about Kennedy sooner I'd have—"

"I'm talking about the Center," Pap insisted. "Like I told you in the messages I left, it's not mine anymore. Your mother bought me out, and when she died, the ownership passed to you. I helped out as long as I could, but I'm an old man. I want to sit back and rest on my laurels. I want to enjoy my twilight years."

Mal scoffed. "Twilight my a—"

"Watch your language, boyo."

Something in Mal loosened at the childhood nickname that only his grandfather had ever used. "I'm not a boy anymore, Pap."

"I know. I just wasn't sure you did." He hefted the suitcase with ease and set it on the floor. "The fact you're an adult is the reason why you need to be here in Cupid Falls, taking care of your obligations. I've put off this trip for too long."

"But Kennedy—"

"No. I'm not getting in the middle of anything. She was a great friend to your mom, and she's been a good friend to me. I don't know what I'd have done without her help these last few months. Your mom set up that new computer system and a new contract system. I don't understand the first, and don't want to be bothered with the second. I've sent everyone over to Kennedy since we lost your mother, and she's taken care of all that stuff as well as the staff schedules. I'm sure she'll show you how it all works. But you might want to talk to her sooner rather than later. You might save yourself some headaches."

"Pap, where are you going?" Mal asked. His grandfather had always done things his own way. When he set his mind on something, there wasn't much that could change it.

"I've rented a cottage on Lake Erie. It's off-season, so the rates were fantastic." He pulled the suitcase out of the room and down the hall.

Mal followed. "You're going to stay on the lake in November? We get snow early and often, but this time of year, Erie gets it even worse." The cold Canadian winds picked up moisture from the open lake and dumped it on the city that sat closer to the lake.

"I don't need a weatherman's explanation of lake-effect snow, boyo. Like I said, it's off-season and I got a killer rate. I've always wanted to spend a winter on the shore. I want to watch the ice dunes form. I want to go ice fishing on the bay. I've worked hard all my life and I deserve to do that."

Malcolm knew his grandfather too well to buy that he was in a hurry to get to some lake cottage in November, and if his grandfather had ever dreamed of ice fishing, this was the first Mal was hearing about it. "There's more to it than that, Pap."

"Maybe, but I'm not willing to talk about it yet, so that's all you're getting out of me. With my going to Erie, you get the house to yourself while you and Kennedy work things out—"

"She told me she doesn't need anything from me for the baby." He could hear the frustration in his voice.

Frustration? That wasn't nearly a strong enough description of how he felt. He felt . . . he felt too many emotions to sort them all out.

"I was talking about you and Kennedy working things out about the Center. As for the baby, I'm staying out of it."

His grandfather had never stayed out of anything. This new hands-off policy was suspect in and of itself.

"Pap . . ." Mal let the sentence fade because he didn't know what else he could say that hadn't already been said.

His grandfather pulled on his coat. "That's it. I'm off. I'll talk to you next week. If you're still in town, I'll come back for Thanksgiving dinner. Well, I will if you cook."

His grandfather had always cooked the holiday meals. Even when his mom was alive, his grandfather had cooked. "Seriously?"

He'd always been able to count on his mother and grandfather. Now his mother was gone and his grandfather . . . was going.

And he was going to be a father.

His roiling emotions gave a mighty twist.

His grandfather didn't seem to notice his inner turmoil. Pap continued, "Your grandmother's cookbook is in the kitchen on the shelf. Help yourself . . . if you stay. If you head back to Pittsburgh, please turn the thermostat down to fifty-five before you go, and set the timer on the front light. Oh, and let Kennedy know. She'll keep an eye on the house and pick up my mail and stuff."

"Pap, I don't know what to do." Those words were hard for Mal to say, but they were the truth. He'd always been a man who knew what he wanted. Even as a boy, he knew what he wanted. And he'd been willing to work for it. He'd worked hard and accomplished all his goals.

Losing his mother hadn't been anything he could plan for or prepare for. She'd always been his touchstone, but an aneurism took her so fast, he didn't even get to say good-bye. One day she'd been going about her life like normal, the next she'd been gone.

He tried to tell himself that it would have been easier if he'd had time to say good-bye, but he wasn't sure that was true. What he was sure of was the fact his world had tilted off its axis. Kennedy had seemed to understand better than anyone, and for one night he'd taken comfort in her arms.

But now this.

He hadn't planned on a baby . . . ever. Nor did he plan to marry. He knew there were happy marriages, but he'd seen more than his share of the other kind. He wasn't someone who liked the odds.

But odds or not, he and Kennedy had created a child.

"I don't know what to say to Kennedy to make her see reason," he told his grandfather, hoping Pap would know and give him a clue.

His grandfather and mother loved Kennedy. They'd mentioned her from time to time over the years, talking about her as if she were one of the family.

His grandfather put down his suitcase for a moment, turned around, and put his hands on Mal's shoulders. "Listen, boyo, I've done everything I can to show you how a real man behaves. You're smart. You've got the tools. You'll figure it out."

"I've already done that. I asked Kennedy to marry me." He paused and said, "She said no."

His grandfather started laughing. "I'm sure she did. Even though I said I was staying out of it, I have one suggestion before I leave. Spend some time with Kennedy. Learn what you can about her. You're an attorney, for goodness' sake. You'd never go into court without knowing your opponent and having a plan."

"Kennedy is not my opponent. I know that much, Pap. Dad never realized Mom wasn't his. I know Mom tried to hide all the times he dragged her into court over me." Mal remembered feeling so guilty, even though as an adult he knew it wasn't his fault. "I don't want that kind of relationship with Kennedy. I won't put my child through it."

His grandfather grinned and patted his shoulder. "See, you're learning already. I have every faith that you'll figure the rest out, too. I'll have my phone. Call if you need me. I'm only half an hour away."

With that, his grandfather picked up his suitcase and left. He simply walked out the door.

Mal stood in the foyer, not sure what to do next.

He heard, rather than saw, his grandfather's car pull out of the driveway, and still he stood there in the quiet house.

The too-quiet house.

When he was growing up, the house had always seemed full, even though there were just the three of them—his mom, Pap, and him. He took a step toward the living room but wasn't ready to face the emptiness and the silence. So he went outside and locked the door behind him.

He looked across the lawn and saw the small bungalow next door.

Kennedy's house.

She'd moved in with her aunt when she was sixteen. He remembered her as a quiet girl. Sort of a loner. They didn't really hang out in the same crowd. Now they were tied together for the rest of their lives.

When Mal thought of home, he'd thought of his grandfather's Cape Cod cottage, of this street, and there had always been an immediate sense of warmth. Peace, even.

He felt neither in the house or on the street at this moment.

He wanted to get in his car and head back to Pittsburgh. He knew who he was there. He knew what was expected of him.

But Pap and his mother had raised him better than that. Since he wasn't ready to face his empty home, he turned and walked down the block.

Amos Greer was opening his mailbox. "Hi, Amos," he called.

"Mal, how's Cupid Falls' own Perry Mason doing? Still haven't lost a case?"

"Not yet, Amos." Most of his job dealt with contracts and deals, not arguing in front of a judge. He'd tried explaining that before, but no one in town really cared.

"How are you?"

The electrician smiled. "I'm well grounded, Mal." He paused and added, "That was some electrician humor."

Mal managed a smile. "Good one." He waved and continued toward Main Street, not really sure of where he was heading. He walked by Kennedy's flower shop and the Center. But he didn't go in.

Instead, he left the building and walked kitty-corner to the next block down on the north side of the street. He stood outside The Cupboard on the wide, creaky wooden porch. Three sets of rocking chairs were placed with wooden barrels between them. There were two checkers games and a chess set. He wondered if Tavi left them out all winter or simply hadn't put them away yet.

Mal looked through the plate glass window that had "The Cupboard Restaurant" painted in the center. He could see Tavi and Jenny Murray navigating the tables. He didn't need to look to know that Gus was in the kitchen, probably cursing up a storm in Greek.

Tavi and Gus's parents were first generation in the US. The siblings had bought McQueen's Cupboard from Terry McQueen. It had been a general store back in the day. Terry had tried to turn it into a gift shop, but they didn't get enough tourists through Cupid Falls to make the business viable, although Pap said that Kennedy, as mayor, was working to change that.

Gus and Tavi had converted the general store into a restaurant. They'd left a lot of the original shelves and cupboards in place and filled with tons of local goods that were for sale. Goodwin's Honey. Maple syrup from the Hastings' place. Some quilts and other hand-crafted items—not enough to compete with the craft shop down the street, but enough to give the restaurant a unique flavor.

Mal went inside. There was a table at the front with one lone occupant. In Pittsburgh, no one would think of asking to join anyone dining alone, but here in Cupid Falls custom would dictate that one lone diner ask another lone diner to sit together. But Mal didn't know this guy, though he looked familiar, and frankly he wasn't in the mood to talk to anyone. All he wanted to do was slink to a back table and brood, but to get back to the booth that he wanted, he had to run the gauntlet.

Table after table called out greeting. There was a certain anonymity in Pittsburgh, but here, everyone knew him—at least they had known him when he was a kid. They seemed to delight in asking him if he'd had any big cases.

"Hey, Mal, did Pap tell you about our football team this year? They almost rivaled your senior year . . ."

"Mal, I was at the high school last week, and our science trophy is still in that big case in the front hall . . ."

He nodded, shook hands, and said his hellos, then finally made it to the back corner table. It was as out of the way as he could get. Jenny came over with her order pad and a smile. "Hi, Mal. I didn't know you were in town. Are you here for a while? Your grandfather must be so happy."

"Hi, Jenny" was his only response to her question, because frankly, he didn't have a clue how long he'd be here. He'd planned to head back to Pittsburgh tomorrow, but that was a pipe dream now.

"Gideon's up front at a table by himself, if you want company. I'm not sure if you remember him. He was Amish and didn't go to high school with us. He's not now, of course. Amish, that is. And Jon said he got a GED. He's a nice guy and did some work for your mom."

"No, I don't think I remember him. I'll just stay here, if that's okay."

"That's fine," Jenny assured him. "What can I get you?"

"Coffee" was all he said.

Jenny's expression said she'd noticed his shortness, but she didn't say anything more than "Sure thing. I'll be right back with it."

She delivered the coffee and took his not-so-subtle hint and left him alone, other than circling back with refills from time to time without any more questions meant to engage him.

Mal sat back and tried to understand what had just happened. He'd left Pittsburgh this morning, driven two hours to get to Cupid Falls in order to take care of the Center. He'd planned to put it up for sale or find a manager. Whichever option his grandfather wanted.

Instead, he'd found out he was going to be a father.

He'd offered to marry the mother of his child and she'd looked almost insulted. She'd told him, in no uncertain terms, *no.*

What was he going to do about Kennedy Anderson . . . and his child?

At that moment, Kennedy came into the restaurant with a little girl who was carrying a brown paper bag as if it were precious. They sat at a big, empty table in the center of the room. Kennedy helped the girl unbundle her coat and hat before she took off her own parka.

He couldn't help but notice how huge she was. Huge with his child.

She wasn't due until sometime next month. *A few weeks,* she'd said. He didn't know how she'd manage to last another few hours, much less weeks.

He watched as Kennedy listened to something the kid was saying with complete attention. She leaned closer, as if whatever the girl was saying were of the utmost importance, then Kennedy nodded.

The kid jumped up from the table and found Jenny Murray and handed her the bag.

How could he have missed the resemblance? That had to be Jenny's kid. She had a bunch, if he recalled correctly. His grandfather and mom were always going on about the town's people as if they wanted to keep him connected. He'd long since learned to tune most of it out.

He had frequently worked on paperwork while they went on and on about who did what, when, and how.

Mal felt a stab of pain. His mother wouldn't be calling him anymore with updates.

He missed her. He could kick himself for all those moments he'd squandered.

"You're looking deep in thought," someone said.

Mal looked up and found Tom Lewis standing next to the table.

"Sorry, I didn't see you come over. How are you?" he asked, rising and shaking Tom's hand. Tom owned a bookstore on Main Street. Tom's Books and Stuff. The *stuff* part of the name was anything that struck Tom's fancy. Toys, puzzles, music. It was one of the newer businesses in town. Mal remembered his mom saying something about the mayor wanting more Cupid Falls residents doing their shopping on Main Street.

Tom had worked at an Erie factory but had been laid off. He said it was the best thing that had ever happened to him. He'd left Erie, moved to Cupid Falls, and had opened his own store. Tom said he wasn't sure he'd ever have been brave enough to leave a secure job, but because he was forced to do something new, he'd found something better. Someplace better. It was actually nice talking to someone who didn't want to talk about high school or his job in Pittsburgh.

"I'm here to have our monthly lunch with the mayor," Tom said. He might not have grown up in Cupid Falls, but he'd become a fixture of the town. "We're discussing the big Christmas fund-raiser."

Well, that explained why Kennedy was here. "Who's the kid?"

"That's Jenny's youngest. Their sitter is sick, and Kennedy's helping out. Rumor has it Cupid Falls has a new deputy mayor for the day."

"Oh." He'd been right. The little girl was Jenny's.

"That's Kennedy for you. She ran for office on the slogan *The buck stops here.* Well, it's not just the buck . . . it's pretty much everyone and everything in town that stops by her place."

"Even kids," Mal said, eyeing Kennedy, who was now holding the girl. How on earth she managed to fit the kid on her lap was a mystery to him.

"Yeah, even kids." Tom glanced back at Kennedy and the girl and smiled, as if the scene pleased him.

And having Tom pleased about Kennedy bothered Mal, though he wasn't sure why.

"Speaking of kids—" he started, but Tom's expression stopped him in his tracks.

"Listen, no one can miss that she's having a baby and there's no ring on her finger, but no one here in town would allow anyone to gossip about her, or put her down." It was a warning, plain and simple.

"I wasn't planning to gossip. But you're right, I couldn't help but notice."

"She's not saying anything and no one's pestering her." Tom's tone was flat and final.

Mal nodded. "Got it."

"Good." Tom glanced over his shoulder at the table, which was filling up with other local business owners. "I'd better get over before they start without me. Good to see you, Mal."

Tom walked back over to the table. Mal recognized everyone except that guy—Gideon, Jenny had said—at the front table and another guy who sat at the table with the group. Elmer and Marge, who owned the grocery store. Vivienne from the antique store. Erik from the pharmacy . . .

Though he noticed all of them, he focused on Kennedy.

She handed out papers and talked for a while. He noticed how often her hand slipped down to her stomach. He wondered if the baby was kicking. He didn't know much about pregnancy. Basically he knew what various television shows had taught him, and that wasn't a lot.

He'd have to research the condition.

No, not the condition. A baby.

His baby.

He felt overwhelmed again at the thought.

His father was letting him help on the Thompson case. He should be at the office in Pittsburgh right now, helping with that research, preparing briefs.

Instead he was here. Not for the day like he'd planned. He was here until he figured out what to do about Kennedy and the baby. He'd have to call and let the office know. He could do some work from here . . .

He stopped thinking about work as he watched Kennedy. She held up a finger, indicating Tavi should wait a moment, then leaned over and listened to something Jenny's kid said.

She didn't seem to mind interrupting her meeting for a kid.

She smiled, nodded, and waved Jenny over. The two of them talked a moment, and Jenny laughed and mussed her daughter's hair.

Jenny went back to waiting tables, and Kennedy put her arm around the little girl and went back to her meeting. As she talked, the girl squirmed her way onto Kennedy's lap again—what little there was of it. She draped herself over Kennedy's stomach and rested her head on Kennedy's shoulder.

Kennedy stroked her hair as she continued her meeting.

Mal felt the tug of a memory. He couldn't have been much older than Jenny's kid. His mom had come to his room in their Pittsburgh home and told him they were moving to Pap's place in Cupid Falls. He remembered being excited until he realized that his mom was talking about the two of them moving and not his father.

She'd hugged him and stroked his head, and she'd promised him that everything would be okay.

Two years later, the divorce was final.

He'd been in second grade.

He'd seen his father on rare weekends and sometimes a week or two in the summer.

He watched Kennedy gently holding the little girl, and he knew that he didn't want that kind of relationship with his child. He didn't want to be an occasional weekend dad.

When the meeting was over and the crowd started to dissipate, the one stranger at the meeting walked over to Kennedy's table and spoke to her. She smiled at the guy, who patted her shoulder before he left. Then that Gideon guy came over and talked to her for a while, too.

She smiled at something he said, and Mal, before he knew what he was doing, got out of his seat and he walked over to the table. "Who's your friend?"

Kennedy looked up and seemed less than enthused to see him.

"Malcolm Carter, Gideon Byler. He's the best carpenter in the area. He's going to do some work for me at the flower shop."

"Mal," he said, correcting Kennedy's introduction. She was the only one in town who insisted on calling him by his full name. He extended his hand to the guy and they shook.

"Nice to meet you," Gideon said. "If you'll excuse me, I need to get back to work."

"Nice meeting you, too," Mal said. There was a trace of a lilt in Gideon's voice that Mal recognized from the local Amish community. He knew they spoke Pennsylvania Dutch at home, and the cadence seemed to carry through to their English as well.

Before he could ask Kennedy about the man who Jenny said used to be Amish, the little girl who'd sat quietly through the introduction tapped on his thigh. "I'm Ivy. I'm five and I'm helping Miss Mayor today. I'm her . . ." She looked to Kennedy.

"Assistant," Kennedy filled in.

"Yeah, that's right. I'm the assistant. Who are you?" Ivy asked.

"I'm Mal."

"Oh." Obviously that was all the information that Ivy required. She turned back to her picture.

"Kennedy, Pap left town this afternoon. I was wondering if you could come over to the Center later and show me the computer system and forms?"

Her eyes seemed a dark grey and her expression said she'd rather have a tooth pulled, but she nodded. "My assistant and I have a few deliveries to make, then we're picking up her brothers at school. Jenny's off work at four, so how about I meet you about four thirty and we can chat for a bit?"

"That would be fine." He wanted to say more. He wanted to talk to her about the baby, about what they were going to do, but before he could formulate what to say, Jenny walked by.

"Hey, here's for my coffee." He handed her a ten-dollar bill.

"I'll get your change," she said.

He smiled and shook his head. "I tied up your table forever. It's your tip. Sorry I was short earlier."

"That was nothing. May Williams was in earlier. Now that woman has given *short* a whole new meaning. She wouldn't know a happy emotion if it bit her on the butt."

He managed a small smile, and as Jenny went to attend to her other tables, he turned back to Kennedy. "I guess I'll see you in a while then."

"I'll be there as soon as I can," she said.

"It was nice meeting you, Ivy," he told Jenny's daughter.

"I know. I'm a nice girl, except when I'm not. Mommy always thinks I'm nice, but my brothers don't. 'Specially when I spy on them. Timmy and Lenny don't like girls, but I'm tricky."

"I'm sure you are," he said and ruffled her hair as he walked past her and smiled. He felt sorry for her brothers. He suspected having Ivy for a little sister might be a bit of a trial.

He stopped on the restaurant's porch and looked through the window, back into the restaurant. Kennedy was helping Ivy bundle back up. The little girl was talking a mile a minute, and Kennedy was giving her every word her full attention.

He couldn't help but remember all the times his mother had come to his games. His mother was not a sports enthusiast. She was more at home with a book than on a bleacher. But she had been at every game. And after each one, she'd listened as he ran through the highlights.

She'd always given him her full focus and made him feel as if everything he said was the most important thing in the world to her.

That's what he saw in Kennedy as she listened to Ivy.

She'd be a good mom.

And all Mal could do was hope he'd be a good father. A present father. Not simply an occasional weekend sort of dad.

He wanted to listen to his kid talk about . . . anything. About friends, about school, about games. He wanted to hear about their dreams.

He wanted to be there if they had a nightmare. He wanted to be there to pick them up and hold them.

Mal had never intended to be a father, but that ship had sailed. Intention or not, he was going to be.

And if that was the case, he was going to be the best father he could be.

Mal let himself back into the Center. He had some calls to make, because it looked as if he'd be taking off more time than he'd anticipated.

He thought about the Thompson case and sighed. There'd be other cases. He only had one chance to make things right with Kennedy, and he wasn't going to blow it.

CHAPTER THREE

Kennedy was exhausted. The last few weeks, she'd gone home after work and crawled into bed for a long nap, emerging sometimes hours later. She'd make herself something for dinner and then collapse again.

She wished she were heading home tonight.

The last thing she wanted to do was see Malcolm.

She'd imagined—hoped, even—that he'd hear her news, visit with Pap, and then go back to Pittsburgh. Leave it to Malcolm to mess things up. He never seemed to do what she wanted.

When she was younger, she'd had the biggest crush on him. She wanted him to fall head over heels for her. He lived with Pap Watson, next door to Aunt Betty's house. In nice weather, she'd arrange herself on the porch with a book or homework, hoping he'd notice her. She'd imagine that he'd come over and say hi.

He occasionally offered her a nonchalant wave, but that was it.

Yet in the fall she went to all his football games. In the winter she tried to be outside shoveling the walk when she thought he'd be coming home.

Weekends she'd help Aunt Betty out at the flower shop because she knew he frequently worked for Pap at the Center.

She did everything she could to put herself in his path.

And he'd never done more than nod or wave at her.

Yeah, Malcolm Carter IV had never once cooperated with what she wanted.

Even now, when she'd stopped wanting anything from him, he still wasn't cooperating.

Kennedy walked across the sidewalk from the flower shop next door to the Center and she let herself in. "Malcolm?"

"In the office," he called back.

She hung her coat on the coatrack, stomped off her boots, and grabbed her file. The sun had come out and sidewalks had almost cleared. What was left wasn't so much snow as slush. That was almost worse. If it got cold tonight, the slush would freeze and she'd have an icy walk into work tomorrow.

Ice and pregnant women didn't mix.

Kennedy balled her hand into a fist and shoved it in the small of her back, hoping to relieve the ever-present ache.

The Center was ideally designed. There were retractable walls that could divide the space into three smaller rooms if need be, but most of the time they were tucked into their pockets, leaving one gigantic room. At the back of the building there was a kitchen to the left and the office to the right.

She headed to the right and walked into the compact space. Malcolm seemed to fill it up in a way that Pap and Val never had. But then again, Malcolm always seemed to fill up whatever space he was in.

Kennedy couldn't help notice him today at the restaurant. He'd sat at the back table, tucked up in the corner as if he thought no one would notice him.

She was pretty sure that would never happen.

Right now, he was hunched over the keyboard staring at the computer monitor. "I can't find the schedule."

"Move over."

He wheeled the chair back a bit, but to her, it didn't feel like it was nearly far enough. She didn't want to be that close to him. But she didn't want him to know that, so she made herself move forward and opened up the schedule. "There you go." She stepped back and pushed against her lower spine again.

Malcolm moved forward and looked at the screen. "It's pretty full."

"Yes. We've been doing some bigger events. I've worked with Gus and Tavi on a few of them. The Cupboard has done a lot of the catering lately." She thrust the file at him. "Here. I've worked up some spreadsheets for you. You can see that the Center's pulling in a nice profit every month. But it has so much untapped potential, it only needs some money invested into the infrastructure and some publicity. We could easily draw some people from Erie or other neighboring towns. Cupid Falls has so much ambiance. I don't think Main Street has changed much since Pap was a kid, other than the names on the storefronts. Really, the Center is the perfect place for a wedding reception. We've got the large lawn behind us, and it's a short walk down the trail to the falls. I can't imagine a prettier place for photos. I—"

He interrupted her. "I don't have time to invest in growing the Center's potential. Pap said he's not interested in running it. He also said you've been doing a lot of the management. Has he compensated you?"

She shrugged. "I helped out, that's all. But I want to talk to you about Pap's retirement. I know you're busy in Pittsburgh and can't put the time and effort that the Center needs into it. So I think you should sell it. If you look at the last page, there's a breakdown on how much the updates will run and what the current market value of the property is."

He glanced at the last page. "You had someone appraise the building?"

She could see him bristle at the thought, so she hastily assured him, "With Pap's permission. You see, I'd like to buy the place. There are a lot of—"

Malcolm frowned. "You've got the flower shop."

Kennedy wanted to snap *thank you, Captain Obvious* but bit her tongue and simply said, "I do have the flower shop. And I've expanded my inventory. We do gift baskets and fruit baskets now, too. But I want to be sure I have an adequate, steady income in place . . ." She let the sentence fade. She'd been about to say *for the baby*, but she didn't want to remind Mal about the baby. She wanted him to agree to sell her the Center and then leave and go back to Pittsburgh. After all, he had big-city law to return to. And he'd barely visited his grandfather, so he wasn't exactly what she'd call father material.

"I've spoken to the bank, and using the Cupid's Bowquet as collateral, I won't have any problem paying you a fair market price."

She waited for his response. Malcolm sat there, staring at her for a long moment that stretched into an *uncomfortable* long moment. She felt a surge of disappointment. He was going to say no.

Well, she'd tried. "Never mind. I can imagine that it would be hard to let go of the place. You're the third-generation owner. I imagine you have so many happy memories here."

Malcolm was still silent, and that silence had now gone from uncomfortable to plain old rude.

She'd said her piece, and he obviously wasn't impressed. If he'd argued or asked questions, she could have countered his concern, but she had nothing to throw at his silence, so she reverted to all business. "That file I opened is in your document section. There's a file for the schedule, and there are files for the specific events. And the other document you really need to keep an eye on is the to-do list. I broke down each event and listed what Pap or I needed to do for it and when. I've included all vendors' numbers and info. If you follow it step by step, you should be fine."

He glanced at the folder again but still said nothing.

Kennedy moved toward the door. "I should probably go."

"Are you hungry?" he finally asked.

Kennedy turned. "Pardon?"

"Have you had dinner?" Malcolm asked slowly, as if he was afraid she hadn't understood him.

She shook her head. "Not yet. I came here right after I closed up the shop and dropped off Jenny's kids."

"You must be starved." He stood. "I noticed you didn't eat much at lunch, between running your meeting and entertaining Ivy."

"I—"

He didn't let her finish her sentence. "I thought I'd pick up a pizza. We could go back to your place and you could lay out your proposal while we eat dinner."

She wanted to tell him that she didn't need someone watching over her. She was an adult. She ate when she was hungry. And she didn't want him in her house. He was staying at Pap's place, right next door, and that was close enough. "Really, I can tell you here."

"Come on, Kennedy." He shot her an award-winning smile that had probably swayed countless female jurors as easily as it had all the girls in high school. "I know you've done business over meals in the past. Just today, by the look of things. We have a lot to talk about and it would be a lot more comfortable at home."

"Then let's meet at Pap's," she tried. If they ate dinner at Malcolm's, she could simply leave at any time.

"You don't want me in your house?" he asked.

"That's not it," she said, though that was a lie.

She didn't want him there. More specifically, she didn't want any memories of him there. It was enough that she had to look at Pap's every day, and visit it occasionally—there were memories galore there. And when she came to work, she still had memories right next door. So, no, she didn't want them at her house. But she didn't want to admit that to Malcolm. "No, of course, that's not it."

"Fine. Why don't you go home, put your feet up, and I'll call Tavi and order us a pizza. Anything special you want on it?"

She hadn't said yes, but that obviously didn't matter to Malcolm. Since she doubted she'd be able to eat any of it with him there, she shook her head. "Whatever you want is fine."

"I'll meet you at your place in about half an hour then," he promised.

Drat. "Fine."

"Kennedy, we do have a lot to discuss, but I'm not trying to make things difficult for you."

If this was Malcolm trying *not* to make things difficult, she didn't want to see what it would be like if he was. "Maybe you're not, but that doesn't mean you don't manage it anyway." She turned around and left as he picked up the phone to call in their order.

Kennedy walked the four blocks east on Collingwood Drive to Aunt Betty's. It was a bungalow and used to be painted grey. Since Aunt Betty hadn't wanted to put money into the home, it had been a peely mess when she passed away three years ago. One of the only changes Kennedy had made to the house was getting it repainted. She'd had them paint it a creamy light yellow. She'd felt guilty because she knew that Aunt Betty wouldn't have approved, but she did think the house looked so much better.

Kennedy looked at the small porch that was on the side of her house closest to Malcolm's. She'd replaced the cushions on the white wicker furniture with striped cream, yellow, and grey ones. They tied in the house color with the grey stone fireplace that was the focal point of the front. They were in the shed out back for the winter, but in the spring she'd pull them back out.

Next door, Pap's house was more of a Cape Cod style. There was no front porch on it. The only thing that broke the flat front were the two dormer windows that poked out of the roof on both the front of the house and the back. The one on the right, closest to Aunt Betty's house, was Malcolm's room. Kennedy couldn't count how many times she'd sat on the porch when she was in high school, watching the light that cascaded from that window, knowing he was in there and didn't have a clue she was alive.

She shook her head. She was glad she'd never mentioned her childhood crush to anyone, not even Malcolm.

Kennedy walked along the porch and let herself in the front door. The small coat closet was on the right. She opened it up and put her parka inside, then kicked her boots off and put them on the plastic mat. She'd left her slippers on the carpet runner but didn't really want Malcolm to see her waddling around in her red-and-black-checked slip-ons, so she took her shoes out of her purse and slipped them back on, then hid her slippers in the closet.

She flipped on lights and sighed as she looked at the living room. It was Aunt Betty's frilly, floral furniture and doily-covered tables, which she faithfully polished every Saturday.

She hadn't changed a thing because it seemed . . . wrong. Wrong to change Aunt Betty's house.

She turned off the lights and walked into the kitchen instead. This was as Aunt Betty had left it, too, but Kennedy wouldn't change a thing in it. She loved the old floor-to-ceiling white cabinets. The soapstone counter was worn in a few areas and dipped severely enough that it made some plates wobble. There were dings and scratches all over it. It looked at home in this kitchen.

The table was a worktable, a place where occupants had prepared meals for decades. It was the equivalent of today's islands. The butcher-block surface was scarred and discolored from years of cooking.

The only changes she'd made in here were adding the desk in one corner and a dark plaid chair with a small end table and lamp in the other.

That chair was her favorite place in the house. She had a view of the backyard. An ancient mulberry tree was outside the window, and every morning she faithfully filled the bird feeder that hung from it. She loved sitting in the chair with a cup of coffee, reading the paper, and watching the chickadees, sparrows, and finches flock to it for their breakfast.

She stared out the window. It was dark now, but the snow that still sat on the grass, and the moonlight shining down through the leafless mulberry branches, allowed her to catch the now-empty bird feeder. They'd even cleaned out the suet holder.

She wondered where the birds slept. She wondered if there'd been enough food to satisfy their hunger. She wondered . . .

She stood there, staring out the window at the dark backyard and wondering all kinds of nonsense.

The doorbell rang and forced her to pull herself away from her thoughts.

Time to face Malcolm.

The advantage to standing at the window was she didn't have to heave herself out of the chair in order to answer the door.

Her hands rested on the baby, who obliged her and kicked. "I love you," she whispered.

She'd do whatever it took to protect this baby. To see her child safe and happy.

"Pizza," Malcolm said, holding out a pizza box that had a bag resting on top of it. "Are you going to invite me in?"

She opened the door wider and tried not to sigh as she said, "Yes. Please come in."

Obviously she hadn't done a good enough job covering her lackluster invitation, because Malcolm said, "That was not the most enthusiastic response I've ever had, but I'll take it."

She ignored his comment. "Come on back to the kitchen."

He followed her down the hall and into the kitchen, where he set the bag and box on the table. He opened them while she got plates, napkins, and silverware out.

"Would you like something to drink? I have milk, ice tea, and water."

"Ice tea?" he asked. "It's got to be thirty degrees out today."

She shrugged. She refused to defend the fact that she liked ice tea year-round. It was none of Malcolm's business. She'd switched to decaf because of the baby, but that was as far as she'd compromise. When she didn't say anything, he finally said, "Water would be great."

She got them each a glass and took the seat across from Malcolm, who'd helped himself to pizza and some of the salad that had been in the bag.

She did as well but didn't take a bite.

"About the Center—" she started.

Malcolm interrupted. "Haven't you ever heard that business during a meal gives you heartburn?"

"No. You're the one who pointed out I had a business meeting today at lunch. I like to multitask. So, about the Center . . . you said you couldn't run it from Pittsburgh, and I know Pap is done working.

He wants to re-retire. So selling the business to me makes sense. I'll pay a fair market value. I've already had the loan preapproved. It has a big advantage for you. You won't have to go through the headache of listing the property. You can go back to Pittsburgh—"

Malcolm interrupted her again, and said, "About that . . ."

"Yes?" Kennedy had a sinking feeling that whatever he was about to say next was not going to make her happy.

"I'm not going back."

Yes, she was right, she was not happy in the least. She thought these awkward interactions with Malcolm had a time limit because he'd have to get back to work. Finding out that they were going to continue was awful.

She didn't say anything because the only thing that came to mind was a groan, and she was pretty sure he'd find that insulting.

"I'm not going back to Pittsburgh until you and I work things out. So there's no urgency deciding what to do about the Center. I'm taking an indefinite leave of absence."

"You're staying here, in Cupid Falls?" She knew that's what he'd said in his roundabout explanation, but she needed to hear him say the actual words.

"I'm staying," he repeated. "I'm staying here in Cupid Falls until we work out a few things like custody and—"

She realized she was holding a slice of uneaten pizza. She let it fall to the plate. "What do you mean, work out custody?"

"Kennedy, this is my baby. I've asked you to marry me. You said no. I'd like to think you'll change your mind, because as the child of divorce I can speak with experience, feeling pulled between two parents sucks. But if not, we'll have to work out something."

"Why? You can go back to Pittsburgh and I'll stay here with the baby. You can visit whenever you want."

Work out custody? That sounded as if he planned to take her to court. She remembered hearing that his father took his mother to court on a regular basis. They were in high school when she'd moved to Cupid Falls, but she remembered Val having to go to court at least once even then.

Val was one of the most reasonable women Kennedy had ever met. Kennedy couldn't imagine that she wouldn't have worked with Mr. Carter.

She didn't want to go through that with Mal. She didn't want to be forced to give up time with her child.

"Look how many months it took me to get home and see Pap," Malcolm said. "I won't let that amount of time go between visits with my child."

Mal watched as the blood drained from Kennedy's face. She gripped the edge of the table as if she were holding on to it like some lifeline. He felt concerned but knew that she wouldn't welcome him rushing to her. "Kennedy? Hey, are you okay?"

"You can't have my baby." Her voice was barely a whisper, and her hands moved from the table to her stomach, covering it protectively as if he might reach over at any second and grab the baby from her.

She looked scared as hell as she repeated, "You can't take the baby from me."

"Kennedy, I'm not taking the baby from you. Calm down." Mal was pretty sure that pregnant women shouldn't be upset like this.

"I won't lose this baby," she said as she squinted her eyes and grimaced, as if she were in physical pain. It took him a moment to realize she was.

This time he didn't care if she minded; he rushed around the table and put his hands on her shoulders. "Hey, are you okay?"

She shrugged off his touch. "Braxton Hicks. It's nothing."

"It damn well isn't *nothing*. That was something." He'd known about this baby less than twenty-four hours, but he already felt scared to the bone that something was wrong with the baby or with Kennedy. "Let's get you into the car. We'll drive you to the hospital and have you checked out."

What if he'd caused Kennedy to lose the baby? "Kennedy, please?"

"I'm fine, really," she said. "The doctor's office is closed, and I'm not driving all the way into Erie to have the doctors there tell me what I already know. It's a Braxton Hicks contraction. I've had a few. This was a bad one."

What did he know about babies? Maybe he was just being nervous, but it didn't seem right. "Why are you having them? It's too early for the baby."

"I don't know. This is my first baby. Women have them. My doctor says they're like practice contractions." She thrust one hand into the small of her back as if trying to push away some pain, and the other lay protectively on her stomach.

Mal could see her hand give a little jump, and he wondered if that meant the baby was kicking. He'd seen shows of men with their hands on a woman's pregnant stomach, feeling the baby move.

He'd like to ask Kennedy if he could feel the baby kick, but he knew she wouldn't welcome his touch.

"I'm fine, Malcolm."

"I can't imagine stress helps." Here he was, pushing her, scaring her, and she was carrying his child. She'd been carrying it all this time by herself. With no help.

"I didn't have a contraction as some sympathy ploy in our argument," she said suddenly. She looked defiant, as if daring him to say otherwise.

"Kennedy, I didn't think you did," he assured her.

"I don't need the courts to do what's right. You'll always be welcome to see the baby, but you're not taking my child away from me. I don't care if you sue me for custody. I'll fight you with every penny I have. The baby belongs here, with me. I saw how it was with your father. It would have been kinder if he'd just backed out of your life altogether. But he didn't. He kept dragging your mom into court over everything. He stayed around but let you know that you weren't his priority. I saw you at games, you know. You'd scan the stands, hoping he'd be there. But he wasn't. If he'd simply let you go and got on with his life, you wouldn't have been looking."

For a moment, Mal was back at school. He was that kid on the court, looking for his father, knowing no matter what he said, he wouldn't be on the bleachers. He'd tell himself his father wouldn't make it and try to steel himself for the inevitability, but every time, he still looked . . . he still hoped. And he was still hurt when his dad didn't come.

He was surprised that Kennedy had noticed. He'd worked so hard to hide his disappointment from his mom and never thought anyone else had seen it. But Kennedy had.

Knowing that she had made him feel off-centered. Like when he was in court and the other counsel sprang something on him.

He couldn't argue her points, except one. "So you think it would be better if my father had deserted me?"

"Maybe," she said slowly.

He knew his father had made things difficult on his mom. According to his dad, he was making sure everything was legal and aboveboard. But Mal knew how much his mother had hated having to deal with the court rather than working it out with his father on a one-on-one basis.

"Kennedy, when your parents left you, was it easier?" he countered.

"They didn't leave me . . . they died." That was all she said, but he could see the pain on her face.

What was with him tonight? He was trained to think first, speak second, but sitting here with the mother of his future child, he was continually sticking his foot in his mouth. "I'm sorry. That was a low blow."

"I suppose in your job you've learned to fight with whatever ammunition you have," she said.

"I don't want to fight with you." That much was honest. Mal hadn't even begun to sort through his emotions and his wants, but fighting with the mother of his child wasn't part of it.

Kennedy didn't say anything.

"Listen, you're right. When Mom and Dad divorced, my world shifted. Mom and I moved here to Cupid Falls. I could blame my father's absences on the two hours' distance, but the truth is, he was absent even when we still lived in Pittsburgh." He paused. "I don't want that with this baby. I don't know how we're going to resolve things, and frankly this is all happening so suddenly, I don't know much right now, but I know that much."

"You can't take him," Kennedy said. "I know *that* much."

He ignored her comment and focused simply on the pronoun. "Is it a boy then?"

"I don't know," she admitted. "I don't want to know until it's here. But *he* sounds better than *it*."

"Oh." He was disappointed. He liked the idea of having a son. But as he had the thought, he realized he liked the idea of having a daughter, too.

Kennedy paused a moment. He could see her thinking, though what she was thinking about he didn't have a clue.

She took a deep breath and then gave the slightest hint of a nod, as if whatever she'd been thinking about, she'd made some decision. "Did you want to know?"

"Know what?"

"The baby's gender. I could ask my OB to tell you, but you'd have to keep it a secret from me. The way I look at it, finding out what gender the baby is will be my ultimate Christmas present to you."

Mal was touched that Kennedy had offered. Actually, he was more than touched. She didn't want to know the baby's gender but was willing to allow him to find out. She was basically offering him the chance to know before anyone else. It was beyond generous.

"No," he assured her. "We'll find out together."

"Really—"

He cut her off. "If you're waiting, I'm waiting. We're a team. And listen, I have no idea what we're going to do, but I'm not taking the baby from you. I'm not taking you to court. By custody, I mean we're going to have to figure out a way to share this baby."

She didn't look convinced, so he said it again. "Kennedy, I'm not taking the baby from you. We are two reasonable adults . . . well, at least I am," he said with the slightest hint of humor in his tone.

Kennedy caught it, because she offered him the barest of smiles and seemed to relax, at least a little.

"We can work out something," he continued. "I'm taking time off and staying here in Cupid Falls while I decide what to do with the Center, and what to do about you and the baby."

That barest hint of a smile was gone, and Kennedy was serious as she looked at some point just over his shoulder. "I don't know what there is to decide. It was a one-night stand, Malcolm. I won't say that this baby was a mistake for either of us, but it wasn't planned.

We never said any vows. Our lives aren't tied. You can go back to your life in Pittsburgh."

"You're right, we never said any vows, but you're wrong saying we're not tied. We are. And it's not a bond that can be broken. We're going to be parents. Intentionally or not, we're bringing a baby into the world. And it's best if we figure things out now, rather than have there be problems later."

Kennedy sat there, looking anywhere but at him. She still had one hand behind her back and the other over the baby. She looked exhausted.

Mal said, "But we're not going to figure out anything tonight, Kennedy. So eat your pizza and then show me what you've done with the baby's room."

He thought she'd argue, but instead she dutifully picked up her pizza and took a bite. "I don't have a baby's room, per se."

"You don't?" Wasn't that what all new moms did? Decorated their babies' nurseries, buying things no newborn would ever notice, much less need. It seemed to him that's the sort of thing he'd seen them do on television.

She shrugged. "I've been busy, what with my business, the town, and the Center."

"Will you show me what you have done after you eat?"

She looked as if she were going to say no, then her expression changed. It looked as if she were having an internal argument with herself. And apparently it was a quick one, because she nodded. "Fine."

She dutifully ate the slice of pizza and a small bowl of salad, then said, "Come on. I'll show you the room and then you can go." She struggled out of the chair.

Mal wanted to offer her a hand but didn't think she'd take it. Instead he joked, "Wow, if I didn't know better, I'd say you don't like me."

Kennedy sighed. "Malcolm, even though we've known each other for years, we hardly know each other."

He started to protest, but she cut him off. "You are simply the son of a good friend. When your mom died, we were both grieving. What happened was more about missing her and looking for a connection than actually having a connection. What we did was stupid and now we're going to have to deal with the consequences." She started toward the stairs.

He followed, trying to think of something to say, but the truth was, she was right. He'd been aware of her back in school, but they didn't hang in the same circles. Then he left for college and . . . he'd been gone ever since.

She was right, they didn't know each other in any real sense, but they would. He'd see to that.

At the upstairs landing, she turned toward the back of the house, where her room had been when she was a kid. She must have made that over for the baby and taken her aunt's master bedroom for herself. That made sense.

She flipped on the room's light.

It wasn't a nursery. "This is your room?"

"Yes. And see, that bassinette is for the baby. Once he's bigger, I'll move him into his own room, but for now, this is practical and makes sense."

"So, the baby's got a bassinette?" There wasn't anything else the least bit baby-ized about the room.

Kennedy looked as if she'd taken offense. "And he's got a dresser full of clothes and diapers and . . ." She crossed her arms over the baby. "I'm not going to itemize the baby's layette. Suffice it to say, he's got more than ample supplies."

"What about bottles and that sort of thing?" Malcolm asked.

"I'm going to breastfeed." She blushed as she said the word and hurried on and added, "So I don't need bottles. See, that's another reason you can't take the baby. He would starve."

"How will you do that and work?" he asked.

"I'm taking the baby with me to work, and I've got a sign for the door that says 'Back in a minute.' I'll be using it a lot more. That won't be a solution for you."

He could see all kinds of flaws in that argument. Even if she breastfed, the baby *could* take a bottle. Or he could wait to share custody until the baby was weaned. But she'd looked so worried before, and he didn't want to start another contraction, so he didn't say anything about it. He simply asked, "What's in your aunt's old room?"

Kennedy looked confused. "Her things," she said, as his question was ridiculous because the answer was obvious.

Her aunt had been dead for years. He couldn't imagine why she left Betty's room untouched. This room was tiny, and looked even smaller from the slant of the roofline. "Why don't you move there and turn this into the baby's room?"

Kennedy paused a long moment, as if she were asking herself that question for the first time. "I don't know. That's her room. I feel funny about changing things."

"She's been gone . . . how long? Years. Maybe it's time."

Kennedy shrugged, then turned and walked back downstairs.

There was nothing for Mal to do but follow. But as he walked by, he took a moment to peek into her aunt's room. It looked as if she could come back at any moment.

The whole house looked exactly the way he remembered it, which meant that Kennedy hadn't changed anything since Betty died.

He wondered why.

"Well, good night then," she said as she stood next to the front door at the bottom of the stairs.

When he didn't move toward it, she opened it.

Mal grabbed his coat and put it on. "We'll talk again soon."

Kennedy sighed for probably the umpteenth time that evening. "I'm sure we will."

The moment he was on the porch, she shut the door.

Mal walked next door; his thoughts were almost as jumbled as his feelings. He had no idea what he was going to do about Kennedy and her baby.

Their baby.

And frankly, even if he could sort it all out and make a decision, he doubted Kennedy would cooperate. If you'd asked him yesterday what he knew about Kennedy Anderson, he'd have said she was a nice woman.

Earlier today, when he saw what she'd done for Jenny and her daughter, he'd still have said as much.

Tonight, after eating dinner with her and trying to talk about the baby, he'd say she had a will of iron. That she had unflagging energy and determination, juggling the town, her shop, the Center, and her pregnancy.

But there were more layers to Kennedy Anderson. He couldn't help but wonder why she'd left the house unchanged. Why she hadn't done more to prepare for the baby. And why she seemed so adamant that she didn't need any help.

She'd been right when she'd said they hardly knew each other.

But he was taking time off and staying in Cupid Falls long enough to figure out what to do about the baby . . . and maybe while he was at it, he'd figure out what made Kennedy Anderson tick.

CHAPTER FOUR

It was a blissfully quiet weekend. Kennedy had been nervous that Malcolm was going to hound her every waking moment, but he left her alone.

She caught a glimpse of him Saturday morning as he walked in front of the flower shop's plate glass window. She assumed he was heading to the Center. She thought he might call her with some questions about it, but he didn't. It was one of the rare weekends that nothing was going on there. Next weekend was the official beginning of the holiday season and there was a big craft show. There were probably a dozen different activities planned between that and the holiday itself. The other big event was the weekend before Christmas. It was the Everything But a Dog Foundation's adoption day, followed by its fund-raiser Christmas ball. A lot of people had started calling it the Bow-Wow Ball, since the proceeds would go to the foundation.

Clarence had taken to calling it the Bow-Wow—both long O's—Ball to tease her. Kennedy would never admit it, but he did make her laugh. From what she'd seen, he made Joan laugh as well, despite his occasional trips to the *froghouse*. Maybe that was the key to a good relationship . . . finding someone who could make you laugh more often than they annoyed you.

On Sunday she went to church, then bundled up and took a walk through town. She took her job as mayor seriously. As mayor it was her job to see to it Cupid Falls grew and thrived. As she walked down the street, past Books and Stuff and the Cupboard, she felt as if she was making headway.

As she walked by the flower shop, she looked across the street at the grocery store. There was an empty storefront next to it. She was actively trying to attract a new business there. She hated looking out her window and seeing the vacant shop. It seemed like so much lost potential.

She walked between the flower shop and the Center, through the snow-covered back lawn, then down the path to Falls Creek. There was a giant glacial boulder at the edge of the water. It gave her the perfect vantage point to watch the falls.

Cupid's Falls was only about six, maybe eight feet high. The water poured from the creek above, down a rocky face, and back to the creek again. Through the years the waterfall had hollowed out a swimming hole beneath it. Where the water fell it was easily seven or eight feet deep, but farther back it was only four or five. She knew that generations of the town's kids had come here in the summer to swim.

Even more had sat on this boulder together. Couples.

She knew the legend of the falls.

She wasn't sure she believed it, but she liked the idea of capitalizing on it as a draw for the town and for the Center. Well, if Malcolm agreed to sell her the business.

Maybe that summed up her problems. She looked at this beautiful place as a business opportunity, not a romantic place of local lore.

She refused to remember standing here with Malcolm after his mother's funeral. How they'd sat side by side on this rock—two people mourning her loss. They'd talked about Val. And how talking led to comfort, and comfort led to that one night . . .

Her hand rested on the baby.

She knew she was more practical than romantic. Maybe that's why that one night felt surreal to her. For one night, she thought maybe there was more of a connection than there was.

After he left, and days turned into weeks without word from him, she knew she'd been foolish to fall under the spell of the local legends and her teenage crush.

And as weeks turned to months, she realized that she was pregnant . . . and it only made her more practical. She couldn't afford to be a lovelorn teen anymore. She couldn't pine over the boy next door. She was a business owner, a mayor, and she was going to be a mother. It was time to put away foolish childhood dreams.

As she stared at the falls, she reminded herself of her practicality. She couldn't help but wonder why that practicality didn't lead her to say yes to Malcolm's proposal.

After all, it would be practical to marry for the baby's sake.

The baby kicked and her hands rested on her stomach.

How she felt about this baby had nothing to do with practicality. It had everything to do with love. Maybe there was something to the legends. She had found the love of her life here at the falls. But it wasn't Malcolm . . . it was their child.

That thought settled something in her that night. And it led to her resolve to get along with Malcolm even if it killed her—and it *might* kill her. She smiled despite herself at the thought.

She'd offer to help Malcolm with the Center's two biggest holiday events, the craft show and the Everything But a Dog events. With Pap, she'd have gone ahead and worked on them, but the Center was Malcolm's, not hers, and not Pap's. She'd offer but let him take the lead.

~

Kennedy felt more settled the next day as she jumped right in at work. It was the beginning of her holiday season at the flower shop. She had a slew of Thanksgiving gift baskets and floral arrangements that were being picked up between now and Wednesday. Then a quiet day off, after which began an even crazier schedule until Christmas.

She was tying a ribbon onto a poinsettia when the antique bell on the door jingled. She hurried out front to see who it was.

"Morning, Mayor. Happy Monday."

"No barking today, Clarence?" she asked with a smile.

The old man grinned back at her. "Nah. Joan said you were too pregnant for me to pick on, so I have to lay off . . . but only until after the baby," he warned her. "She was real fond of the frog."

"So you're out of the froghouse?" Kennedy laughed again at the expression.

He nodded. "For now. Probably not for long. You keep your eyes out for other stuff for her, okay? If you see it, it's best to get it and stock up."

"I will. But if you're not in the froghouse today, what can I do for you?"

Clarence's expression sobered. "It's a mayor thing, not a floral thing."

"I'm listening."

"It's about May Williams. She was at my door at six this morning, complaining that I hadn't shoveled yet. Now, Mayor, I keep my sidewalk clear. I shoveled last night before I went to bed. But it was six a.m. I hadn't even started the coffee yet. I told the old bat to go away. I told her that I'd get to it when I woke up, but she said she was going to report me to the police. Now, Jonny, he's a nice boy, but I don't know him well, so I came to you. I don't want him arresting me. There was less than an inch on the ground, and I swear, I'd have cleaned it off as soon as I had some clothes on and a cup of coffee under my belt."

"Listen, Clarence, I'll give Jon a call. I don't think he'd really arrest you, but I'll see to it."

"Thanks, Mayor. If May's not careful, I'm going to press charges. She's disturbing my peace."

The bell on the door rang and Kennedy barely resisted the urge to sigh. "It's all right, Clarence."

"It most certainly is not all right," May Williams said as she stormed into the shop. "I went for a walk this morning, and no one had shoveled."

"May, if you'd waited even an hour, most people would have shoveled."

"I'm accustomed to walking early. Even though June died, I still enjoy those early morning walks."

With a burst of insight, Kennedy realized that May had become a huge pain in her butt late last spring, right about the time the aging dog, June, had passed. May was probably lonely.

The bell rang again.

This was not what Kennedy needed. She had a bajillion orders to fill, calls to make, and . . .

Malcolm walked in. "Good morning, Mayor."

She remembered her resolve and forced a cordial smile and said, "Good morning, Malcolm."

"You don't need to walk that early," Clarence said loudly to May. "There's no dog whining to get out, so you could wait until a man had a chance to put on his pants and make his coffee."

Kennedy saw May's eyes well up with tears.

Before she started to cry in earnest, Kennedy turned her back on Malcolm and said, "May, let's make a deal. I'll have Clarence talk to the neighbors and ask that everyone has their sidewalks cleared by eight thirty. Most of your neighbors are up by then and already on their way to work. On snowy mornings, you'll hold off your walk until then."

Any fight the older woman had seemed to drain out of her at the mention of her dog. "Fine," she said, without the slightest bit of *humph* in her voice.

Kennedy knew she was right about May's behavior having to do with losing June.

Clarence seemed to realize he'd gone too far with the mention of May's dog, because he said quietly, "I'm sorry about June, May."

May sniffed.

Kennedy said, "I'm sorry, too. I know that you can never replace June, but we have that nonprofit organization, Everything But a Dog, coming to town right before Christmas. Vancy Salo has been working in Erie with dog adoptions. She's bringing a bunch of animals with her. Why don't you think about adopting a dog? It would be a lovely Christmas present for yourself."

May sniffed. "I'm not sure I'm ready. I had June for fifteen years. How can you simply replace a companion like that?"

"June had a wonderful life," Kennedy said. "I remember all the sweaters you made him. He was so loved. If you won't do it for yourself, think about a dog that's been abandoned. A dog that's never had a family and known that kind of devotion. Maybe you could do it for the dog?"

May Williams—griping, nagging, annoying May Williams— sniffled, and Kennedy found herself putting an arm over the older lady's shoulders. "You'd be saving some dog's life, May."

"When you put it that way, it would be the right thing to do."

"It would," Kennedy agreed. "And I have a favor. I hate to ask, you know that, but I could go into labor any minute. I really need a team who's able to step in and fill in for me if I do."

May nodded and said, "What can I do?"

"Do you think you could help us out with the adoption day? I know that the ladies at Everything But a Dog would love to have someone local working with them. They've had adoption days all over Erie, but this will be the first one in the county. And if I should go into labor, I'd need to count on you to handle everything." She leaned closer and whispered in May's ear, "Malcolm might be an amazing attorney, but he won't be able to handle an event like this on his own."

Tears forgotten, May smiled and sounded genuinely happy as she said, "Why, Kennedy, I'd love to help."

"Wonderful. I'll get you Mrs. Salo's number. She'll tell you to call her Nana Vancy. Everyone, even her kids, uses that name."

Crotchety, complaining May Williams laughed. "Well, that's a lovely name."

Clarence said, "After you talk to this Nana Vancy, if there's more than you can do alone, you let me and Joan know. We can help. Maybe if Joan got a dog, she'd lay off buying the frogs."

May smiled. "I will. Maybe we can put up flyers and . . ."

Kennedy copied Nana Vancy's number down for May and watched in amazement as Clarence and May left, talking excitedly over plans for the event.

"Nicely done, Mayor," Malcolm said. "You handled them with the wisdom of Solomon. I remember May's dog, June. I don't think he liked those sweaters as much as she did, and I'm pretty sure being named June didn't sit well with him, either."

Kennedy turned around and saw Malcolm leaning against the wall, looking for all the world as if he enjoyed the show.

"You. I forgot about you." Kennedy generally loved Mondays, but she was not loving this particular one. She remembered her resolution and forced another smile. "What can I do for you, Malcolm?"

"I came for three reasons." He held up three fingers.

"Shoot." She waited for him to tell her that he was suing her for custody of the baby and hand her a bunch of legal papers. She felt a sick feeling of dread spread over her.

He bent down his ring finger. "First, I came to see if we could get together this week and go over the events? I'd like you to talk me through what I need to do for next weekend's craft fair."

"Sure. I'd already decided to ask if you'd allow me to help with it and with the Everything But a Dog day, too. Secondly?"

He bent down his middle finger. "Thursday's Thanksgiving. Pap is coming home for the day. I thought we could have Thanksgiving dinner together and tell him he's going to be a great-grandfather. He knows, but I'd like to make it official."

If he'd simply asked her to dinner, she wouldn't have felt bad saying no. Normally, she took Thanksgiving to recover from the first week of the shop's holiday craziness. She'd spend the day in pj's, watch the parades, and make herself a turkey breast. That was before she'd been pregnant and exhaustion was pretty much her constant companion. She needed a day off. But if Malcolm was asking her for Pap, she had to go. "Fine."

"I'm cooking. You're going to sit back and be waited on."

She should fight and assure him that she was capable of cooking, but to be honest, she knew she was going to be done in by Thursday.

"Fine," she said, and realized how ungracious she sounded, so she added, "thank you."

"Lastly." All three fingers were down now. He didn't say a word, but jerked his head in the direction of the delivery truck that pulled up outside. "I came to carry your order."

She remembered him yelling that first morning about her shoveling the dusting of snow, and she'd mentioned that she carried in orders and he'd had a cow. "How did you know it came now?"

"I knew you got them about this time because I asked Pap."

"I don't need you to—"

He cut her off again. "You don't need anyone. I know. You've made that clear. But I'm here anyway so you might as well let me help. I mean, if Clarence and May can work together, then certainly you can allow me to help a little. Think of it as me paying you back for all you do at the Center."

She sighed. "Fine. But only because I have about a dozen orders that need doing yesterday."

True to his word, Malcolm helped unload the shipment while she checked it. When everything was put away, she thought he'd stay and be underfoot, annoying her with talk and questions about the baby, but he simply said, "I'll see you tonight."

"I'll come over to the Center after I close up here."

"I can't wait," he said.

She could, but she didn't say so. Instead she said, "Great." She knew that the word came out with very little enthusiasm. But frankly, *very little* was more enthusiasm than she actually felt.

In her mind's eye, she'd run through telling Malcolm about the baby a dozen times. In her fantasies, his reactions ranged from benign indifference to out-and-out disbelief.

But no matter what his initial reaction was, in every scenario he'd left and gone back to Pittsburgh almost immediately.

And in most of those fantasies, he sold her the Center.

None of those scenarios matched what had happened.

All day long, as she made floral arrangements and a few fruit baskets, her thoughts kept coming back to the realization that nothing was going the way she'd imagined.

Thanks to Malcolm Carter the freakin' Fourth.

Oh, no, she hadn't thought about it before, but if she had a boy, would he expect her to name the kid Malcolm Carter V? No way was she heaping that name or the expectations that went with it on any child.

She didn't remember much about Malcolm's father, Malcolm Carter III.

She did remember him at Malcolm's graduation. Everyone in town turned out each year to see Cupid Falls' newest graduates. Malcolm had been there, looking so handsome in his cap and gown.

She'd long since given up hope of him noticing her by then, but she couldn't seem to help noticing him. His mom and Pap had smiled as they hugged him and offered him words of congratulation. Their pride had been palpable.

Then his father—who'd made it at the last minute—had walked over and joined the group. From her vantage point a few feet away, she saw Malcolm open his arms, as if expecting his father to hug him as well. Then after a few awkward seconds, his arms fell back to his sides and his father patted his shoulder. Even that seemed awk-weird.

She smiled as she thought about her teenage version of the word.

She'd used it so often Aunt Betty threatened to fine her if she didn't stop.

She hadn't thought about that in years.

"You can use whatever odd words you want, as often as you want," she whispered to the baby.

She wished she had something else to do around the shop, but she didn't. So she bundled up and walked over to the Center.

It was unfortunate that Malcolm worked next to her all day, then lived in Pap's house next to her all night. Well, at least until he went back to his life in Pittsburgh. He had to go soon. A lawyer couldn't take an indefinite leave. He had clients, responsibilities. That was his excuse for not coming home for so long. It made sense he'd have to get back.

She let herself into the Center and called, "Malcolm?"

"In the office."

He looked up as she walked in. "You okay?"

"Long day." She wanted to finish this and go home and collapse. She knew she'd have to take off some time after the baby came. She'd fretted about it for months and finally had teamed up with a florist in Erie. Calls to her shop would be forwarded to them, and they'd fill the orders for her. It was a huge hit to her bank account, but she'd been squirreling money away since she'd found out about the baby. She'd be fine. She had to imagine that working with a baby at the shop had to be easier than working when she was as big as a house.

"Sorry to make to make your day longer," he said, sounding genuinely contrite.

"No problem," Kennedy said, even though it was. "Did you look over my proposal?"

"I did. Have you thought about mine?" He didn't clarify.

Kennedy didn't really need him to. "Malcolm, I have. But I can't come up with one good reason for us to marry."

He looked as if he were searching for that reason and finally said, "We should marry because we're going to be parents."

"You've said that before." She didn't know much, but she knew marrying for the sake of a baby couldn't work.

As a florist, she was sort of a bartender of relationships. She knew who was in the doghouse, or *froghouse* in Clarence's case. She knew who sent sweet gifts just because. When they came and ordered flowers, most people shared the reason. She knew what she wanted in a relationship of her own, and being with someone for a baby's sake wasn't on the list. But even without all that, she knew there was only one reason to marry—only one reason that could possibly make two people joining their lives together work. And because they were going to be parents wasn't it. Practicality wasn't it.

She shook her head. "Thank you for asking, but the answer is still no. But what about my proposal to buy the Center?"

Malcolm's eyes narrowed as if he were trying to think of some lawyerly response. "I'd consider giving it to you as a wedding gift."

She laughed as if she thought he meant it as a joke, though she wasn't quite sure that he had. "You can't buy me, Malcolm. This isn't some contract negotiation where you can find the proper terms to make me do what you want."

"I'm a lawyer. Negotiating is a big part of that."

She was insulted. If she wouldn't marry him for a baby's sake, why would he think she'd marry him to get the Center? "Well, good try, but no."

"I'll ask again," he said. "To clarify, that's a promise, not a threat. I really think that being married is the right thing to do for our child."

Kennedy thought about making some retort, but in the end she decided it was safer to change the subject. "About the upcoming engagements. Most of the receptions and parties are easy. You unlock the door, then come back when it's over and lock it again. Most people handle their own cooking and stage the facility on their own. Cleanup is also part of their contract. But we provide any and all if they're willing to pay for it. Tavi and Gus have been doing the catering for us, and I have a list of kids I hire—well, you hire—to set up or clean up when necessary."

She pointed to the lists on the wall. "And that's our cleaning crew and . . ."

Half an hour later, Kennedy was pretty sure Malcolm could handle the upcoming events. He'd worked at the Center often enough as a kid. He needed to get caught up on the new procedures his mom had set up. Everything was simple, once you understood it. She was pretty sure he could handle things on his own. "Your mom really streamlined Pap's system."

He looked at the laminated lists on the wall. "She did."

Kennedy had bought Val her own laminator last Christmas. Malcolm's mom had fun using it all over the office. She'd call and fill Kennedy in on what new item had benefitted from her new toy.

Kennedy felt a pang as she realized Val wouldn't call her again.

Malcolm's expression looked as if he was missing her, too.

"Sorry. Does it hurt to talk about her?" she asked.

He thought a moment, then shook his head. "It did. At first it hurt so much. Something would happen and I'd reach for my phone to call her, and realize I couldn't. I'd call Pap, and he's always been so supportive, but he's not Mom."

"She was a special lady," Kennedy agreed. "After I got home from college and moved back in with Aunt Betty, Val found me sitting on the porch reading a book. She said she was baking her world-famous oatmeal cookies and could use a hand. She asked if I'd be interested."

"She taught you to make her cookies?" There was a gleam in his eye she'd never seen before as he asked.

Kennedy nodded. "She taught me a lot about cooking."

"Me too. I'd call and ask how do you make this or that, and she'd help me through it, but I never asked about the cookies. She always had a plate of them when I came home. So I never needed to make them on my own. I missed finding them waiting for me when I got here the other day."

Without thinking, Kennedy reached over and placed her hand on his.

He finished, "It really didn't feel like coming home at all."

"I'm sorry," she said.

Val had always been the picture of health. The night before she passed away, she'd gone to the movies with Kennedy, like they did most Mondays.

Then Tuesday morning, Pap had called with the horrible news. He'd sounded so confused. *She'd slept in. That's all I thought. She'd slept in. Only she wasn't sleeping,* he'd said over and over.

Kennedy had hurried over and was there when the ambulance came. The doctors said it was an aneurism. They said there was no way anyone could have known. Knowing there was nothing they could have done didn't ease the pain.

Malcolm looked as lost tonight as Pap had looked that morning.

She missed Val so much. She could only imagine how much more Malcolm was suffering. She almost leaned over to hug him but pulled herself back and pulled her hand back as well.

He shot her a questioning look.

"This is what got us in trouble in the first place," she said. "I think we better stick to talking about business—"

He added, "Or the baby."

"Or the baby," she agreed. "We'll stick to the present or even the baby's future. The past gets us in trouble. But it was nice to remember her." Val had been a friend. A mentor. And whenever Kennedy realized that Val was this baby's grandmother and that the baby would never know her, she cried.

She blamed pregnancy hormones for the tears welling in her eyes as she said, "Val was an amazing lady."

"Yeah, she was. When I was younger, the fact our names rhymed presented all kinds of confusion."

When they were kids, she'd thought of him as Mal, but she'd referred to his mom as Mrs. Carter then. Later, he was Malcolm to her, and Val was Val, so there was still no rhyming. "I never really thought about it, but I can imagine it did. Why didn't they name you something else?"

"Mom wanted to," he said. "Dad insisted his son would carry on the family name. He always referred to me as Malcolm and her as Valerie. He insisted it wasn't a problem. The rest of the world called us Val and Mal. Except you?" He turned the statement into an almost question.

Kennedy found herself answering. "I don't know why. Malcolm seems more lawyerly. It seems like a serious name. A name to be reckoned with. Mal seems like a young kid or the captain of a starship."

"Huh?" he asked, looking confused.

"You never watched *Firefly* or *Serenity*?" Kennedy was a sci-fi geek. She didn't go around wearing costumes and didn't speak Klingon, at least not in public, but she loved all things science fiction.

"No, I've never seen them," Malcolm said.

"You've missed out. And speaking of out, it's time for me to go. I think you're caught up on how things run here. If you run into any trouble, holler. And I hope before you go home to Pittsburgh you consider my offer on the business."

She rose with difficulty and asked, "Just when are you leaving?" She tried not to infuse too much hope in the question, but when Mal frowned, she wasn't sure she'd succeeded.

"Like I said," he said slowly, "I'm not leaving until we've worked things out. My father's none too happy about it, but I know I can't go yet, Kennedy."

"Oh."

He offered her a small smile. "Don't sound so enthused at the thought of my staying here."

She didn't want to tell him how absolutely unenthused she really was, so she simply said, "I really need to head home."

71

Malcolm sprang from his chair with ease. "Wait a minute while I lock up and I'll walk back with you."

"It's okay, Malcolm. It's only four blocks. Just because I'm pregnant doesn't mean I'm incapable of looking after myself."

"Kennedy, were you always this prickly, or is it the pregnancy?" Before she could answer, he added, "I'm heading home anyway and it doesn't make sense to walk separately. I mean, I could follow behind you, but that looks a bit stalkery, doesn't it? And what if May saw me skulking after you? She'd be calling the cops for sure."

There was no way to say no and not sound rude, so Kennedy resigned herself to walking home with Malcolm. She waited while he turned off lights and locked the back door.

He offered her his arm as they approached the snow-dusted sidewalk.

"I'm capable of walking on my own, Malcolm. I'm pregnant, not an invalid." She realized that did sound prickly. She was pretty sure it wasn't the pregnancy, but Malcolm who brought it out in her.

He dropped his arm.

They walked side by side down Main Street to the corner and turned onto a residential street. It was seven on a November evening, so it was already dark and the lights from the homes spilled out the windows.

Kennedy walked this way home every day. She knew the houses, knew each family.

"Mr. Peterson's sidewalk's cleared," she murmured more to herself than Malcolm.

"And that's a good thing?" he asked.

"It means I won't get a visit from May Williams tomorrow complaining. Well, she might complain, but it won't be about his sidewalk."

"May has always been a spitfire. She rented the Center once for some party and my mother swore that she'd never make that mistake again. If May asked about a date, we'd be booked or closed for repairs. She said she'd paint the place herself in order to escape May's nitpicking."

"That bad?" Kennedy asked.

"She made my mom dust the ceiling."

"Pardon?" She laughed. She could almost hear Val complaining about dusting a ceiling.

"May claimed the ceiling was dusty and she didn't want dust dropping in her food."

"Oh, I can so imagine her tone. 'Val, your ceiling is dusty. How do I know? Why, I saw a dust mote float to the floor. Yes, only one, but if there's one, there's more. What if that piece of dust fell on my cucumber sandwiches?'" Having dealt with May on a regular basis since becoming mayor, Kennedy was pretty sure she'd nailed her impression of her.

Malcolm burst into out-and-out laughter. "Yes, that was about it."

"She's been really difficult lately. I really think it has to do with her losing June. I'm hoping I can convince her to adopt a new dog at the Everything But a Dog event."

"I'm not sure a dog will be enough," he teased.

His shoulder brushed hers as they crossed the street to the second block. Kennedy felt an urge to lean into it. But she held herself back. *Present or future*, she reminded herself. Talking about the past was obviously trouble.

She searched for something innocuous to say. "It's a beautiful night" was the best she could come up with.

"I always liked walking at night," Malcolm replied. "I forget how much when I'm in Pittsburgh. I leave for the office in the morning, come home, pull in the garage, and go straight inside. I'm always so busy that I forget to take a break and get outside."

"I live so close to work, I rarely drive. I can stop in at Elmer's Market and get any groceries I need over lunch."

She contrasted the life he'd described in Pittsburgh and her life here. His seemed incredibly lonely to her. "I can't imagine never going outside and not being able to walk to things. I can go weeks without using my car. That's one of my favorite parts of Cupid Falls. It's a green thing."

She made a mental note to try to think about a green campaign for town. She'd heard the term *ecotourism* bandied around. She'd have to explore the idea. After all, they had Lincoln Lighting now. It made LED lights and had started making solar panels, too. That was as green as green could get. She was always looking for angles to promote Cupid Falls, so she filed it away and concentrated on Malcolm.

"Mom used to walk me to school every day, then pick me up. Until I got so old that I told her it was embarrassing. I wish I'd have realized . . ." He stopped, as if there was so much he wished he'd have realized that he couldn't list it all.

"Your mom and I walked home in the evening together. Pap came along if we went in the mornings, but he was gone by the time she closed up the shop. We walked home most nights on this same route."

Malcolm didn't say anything.

"She used to talk about you, you know. She was so proud of you." But it was more than that. Val used to tell Kennedy every detail of Malcolm's life. When he graduated college, when he got accepted to law school. She shared the big moments in his life in the most minute of details.

Kennedy wouldn't let him know how much she knew about him. She knew about his first big heartbreak.

She knew how much Malcolm wanted to please his father.

She knew that Val had worried that he felt torn between his parents. Val had always tried to shelter him from her difficulties with his father.

Kennedy wanted to reach out and take Malcolm's hand.

Present or future, she scolded herself. She couldn't allow herself to get lost in the past and feel bad about things she couldn't change.

"I love how quiet it is this time of night," Kennedy said, trying to place them firmly back in the present.

"I like how the houses are all lit up. You can imagine the family all coming together after a day of school or work," Mal said.

Kennedy caught the beginning of the fantasy and added, "Sitting down and sharing their day as they share a meal."

Malcolm must have sensed the rhythm. He added, "Maybe the neighbor runs over for sugar."

"No, that's cliché," Kennedy scolded. "Maybe the neighbor runs over for cinnamon."

"Cinnamon?" Mal asked with a chuckle.

"I was thinking about your mom's oatmeal cookies, and she always claimed the cinnamon was the trick." What was wrong with her? Thinking about Val, about their loss, got them in trouble.

"Oh, great," Mal said, a note of teasing in his voice. "I'd forgotten the cookies, but now I'm pining for them again."

Kennedy pulled the conversation back to the present. "About our fictional family, maybe the dog's jumping up on them, begging to go for a walk."

She pointed across the street at Lamar Thomas. He was a big, burly man. His father was a fisherman back when Lake Erie was populated with fishing boats. Lamar's father had fished, even through retirement, even as the number of fishing boats dwindled.

Lamar had grown up on the boat, and now he was Cupid Falls' street department. A department of one. He did more than plow and maintain . . . he was a general handyman. Kennedy had never asked Lamar to do something and not had him find a way to accomplish it.

"Hi, Lamar. Hi, Otis." Otis was his aging cocker spaniel.

"Good evening, Mayor. Mal," he called back as they passed.

Mal looked back at the man and his dog. "Do I know him?"

"No, I don't think so. He moved here from Erie."

"But he knew my name," Mal said, glancing back again.

Kennedy laughed. "You've been in Pittsburgh too long. You forget what it's like here in Cupid Falls. Everyone knows everyone, even if they don't. And everyone knows everyone's business, even when it's none of theirs. You have always been the subject of a lot of the town's talk. Malcolm Carter the Fourth, Esquire. It's a 'local boy moves to the big city and makes good' sort of thing."

He glanced back again, but Kennedy didn't need to in order to know Lamar had long since turned the corner with Otis and headed home. Malcolm was still quiet, which made her nervous, so she blurted out, "Did you know Lamar means 'from the ocean'?"

"No."

"Lamar's father said he didn't know a name that meant 'from the Great Lake,' so he went with Lamar."

Malcolm still didn't say anything.

"His dad retired last year and moved in with Lamar. They're building a boat in Lamar's backyard."

"A boat?" he finally asked.

Kennedy nodded. "It's a small model of the *Brig Niagara*. To scale and everything."

"Oh."

Kennedy couldn't remember ever being so happy to see home. The timer had turned on the porch light for her, and Aunt Betty's house looked welcoming. "Thanks for walking me home."

She fled into the house. Malcolm stood and watched as she hurried inside, closed and locked the door behind her. She peeked out the window. He was still on the sidewalk. He looked like he was lost in thought. After another moment, he turned and walked the final few steps to Pap's house.

They'd talked about coming home to families at night, but neither of them was coming in to anything more than an empty house.

Kennedy hung up her coat.

She needed to make dinner. Maybe an omelet.

But more than that, she was thinking about making cookies.

Oatmeal raisin, with lots of cinnamon, to be exact.

CHAPTER FIVE

Mal was up early on Thursday to start the turkey. He'd put it in the brine solution yesterday. He remembered helping his mother with holiday turkeys. She used to squeal like a girl when he pulled the neck out of the cavity for her. *It's so gross*, she'd cry.

There had been no one around yesterday when he'd prepped the bird.

He realized that he'd missed Thanksgiving with his mom last year. He wished more than anything he could go back in time. He'd have come down the day before Thanksgiving and prepped the bird for his mom. He'd have hung out in the kitchen and helped with the rest of the cooking.

But there were no do-overs.

Maybe that's why he was still in Cupid Falls. He wanted to do things right with Kennedy and the baby the first time around.

He glanced at the plate of oatmeal cookies Kennedy had left on his porch.

There was no note. Nothing to indicate they were from her. But the minute he'd opened the plastic container he'd known.

And the gesture touched him. It also made him feel hopeful they'd make things work out, though he wasn't sure how.

For a man who spent a great deal of his life meticulously planning cases or even writing contracts, he still didn't have any solid idea what to do about Kennedy and the baby. He hoped that if they spent time together she'd see that he was right, they should get married for the baby's sake.

He popped a cookie in his mouth before getting to work on the dinner, and for a moment, all his confusion gave way to the feeling of being home.

He closed his eyes, and for that one moment, he felt his mother's presence.

When he opened his eyes, he realized there was one thing he could do for Kennedy—he could feed her a Thanksgiving dinner to remember.

He pulled the bird from the brine and saw that the light had gone on in Kennedy's kitchen.

He glanced at the clock. It was only six. She didn't have to work today, so this was awfully early.

He wondered if she was okay.

If the baby was all right.

Maybe it was kicking. Or maybe she was having more of those Braxton Hicks contractions. He'd been reading up on pregnancy and knew a lot of women experienced them, but he worried.

He knew that stress wasn't good for Kennedy or the baby. He patted the turkey dry.

He was certainly giving her stress, but he couldn't walk away like she wanted. He started spooning the stuffing he'd made into the bird.

So what was he going to do about Kennedy?

That was the question he needed to answer.

He finished up with the turkey and put it in the oven after he'd pulled out the pan of cinnamon rolls. They were another part of his mother's Thanksgiving tradition. She'd get up early to cook, and the cinnamon rolls were her reward.

The light was still on in Kennedy's kitchen.

He looked at the cake pan full of rolls and took half. He put them on a plate, then pulled on a pair of Pap's old boots at the back door and tucked his flannel pajama pants into them. He flipped the hood of his sweatshirt up over his head as he made a dash from his back door to Kennedy's. It hadn't snowed in a couple of days, but it was cold enough that the grass in the back was frozen hard, so the sprint was easy.

He knocked softly.

Kennedy came to the door with a smudge of flour on her nose, her hair in a braid down the back, and a bathrobe covered in balloons. "Malcolm, it's only six. What are you doing?"

"I was starting the turkey and saw your light on, so I brought you these." He thrust the plate at her. "If you let me in, they'd stay warm."

"I just put the pies in the oven."

"Then this is perfect timing. You can invite me in and we'll have a cup of coffee and a cinnamon roll before I head back over to clean up this first batch of dishes."

"Malcolm—"

He interrupted her. "Kennedy, it's a cinnamon roll and coffee. Think of them as a payback for the cookies."

She didn't acknowledge the cookies, but she did open the door wider and let him in. "Have a seat. It'll have to be decaf."

"That's fine. I switched over the other day." He sat down at the counter.

She turned around as she poured coffee into two mugs. "Why?"

"I handed you the decaf and looked at mine and felt guilty. I figured if you couldn't have caffeine, then I shouldn't, either. Sort of a misery-loves-company sort of thing."

She set the mugs down on the counter, then sat down. "You don't have to do that."

"Kennedy, I left you alone for most of this pregnancy. The least I can do is give you what little support I can." He nudged the plate toward her. "So now I drink decaf and bring you cinnamon rolls."

She laughed and took one. "They are still warm."

"Mom and I used to try to time it. The rolls came out as the turkey went into the oven. Then we'd celebrate. I don't think they'd taste the same if I ate them by myself, so you're doing me a favor."

She chuckled and took a bite. "They're so good."

"Mom made hers from scratch. Mine came from a can."

"Well, they're still good. Your mom would be pleased you're carrying on the tradition."

He took one himself. "I wish I'd been with her last Thanksgiving."

"Malcolm, she understood. There was so much pride in her voice every time she talked about you."

"Still . . ."

She set down the roll and said, "Do you know what she said once?"

"What?"

"She said you were the son that every mother wished she could have." Kennedy patted his arm. "She loved you, she was proud of you, and she knew you loved her. That's something to take comfort in."

"Thank you." He reached over and wiped the flour from her nose. "Flour," he explained as she shot him a questioning look. He pulled his hand back.

Kennedy reached up and rubbed her own face as they finished their rolls in companionable silence.

Mal felt . . . a bit more settled. His mother knew he loved her. He still wished he'd been around more, but she'd understood.

"I was thinking about do-overs this morning," he said.

"Do-overs?"

"If I could go back, I'd do things differently. I'd come home more often. Not just on special days, but just for the heck of it. I'd surprise Mom. I'd show up at the Center and walk home with the two of you, like we did the other night."

"She'd have loved that." Kennedy smiled, as if imagining the scene with him.

"That's what I want you to know," he said softly.

"There are no do-overs?" she asked.

"That's right. You and me . . . we didn't plan on being in this position, but here we are. We need to get this whole parenting thing right the first time, because if we screw it up, we can't go back and fix it. If we screw up, it will be our child who pays the price."

He waited for Kennedy to say something. To agree. When the silence dragged on too long, Mal decided to say it all at once. "That's why I asked you to marry me. Our child deserves to have two parents. I can't tell you how many times I wished my parents were still together so that I wouldn't always feel as if I was being disloyal to one of them. If my dad made arrangements to have me in Pittsburgh and I didn't really want to go because I had something going on in Cupid Falls. Or if I was in Pittsburgh enjoying myself, I'd feel guilty knowing Mom and Pap were here missing me."

"You couldn't ever make both of them happy," she stated, not asked.

That was an understatement. "No. So I tried to make them both proud. I did well in school and played sports, but nothing I did ever felt like enough. Nothing could ever change the situation."

"Malcolm . . ." She reached across and touched his hand. For a moment, he thought she was going to hold it, but she pulled her hand back and said, "When I was young, I had a crush on this boy. I wanted him to notice me, to fall madly in love with me, and to realize he couldn't live without me."

"Did he ever notice you?"

Kennedy shook her head. "No. But the point is, I learned that I'm okay on my own."

She busied herself with spreading more butter on her cinnamon roll, and Malcolm realized that it was more than that school crush. She'd lost her parents and found herself living with her aunt.

He remembered her aunt. She was a no-nonsense woman who didn't seem overly inclined to shower Kennedy with love and affection.

Kennedy had been alone, looking for someone to love her. And she'd fallen for some guy . . . some guy who couldn't see what an amazing woman she was.

Mal wish she'd told him the guy's name. He wasn't the kind to seek out someone and punch him for something that happened in high school, but he wouldn't be opposed to accidentally stepping on the idiot's foot.

He smiled at the thought.

"What?" Kennedy asked.

"I was thinking that you and I might not have all the answers, but we both agree on one thing."

"What's that?"

"The baby is the priority. If we can always remember that—always put him first—we won't get too far off track."

This time she reached over and didn't just brush her hand across his . . . she held it.

"I think you're right."

The timer buzzed and she pulled back her hand. "The pies should be done."

Mal glanced at the clock. "I better get back and check on the turkey."

"Thanks for sharing," she said, gesturing to the rolls.

He nodded. He wanted to thank her for sharing, too. He knew they weren't any closer to figuring out how to share their child, but after their exchange, he felt pretty sure that given some time, they'd figure it out.

～

It was just after one that afternoon when Kennedy walked over to Pap's house. She was holding two pies and waiting for Malcolm to answer the door. He'd only stayed a half hour this morning, but that half hour had shaken her.

There was something so . . .

Intimate. That was the word.

There was something so intimate about sharing coffee and cinnamon rolls with him while she was wearing a bathrobe.

Sharing decaffeinated coffee.

He'd switched because she had. That touched her.

She felt as if they'd built some connection, and she wasn't sure she wanted to do that. If she had a connection to Malcolm, it might make things harder since he wanted to be involved with the baby. Keeping things civil but distant. That's what she wanted.

This morning threw that off. She wished she'd said no to dinner, but since she hadn't, she was going to try to build that relationship. Civil. That's what she was going for. So she pasted her best flower-shop-civil smile on her face in preparation—she'd used it a lot with May. But it wasn't Malcolm who opened the door, it was Pap Watson.

"Pap, you're back," she said with genuine delight as she set the pies down on the small table in the entry and hugged him. It was an awkward hug because the baby had pushed her stomach to ridiculous expanses.

"I am back. Course, I'm heading back to Erie right after dinner. I've got plans at six, that's why we're eating in the afternoon here."

"So who is this mystery woman?" she asked as he shut the door and she started to debundle. Most years she didn't mind cold-weather layers, but this year it was one more thing to try and work around. "She must be pretty special."

Pap's eyes narrowed. "How do you know there's a woman?"

"Look at you. No flannel. No worn jeans. You're all spit and polish. You look dapper, Pap. Of course there's a woman."

"Did anyone ever mention you're a sassy girl?" He said it with a grin, so she knew he was teasing.

"You might have, once or twice." She kissed his weathered cheek, then stood back and looked at him. She realized that this was the happiest she'd seen him since Val had passed. "I'm so glad. You deserve to be happy."

"Everyone does, sweetie. Not everyone manages it, though. I'm lucky. I'll introduce you to her at the Bow-Wow Ball. I still say that's a lame name for the fund-raiser."

"Don't look at me. Clarence Harding started it when he heard the proceeds for the Christmas Ball were going to the Everything But a Dog Foundation. He barks every time he comes into the floral shop, no matter how many times I've told him it's Bow . . . long *O*. Bow as in Cupid's bow and arrow."

Pap laughed. "Kennedy, you are an original."

"I'm doing my best to promote the town. Did I tell you that Aggie Samuels requested a variance so she can open a business in the residential part of town? The Cupid Falls Bed and Breakfast. How wonderful would that be? And I think I've found the money to expand the trail to the falls into a real bike path. Next summer we can have tours. Gus mentioned buying some bikes and maybe eventually some Segways and renting them out from The Cupboard's old barn . . ."

∼

Mal stayed in the kitchen cooking as he listened to Pap and Kennedy catch up. Her enthusiasm for the town was only rivaled by her plans.

He'd found a notebook where Kennedy had obviously jotted down ideas for the Center. There was a bunch of pages with a *VD Ideas* header. It had given him a start until he realized she meant Valentine's Day.

"Should we help Malcolm?" he heard her ask.

"No, that boy is just like his mom. He doesn't like company when he cooks," Pap said.

That wasn't quite true. Mal did like company—he used to enjoy cooking with his mother, and he was pretty sure that he'd enjoy cooking with Kennedy. But he'd rather she sit down and put her feet up. She'd been up early this morning baking pies, and he couldn't help but notice the plethora of fruit baskets, gift baskets, and flowers that lined the counter of her shop yesterday. She had to be exhausted.

The doorbell rang again.

Malcolm heard Pap go to answer the door. Kennedy came into the kitchen. "I brought the pies."

"Thank you." He nodded at an empty corner of the counter. She set them down.

"How're you feeling?" he asked as he mashed the potatoes with a hand masher. "Yesterday must have been crazy for you."

"I'm fine," she said in a tone that didn't brook any further comments.

He switched topics. "I'm going to tell Pap about the baby at dinner. He knows, but I don't think he'll acknowledge it until we make it official."

She nodded. "Fine. But you don't have to."

"Kennedy, I—"

Pap came into the kitchen, interrupting what was sure to be an argument. "Look what the cat dragged in . . . or rather who."

Mal liked to think that being an attorney had taught him to be prepared for the unexpected and that he was prepared for most contingencies. Well, unexpected was one thing and his father walking into the kitchen was entirely another. He wasn't sure he could prepare for a contingency like that.

CHAPTER SIX

Mal tried to see his father through Kennedy's eyes. Malcolm Carter III was a tall man. His dark hair had faded to a steely grey that perfectly matched his eyes. Today he wore a pair of black slacks and grey shirt and no tie. That was Senior's version of dressed down.

He glanced at Kennedy, who was frowning at his father.

"Dad, what brings you to Cupid Falls? I thought you said you were spending the long weekend prepping for the Montgomery case?" He loved his father, but he knew his grandfather and father were like oil and water . . . they didn't mix at all. And from Kennedy's expression, she wasn't pleased to see him, either.

Frankly, neither was he. Having his father in Cupid Falls had never been a good thing. They got along so much better in Pittsburgh. They were colleagues there. They had business in common. Here? They were simply father and son, and they'd never quite figured out how that should work.

"It's Thanksgiving. I thought I'd give the whole family holiday a try."

That was a first for his dad. Mal hated to be cynical, but there was something more going on here.

Kennedy stood, and Mal saw his father's expression of shock as he took in her condition. "And this is?"

Before Mal could introduce her, she said, "I'm Kennedy Anderson. We've met before, Mr. Carter. I was your ex-wife's friend, and I think I'm your son's friend as well."

She glanced at Mal, and he smiled at her description of their relationship, hoping that reassured her that he thought it was a fair description.

"Kennedy forgot to add that in addition to being my friend, she's also going to be the mother of my child." He turned to Pap and said, "Sorry. We meant to announce it at dinner. I know you already knew." Before his grandfather could protest, Mal added, "Or at least suspected, but we wanted to make an official announcement."

Pap walked over and hugged Kennedy. "I'm thrilled. I'm going to be a great-grandfather. Did I say *thrilled*? That doesn't even begin to cover it. I'm beyond thrilled."

Senior stood there, stunned into unfamiliar silence.

In for a penny, in for a pound, Mal thought and added, "And in the interest of honesty, I've asked Kennedy to marry me, but she's said no. I plan to ask again, and I won't be back in Pittsburgh until things are settled here, sir."

"What have you done?" his father finally asked. "I would have thought you'd have learned from my mistakes. I came here on a case and met a girl I thought I couldn't live without, so I married her and brought her home to Pittsburgh with me. I thought love trumped everything. I should have known better. Valerie wasn't interested in being an attorney's wife or living in the city. She missed this ridiculous small town. But by then, I was trapped. Tied to her and this place because of you."

Mal was accustomed to his father's shoot-from-the-hip blunt ways, but try as he might, he couldn't manage to avoid his father's direct hits—they still hurt after all these years. "Gee, thanks, Dad."

"That's not what I meant, Malcolm." His father sighed. It was a sound of pure frustration. "I simply meant your mother and I were never suited for each other. I think we did really love each other once, but our differences were too great. She couldn't understand my need to work, and I couldn't understand . . . her. I never really understood anything about her. The only thing that held us together for the five years we managed was you."

"Aka, the mistake." His father looked as if he wanted to say something else, but Mal cut him off. "Senior, I think we should stop talking about the past. It's only going to lead to trouble." He shot Kennedy a look and she smiled. "We'll concentrate on the present and the future. And at the present, this turkey is almost ready. Kennedy, why don't you set a place for my father? Pap, why don't you take him in the dining room before he puts his other foot in his mouth."

Pap led the uncharacteristically compliant Senior out of the room.

Mal turned to the mother of his child. "Kennedy, I'm sorry."

She shook her head. "You have nothing to be sorry about."

"I do. I shouldn't have announced the baby that way. My father does have a way of putting me on the defensive. It's a great trait for an attorney, but he can't seem to turn it off outside the courtroom, and it's not quite the great trait in a father."

"It's fine. You were bound and determined to announce it one way or another, so it doesn't matter."

"You wouldn't have announced it?" he asked.

"No. People in town have accepted the fact that their unwed mayor is pregnant. I don't think we need to complicate the issue by telling them their golden boy is the father. I'd hoped to tell you about the baby, then have you head back to Pittsburgh and get back to your own life and leave me to the baby."

He placed the turkey on his grandmother's platter. "I think I'm insulted that you think I'd walk away."

Kennedy sighed. "That sounded harsher than I meant. It's just that . . ." She paused.

Mal was getting used to Kennedy's silences. As a lawyer he understood the need to sort out your arguments, but he didn't want to argue with Kennedy. He actually preferred her when she occasionally let some uncensored comment escape. He might not like what she said, and it might even sting, but at least it gave him a bit of true insight into her—into the woman who was going to be the mother of his child.

She finally continued, "Maybe your father summed it up. Your parents loved each other, but they were too different. Their love couldn't bear the weight of those differences. I think we're friends—or at least on the way to being friends. If love couldn't make their marriage work, then what chance does almost-friendship have?"

And with an attorney-worthy bit of summation, she'd hit the nail on the head. She was right about that, so why didn't he care that she was right? Why did he want to ask her again, right now, to marry him?

And why did he wish she'd say yes?

"Kennedy, I—"

"I'd better go set your father's place," she said as she fled.

~

Kennedy wasn't sure what Malcolm had been about to say, but she had a feeling whatever it had been was best left unsaid. Facing his father was preferable. She set the plate and silverware down in front of Malcolm's father.

"How are you feeling?" he asked politely.

"I'm fine. Thank you, sir."

There was an awkward pause, and then he asked, "When are you due?"

Her hands fell to her stomach. The gesture had become more and more common because her stomach was so huge there was nowhere else for her hands to rest. "I'm due in a few weeks."

"And you just let my son know now?" There was censure in his voice.

Pap cleared his throat. "I think we should all remember that this is a holiday. And holidays are about families. Like it or not, that's what we are. Senior is the father of my grandson, and Kennedy, you're the mother of my great-grandson, and a good friend to boot. This baby is going to tie us all together as a family from this point on. And I refuse to let him ever feel as if he, or she, is responsible for any fights between us."

"I agree," Malcolm said as he walked into the room with a turkey on a platter. "We might not be a traditional family, but the four of us are a family. We're all tied to an unborn baby—a baby who didn't ask to be born. And we will all put the baby's needs and wants first. We will never make him or her feel as if they are anything but a joy to all of us. And if anyone"—he looked at Senior—"can't abide by that one, very important rule, then they should get out. And get out now."

His father looked as startled as Kennedy felt by the ferocity in Malcolm's voice.

Mr. Carter said, "I—"

But Malcolm interrupted him. "Right now, the only appropriate discussion is how amazing my turkey is, and possibly a list of things we're thankful for. You can all think on that and put together a list as I bring in the rest of the dishes."

Kennedy watched Malcolm make half a dozen trips to and from the kitchen. His expression said, more clearly than words, that no one should offer to help, much less talk to him.

She looked at his father, whose anger was palpable. She had a feeling Malcolm Carter III was not accustomed to being spoken to in that manner, and he wasn't overly fond of the experience.

Finally she looked at Pap, who grinned and winked at her.

When all the serving dishes were on the table, Malcolm sat down.

"I'll go first," he said. "I'm thankful that I'm going to be a father. It's something I didn't plan and I've hardly had time to adjust to, but I'm thrilled. I'm thankful that my child will have a mother like Kennedy. Someone who works hard for what she wants and has an innate kindness. I'm thankful to be sharing this meal with everyone I love. I'm thankful that a simple plate of oatmeal cookies finally made me feel that I'd come home."

Kennedy wasn't sure what had prompted her to make the cookies for Malcolm, but she was suddenly glad that she had.

Pap said, "I'm thankful that while I might be old, I'm still young enough to appreciate a fine woman when I see one and snap her up." He winked at Kennedy again. "And I'm thankful that because of my age, I realized that as you get older you never find yourself wishing you had more time to work, you find yourself wishing you had more time for the people in your life. I'm also thankful that my grandson came home to take care of business and that Kennedy will help him as much as she's always helped me. Finally, I'm very, very thankful I'm going to be a great-grandfather."

Everyone looked at Kennedy. She'd never done anything like this with Aunt Betty during the holidays. Her parents hadn't done this at Thanksgiving, but to this day she could remember them being happy about the smallest things. Her father would show up with daisies and her mom would act as if he'd given her a diamond. She'd buy him a new shirt and he'd act very much the same.

She'd asked her mom about it once, and she'd said, *If I can be thankful and happy about the smallest things in my life, imagine the joy I feel over the bigger things, like having you as a daughter. Life's too short not to appreciate all the moments.* She missed her parents so much, even after more than a dozen years. In a few more years she'd have lived half her life without them. And she felt a wave of kindredness with Malcolm and Pap.

She cleared her throat, trying to push back all the emotions that sat so close to the surface, and managed to say, "I'm so thankful that the baby's healthy and will be here soon. And I'm thankful to be here . . . to feel like I'm part of a family for the first time in a long time."

They waited as if they wanted her to say more, but Kennedy was done.

Everyone turned to Senior. "I'm thankful to be having dinner with my son and *his* family" was all he said.

Malcolm's sigh was audible. But he smiled and said, "Let's eat."

Somehow Kennedy got through the dinner. It was a shame that it was so long and arduous, because under other circumstances, she'd have enjoyed it very much. Malcolm was a good cook. Kennedy dutifully put bite after bite in her mouth. She wished Malcolm's father were anywhere but here.

Everyone except Mr. Carter tossed out a few conversational gambits, but they all faded or simply fizzled almost as soon as they started.

When the meal finished, Kennedy managed to resist the urge to clap with joy.

"Go sit down in the living room, Kennedy," Malcolm said. "The guys are going to clear and do dishes. Your only job today is to rest. I'll call you for dessert."

"Normally I'd argue, but yesterday was exhausting, so I'll meekly go kick up my feet."

And while yesterday *was* busy, Kennedy acquiesced more because she welcomed a break from Mr. Carter.

She went into the living room and sat down on the couch she'd sat on a thousand times with Val. Malcolm's mother had a collection of old teacups. She had loved having a reason to make tea and drink out of her fancy cups.

Kennedy hadn't had a good cup of tea since Val had died. She could blame it on the pregnancy, but the truth was, having tea was something she did with Val. She couldn't bring herself to do it solo.

Mondays were the worst days. Kennedy would be in the middle of making a flower arrangement and think, *It's Movie Monday*, and then remember it wasn't. Or she'd hear movie reviews on the radio and think about telling Val about which ones sounded good. And every time she remembered that she'd never have another Movie Monday with Val it was like a punch in the gut. She hadn't gone to a movie in the theater since Val's death. She just couldn't face going without her.

Kennedy's hand strayed to her child. Val's grandchild. Her parents' grandchild. The baby would never know any of them.

Kennedy looked around the room, her hand still protectively covering her unborn baby. There were so many pieces of Val here.

Kennedy remembered buying the red throw on the back of the recliner. She'd given it to Val for a birthday. Malcolm's mom loved things that were soft, and this was like butter. Kennedy struggled up off the couch and ran her hand over it as she passed by the chair on her way to the mantel and the pictures that lined it. She'd seen them a million times. Malcolm as a baby. He wasn't on a bearskin rug, but rather on a plaid blanket that was still folded at the end of his boyhood bed. Pap and Val dancing at the Center. Pap and his wife on their wedding day, posed in front of the falls. Pap, Val, and Malcolm on his high school graduation day.

Kennedy picked that one up. She thought again about that awkweird graduation, Malcolm craning over his shoulder to look for his father.

She knew he was watching because she'd watched, too. She'd been keenly aware of his disappointment. She'd shared it in a way. Aunt Betty had been there for her, but she'd wanted her parents there as much as Malcolm had wanted his dad. She'd felt a certain kinship with him. She knew what it was like to want what you couldn't have.

Even after Mr. Carter finally showed up, he hadn't sat with Val and Pap. And later, he'd kept his distance.

She noticed something she'd never seen before in that graduation picture. There she was in the background. She was sitting in a folding chair, looking at the family as someone snapped the picture.

That was pretty much the story of her life. In the background. Always one step removed from everyone.

She put the picture back and her hands fell to her stomach again. The baby gave her a satisfying kick.

Soon she'd have a family again. She hadn't felt she belonged to anyone since her parents died. Oh, Aunt Betty was family, but she had looked at Kennedy as more of a burden—a burden she had to bear. And once Kennedy grew up, she'd looked at her as help, and later yet, as a colleague.

"Kennedy, are you okay?"

She whirled around and found Malcolm staring at her from the doorway. "I'm fine. Thank you for asking."

Malcolm came over to the hearth and looked at the picture. "I miss her so damn much."

"Me too. I was thinking that I hadn't been to a movie since she died."

"Movie?" he asked, standing next to her and looking at the pictures.

"Your mom and I had a standing date on Mondays. *Movie Mondays*, she called them. We saw wonderful ones, and sometimes we saw really bad ones. We gorged ourselves on popcorn until we were stuffed. But afterward we'd still go out to dinner, complaining the whole time about how full we were, and we'd discuss the movie. And we laughed. That's what I remember most about Val . . . her laughter. I miss it."

"Me too," he said, gently touching the picture of his mom as a girl at the falls behind the Center. She was wearing overalls and a Huck Finn hat and had a fishing pole slung over her shoulder. She'd told Kennedy that she hated fishing but had loved going to the creek with her father. "I never knew about your movie dates."

"We spent a lot of time together. She was my best friend." Kennedy had worried early on that her friendship with Val was an offshoot of her girlish crush on Malcolm, but soon that worry wasn't even on her radar. She loved Val for all the reasons everyone in town loved her—because it was impossible not to. She loved Val for simply being Val. Their May-December friendship might have seemed odd to some people, but maybe they each filled a void. What they had was different from a mother-child relationship—not more, but certainly not less. *Friends* was the best description Kennedy had, though she wasn't sure it truly reflected what they'd had.

Malcolm studied her a moment, then nodded. "Are you up for dessert? I'm sorry about my father. I know he's a hard man, but—"

She interrupted his apology. "Malcolm, what he is, what he says, it's on him. You don't ever need to apologize for either. And I'm tougher than I look. I can handle your father."

He smiled. "So much of who he is makes him a great attorney, but sometimes that gets in the way of him being . . ."

Kennedy thought about helping Malcolm fill in the blank by saying a *human being*, but that sounded cold, so she said, "It gets in the way of him being warm and cuddly?"

Malcolm laughed. Genuinely laughed. "Yeah, I'm pretty sure that's a description no one has ever used for my dad."

He wrapped an arm around her shoulder and hugged her to him as he led her back to the dining room.

Kennedy thought about wiggling away from his touch, but this once, she sensed they both needed to feel connected to someone else, so she let it be and let him lead her back to the dining room.

⁓

Mal watched as Kennedy finished her pumpkin pie, then said, "I really need to go now. Tomorrow is going to be crazy, and I want to nap today in preparation for it, because there will be no napping for a few days."

He was sure she did need to nap, given her condition. But he was equally sure she was ready to get away from his father. Frankly, he didn't blame her.

"Thanks for coming," he said as his father scowled.

Pap stood as well. "Hold on, Kennedy, I'll walk you out." He smiled at Mal. "You are still one of the best cooks I know."

"I learned from the best," Mal said.

"You did." Pap joined Kennedy in the doorway. "Don't get up. We know our way out, don't we, Kennedy?"

She smiled and linked hands with his grandfather. "We'll be fine. Thanks again for dinner, Malcolm. It was wonderful."

He heard their voices murmuring as they went toward the front door, though he couldn't tell what they were saying.

Moments later the door opened, then shut.

His father sat there, saying nothing.

"Thank you for coming," Mal said stiffly.

"You're going to give up everything you worked for, aren't you? You'll throw away your career and the position you've earned because of a fling with the girl next door?"

"It's a sabbatical, sir. I'm not walking away from anything."

"I see how you look at her. Every time she moved her hand to her stomach, you melted. You want to win. And you think getting this girl to marry you will be winning, but it won't. Marrying someone because you 'should' never works out. Not for you. Not for Kennedy. Not for the baby."

"I think we could build a good life. Kennedy is smart. She can do anything. Adjusting to life in Pittsburgh might be tough at first, but—"

"Wait, you think you can get her to move to Pittsburgh?" His father scoffed. "Never going to happen. She's the mayor here. She's a business owner. She has friends here. What could you offer her in Pittsburgh?"

Before Mal could answer, his father continued, "Nothing. You don't love her. I've known women like her—your mother was like her. That's what they want. Love. If you could love her, she might find happiness in Pittsburgh, but son, you're like me. You're married to the job. You like her. You want her. You might even be compatible with her. But that's not enough for her. And staying here with her? That won't be enough for you. I've seen you at work. You thrive on it. You could have a successful practice in this Podunk town, but you would never have the kind of practice I'm offering you."

He pushed back from the table. "I'll give you until the new year to figure it out for yourself. Either come back in the office by then, or don't come back at all. And if you don't come back, and then you realize I was right, it will be too late. I don't give second chances."

Mal watched his father leave. He tried to be concerned about his job, and realized he wasn't. For as long as he could remember, he'd wanted to be an attorney and work for his father's firm. To be honest, that's what his father had planned for him, and Mal had grown up with that assumption.

He wasn't sure what he'd thought would happen when he actually worked with his father. Maybe he'd thought if they were together on a daily basis, they'd develop a better relationship. A closer one.

He wasn't sure. But it was obvious that these last few years of working together hadn't worked. They had a business relationship. But they rarely shared so much as a meal with one another.

If he didn't work in his father's firm—if they didn't have business to bind them—what would they have?

He didn't know. But he had a month to decide what to do about his job.

By then Kennedy would have the baby, and maybe she'd think differently.

CHAPTER SEVEN

The next night, Kennedy let herself into her quiet house and breathed a sigh of relief. Black Friday had been crazy at the shop. She had a lot of holiday season orders, and it seemed like half of Cupid Falls had stopped by to see how her holiday was or to tell her about theirs.

She was late getting home but was thankful to close the door on the town. She hung her coat on the hook and went to lean down and take off her boots. She couldn't manage it. It had been an awkward endeavor for a while now, but tonight she seriously couldn't get her foot close enough to her hands, no matter how she twisted and turned. She hooked her left toes at the back of her right boot and pried it off that way. She put on a slipper and then did the reverse on her other boot.

It was official. She'd reached dirigible dimensions, which sounded nicer than saying she was a blimp.

She turned on the living room light and glared at the room, as if it were its fault it was so fussy. She'd never liked her aunt's decorating style, but until Malcolm asked about the baby's room, she'd never really thought about changing anything.

Maybe because this house had always been Aunt Betty's. It had never been *their* house—it had never been Kennedy's home. But

Aunt Betty was gone, and if this house wasn't home, Kennedy didn't know where she'd ever find one.

She suddenly didn't think she could spend one more evening sitting in *Aunt Betty's* living room. Her aunt was gone . . . but Kennedy wasn't.

She went to the basement, brought up a bunch of boxes, and got busy. Aunt Betty had been a collector of bric-a-brac, and the shelves on either side of the fireplace were full of *stuff.*

Kennedy grabbed a stack of newspaper and began wrapping them up and dropping them in the box. Soon all that was left on the shelves were books . . . which in her opinion was what the shelves were for.

She dusted and couldn't help but run her fingers along old favorites. They were all old hardbacks. Grace Livingston Hill was Aunt Betty's favorite. The copies were old and the slipcovers were yellow, but she remembered reading *The Spicebox* and *Miranda.* L. M. Montgomery's Green Gables books. Louisa May Alcott. Gene Stratton-Porter. She pulled out *A Girl of the Limberlost.* Oh, how she'd loved that book.

Yes, the books would stay. She'd found comfort in them when she'd first come to live here. And they felt like old friends on the shelf.

Next, Kennedy made a pile of doilies. And pulled the slipcovers off the furniture. Revealing the dark brown upholstery that her aunt had hated. But Aunt Betty hadn't believed in buying nonnecessities, so she'd sprung for slipcovers.

Aunt Betty had loved the pastel flower-covered pieces of polyester. But the original earth-toned wool suited Kennedy better. It looked warm and inviting.

She went up to her room and brought down her favorite afghan. Her mother had made it. Browns, oranges, rusty red stripes.

She put it over the back of the couch. It looked perfect.

She stood back and admired the room.

The fussy, flowery, dust-magnet room had been transformed into one that was warm and inviting. It seemed to beg her to light a fire, pull an old favorite book off the shelf, then cuddle up under the afghan her mother made.

But not now, she told herself. Now, she was on a mission.

She went into the dining room and decluttered it as well. She tore off the tablecloth and the plastic her aunt had kept, and revealed the dark, rectangular table. Her aunt thought it was too dark, but Kennedy loved it.

She pulled down the heavy drapes and sheers, leaving just the louvered shutters. She knew that tomorrow, when the sun spilled through the slats, the room would look beautiful.

She left her grandmother's china in one corner cabinet and Aunt Betty's collection of Hall's Autumn Leaf dishes in the other.

Kennedy glanced at the clock, and it was already eight thirty. So she grabbed a sandwich and a big glass of water and went upstairs.

She stared at her aunt's room. This was going to be more than she could complete tonight, but she could start.

She emptied her aunt's clothes into garbage bags, cleared out more knickknacks. She took the pastel flowered bedspread off, along with the clashing flowered sheets—she'd donate those, too.

The furniture itself was beautiful. Most of the pieces in the house were inherited. Aunt Betty was her mother's sister, and she'd told Kennedy the bedroom set had belonged to her parents—which meant the furniture had belonged to Kennedy's grandparents.

It wasn't precisely her style, but Kennedy decided to use it. There was something comforting in knowing that the furniture was a part of her family history.

She loved that sense of time it represented.

Malcolm had asked to help her, and she decided she'd ask him to move her old bedroom set down to the basement. She'd store it until the baby was ready for real furniture. She'd set up her old room as a nursery.

Maybe Malcolm would go shopping next week for the nursery with her.

She'd get herself a new mattress and move in here.

She thought about starting to move her clothes over, but her burst of energy had finally ebbed.

She decided to go downstairs and pull out one of those old favorite books, light the fire, and give the *new* living room a try.

She was halfway down the stairs, carrying her plate and cup, when the doorbell rang.

She peeked out the window before she opened it. "Malcolm?"

"I saw the light on in your aunt's room and . . ." He shrugged. "I hadn't seen it on since I got home and I wondered if there was a problem. It's after nine. Normally the house is pretty much dark by now. I wondered if there was a problem with the baby, or if my father had upset you yesterday, or . . ."

"I—"

He interrupted. "Never mind. That sounded stalkerish. It's just you live next door and there's a certain rhythm over here. Your light in the kitchen is always on when I get up. You tend to walk home from the store in the evening, so the lights go on here between five and five thirty." He paused and laughed. "I'm not helping my case. It's only I noticed. And I worried after yesterday."

Once upon a time his pronouncement that he noticed her would have set her heart racing. Now, she knew he was saying he worried about the baby.

"I'm fine. As a matter of fact, you inspired me."

"I did?" He looked puzzled.

"When you asked to see the baby's room. You seemed surprised that I hadn't taken over the master bedroom, that I hadn't made any changes."

"You said it was your aunt's room."

"It was. But I realized, it isn't anymore. This is my house now. My home."

She nodded that he should come in, and she reached around the corner of the small foyer and turned on the light. "I was going to start a fire and try it out."

Malcolm kicked his boots off and stepped into the living room. "When did you find time to redo the room?"

"I didn't redo it so much as declutter and . . . deflower." She felt her cheeks warm as she realized how that sounded and hurriedly continued, hoping Malcom hadn't noticed. "I might work in a flower shop, but I don't think I need to have every inch of my home covered in them. There are lovely family antiques in the house. It's easier to see them without slipcovers and doilies."

"Kennedy, this looks amazing."

She felt a rush of . . . pride? No, satisfaction.

He walked over to the bookcase. There among the old books, he zeroed in on her yearbook. He flipped through the pages and landed on the second and third pages of the seniors. "Wow, we were young."

She stood next to him and peered at the book. She was on the left-hand side, he was on the right. Anderson and Carter. Only one letter away.

He ran a finger over where he'd signed her yearbook. *Have a great summer. Mal.*

She had signatures from most of her class that were generic like that. *Best of luck. Enjoy college. Stay sweet.* She didn't mind that most of the class didn't know her well enough to write anything more personal. But Malcolm . . . she'd hoped that somehow, he'd noticed more about her.

He could have said, *To the girl who read a lot of books on her porch. To my neighbor. To the girl who came to all my games.*

Have a great summer.

She took and shut the yearbook and put it back on the shelf. Then pasted a smile on her face and tried to switch the subject from her lame past. "I'm starting to clear out the master bedroom for myself, and I'm planning to set up a nursery in the other room. I wondered if you'd like to go shopping for furniture for the baby with me next week?"

"I'd love it, Kennedy. Really, I'd love it. I know it's only been a few days, but this baby has already taken up all my thoughts. I want it to be happy. I want him or her to know the same kind of childhood I knew here in Cupid Falls."

That sentence made a tension she hadn't even realized she had loosen. He was talking about the baby growing up here. With her. In Cupid Falls.

"Carefree summer days," he continued. "Snowy school days filled with study and friends. I hope they play sports. I don't care what. I want to go sit in the stands and cheer for them."

Like his father had never cheered for him, she thought, but didn't say.

"And if they don't play sports, I'll go watch plays, or concerts, or even debates. I want to be an active part of their life. I know Pittsburgh is two hours away, but I want you to know I'll do a better job of being part of the baby's life than my father did with me."

She waited to feel more relief; after all, Malcolm was talking as if he was going back to Pittsburgh and leaving the baby here with her. She felt a quick stab of sadness, then forced herself to look on the bright side. He was talking about leaving the baby here with her.

That's what she wanted, wasn't it? "So, you're not suing me for custody?"

"Kennedy, no, I'm not. I won't ever do that to my child. He or she needs to feel safe, as if they belong somewhere. Have you thought about my proposal?"

She waited, wondering if he'd give her another reason why they should marry, but this time, he simply waited.

"No. I mean, yes, I've thought about your proposal, but no, nothing has changed. But thank you for asking," she said, just as she'd said every time Malcolm had asked.

"I hope you change your mind, but even if you don't, I won't sue. I'll want time with the baby. We'll have to work out visitation. Here when they're little, but maybe some time in Pittsburgh when they're older. But I'll be the one doing the bulk of the to-and-from. They need to be able to be part of the activities here. To hang with their friends on weekends. To simply be a kid."

Despite the fact she wouldn't marry him, she knew that he would be an entirely different father than his own father was. "You will be a wonderful dad."

"Thanks. My father gave me until the new year to get things worked out with you and get back to work. It means I'll be here when the baby's born. We have time to get things worked out. And maybe I'll convince you to say yes to my proposal. I am an attorney. Convincing people is what I do."

In her childhood fantasies, she'd imagined Malcolm falling head over heels in love with her. She imagined them going to college together, and then he'd propose because he loved her. She'd say yes, of course . . . because she loved him.

Even though she'd long since outgrown that girlish crush, she knew she could never settle for less than that. She'd been Aunt Betty's obligation. She wasn't about to become Malcolm's.

She'd worried that he'd take the baby from her, but looking at him now, in the room she'd redone, she knew she was wrong. And she suddenly felt very optimistic that they'd find some way to work together on this baby's behalf. "Not going to happen. Tell you what, I was going to light a fire and read a book, but what if I light a fire, we get some cocoa, and plan the baby's nursery together?"

"I can't tell you how much I'd like that."

She looked at her child's father and realized that this was a start.

Because of the baby, they'd be working together for the next eighteen years.

Well, no, for the rest of their lives.

And she suddenly felt optimistic about their future.

~

Mal went home and up to his room. He pulled his own yearbook from the shelf in his childhood room and flipped to the same page he'd just looked at with Kennedy. He knew if he'd signed her yearbook, she'd signed his. There in the margin, to the left of her picture, she'd written, *Mal, good luck at Pitt next year. Someday you're going to make a great lawyer. Kennedy.*

He'd always said he was going to be a lawyer like his father, but he couldn't remember ever having a conversation with Kennedy in school.

He remembered seeing her around. He'd come home from practice and she'd be on her porch reading, or he'd see her at the flower shop, helping out her aunt.

She was just the girl next door. *Have a great summer*, he'd said. Hell, he hadn't even written her name. Just *Have a great summer. Mal.*

She'd known he planned to be a lawyer. Not that it was a state secret. He'd always said as much. But she'd known . . . and she'd believed in him.

Mal suddenly felt as if he'd missed something important all those years ago.

CHAPTER EIGHT

The next morning was the big Christmas craft show.

Malcolm felt optimistic as he walked through the main room of the Center. Kennedy had let him help plan the baby's nursery. He was making progress with her.

Progress toward what, he wasn't sure, but it was still progress.

Interior design wasn't anything that had ever interested him. His condo in Pittsburgh had a design . . . it was called "go to the store and buy what you need." A couch, a table . . . it was an interior designed by necessity. But planning for the baby? Well, that was fun. He was actually excited about going shopping for the furniture next week with Kennedy. He loved her idea of an alphabet wall. She wanted to collect letters and put them up. Any kind of letter. Wooden ones. Old signs. Ads. He was on the lookout.

He forced himself to pull his thoughts away from the baby and Kennedy and concentrate on this weekend's craft show. The Center was filled with table after table of stuff. Crocheted and knitted stuff—he knew there was a difference, that you did one with one hook and one with two needles, but for the life of him it all was made of yarn. He couldn't tell which was which.

There were a lot of tables of woodcrafts. Carved stuff and small furniture.

There were tables of paintings and photographs.

There were tables filled with doll clothes, dog paraphernalia, and ornaments. Wow, there were so many types of ornaments. Clay figures holding local college banners. Pinecones with ribbons. Some kind of thread snowflakes.

Some of the local Amish women had a long table along the side with quilts and a pile of quilted Christmas tree skirts. Mal had grown up with the Falls Creek Amish community at the outskirt of town. When he was younger, the community had mainly farmed, but as he'd grown older, he'd noticed that a number had started businesses. Simple Treasures craft store sat at the edge of town, and after he'd left for college, an Amish restaurant across from it, Simple Food. He recognized the oldest lady in the group. Annie Byler was Pap's age and owned Simple Treasures. She was small, round, and always wore a smile.

"Hi, Miss Annie," he called.

"Hi, Mal. Are you home to stay?" she asked as he looked at the quilts.

"No. Just an extended visit."

"It is always good to see you," Annie said.

He didn't want to answer any more uncomfortable questions, so he kept walking and stopped at a girls' scouting table. They had small silver circles with tin punch designs. He held up a tree. "This is very pretty, girls."

A young girl with a long braid down her back nodded excitedly. "We made 'em from juice cans. Mrs. Corbin had us all buy frozen juice and save the lids for months. We got all our families to do it, too. My grandpa said he never thought he'd say it, but he's tired of juice." She laughed, as if everything her grandfather did was a particular delight to her. "But he drank it anyway."

He held out one with a Christmas tree poked out. "How much?"

"Two dollars," she said.

Then he spotted one with a very good baby buggy on it. "I'll take this one, too."

"That one's for a baby's first Christmas. You can write their name on it with a marker. They make markers that are all glittery so it'll look cool," a redhead told him, as if she was afraid that he would use the wrong, nonglittery marker.

It suddenly occurred to him that the baby would be here in time for Christmas. This would be their first Christmas. "That's a great idea."

He paid for his ornaments, put them in his pocket, and vowed he'd find a glittery marker to write the baby's name on the ornament.

He was going to be a father by Christmas.

His father had given him until the new year to get back to work, but he knew that Senior expected him home sooner. But leaving and going back to work in Pittsburgh had lost some of its allure. The thought of not being here and seeing his child daily . . . was almost a physical pain.

But Malcolm realized it was more than that. He'd miss seeing Kennedy, too.

He scanned the crowd, trying to pinpoint her. She seemed to be everywhere. He wanted to tell her to sit down and let him handle things, but she'd said she'd arranged the day, and he knew she felt that it was her responsibility.

She'd closed the flower shop early and said not to worry because she'd set up a table. It was filled with poinsettias and Christmas arrangements. Some young kid he didn't know was manning Cupid's

Bowquet's table for her while she stopped at all the other vendors and talked to everyone.

Some might say she was campaigning, but a lot of the vendors were from out of town. They'd come in for the craft show. And he didn't think Kennedy ever campaigned. People simply naturally flocked to her and trusted her judgment.

"Mal Carter, how are you?" Clarence Harding asked. He was holding a huge collection of shopping bags. He must have seen Mal eyeing them, because he said, "This is my duty when shopping with Joan . . . holding her bags. Turns out it's a task I'm good at." So saying, he set them down on a bench.

"So how are you?" Clarence asked again.

"Fine," Mal said, but what he really wanted to say was *I'm going to be a father by Christmas*. He didn't think Kennedy was ready to tell the community. She hadn't seemed overly keen on telling his grandfather. And given the way his father had reacted, he suspected she needed some time before they told everyone else that he was the baby's father.

So all he said to Clarence was "Hope you had a nice Thanksgiving."

"Well, it wasn't bad, once I scraped all the burnt bits off Joan's bird. She's not much of a cook, my Joan." It might have sounded like a slam, but the look on Clarence's face said he didn't care if his wife could cook. Clarence added, "She's around the other side, if you want to stop and say hi. She's selling Christmas frogs and shopping in between sales. I'll be lucky if we break even."

Mal started to ask what a Christmas frog was, but Clarence said, "Don't ask. That woman's got tadpoles on the brain."

Clarence grinned as he said the words, and Mal could see that he didn't mind his wife's tadpoley brain any more than he minded holding her bags.

How did that work? Seeing past someone else's peccadillos and loving them despite them . . . or maybe because of them?

His parents had minded just about everything about each other.

His mother had minded that his father worked so much, that he put his career before his family.

His father had minded that while his mother might live in Pittsburgh, her heart was in Cupid Falls.

Some people might think all their *minding* would have ended with their divorce, but there were so many more differences that they had *after* they'd separated. He frequently felt as if he was the main reason.

To his mom's credit, she always tried to include his father. She sent him report cards and monthly schedules with all Mal's activities listed. His mother invited his father to holidays and birthdays.

His mother loved being around people, and people seemed to sense that and flock to her. Her funeral showed just how many friends she had. To the best of his knowledge, his father had colleagues and clients, but Mal couldn't think of any friends.

His father golfed and read.

His mother bowled, loved movies and television.

His father's place was spartan and organized.

His mother had always liked her home to look lived-in.

His mother was quick to hug and equally quick to forgive.

His father . . . wasn't.

Mal looked at bag-holding Clarence, who didn't mind his wife's frog obsession. He'd seen the two of them together and knew they functioned as a single unit. A happy couple.

How did they do it?

"You okay, Mal?" Clarence asked.

"Yeah, I was thinking maybe I'd go find Joan and get one of those for my—for Kennedy's baby."

Clarence might be the town joker, but his eyes narrowed. "You do that." There was no trace of a smile. No joke as he stared at Mal.

Mal hated keeping his impending fatherhood a secret, but he wasn't going to push Kennedy into it. He'd wait for her to make that first move.

"I'll see you later, Mal," Clarence said.

Mal nodded and wondered if Clarence had caught his slip. Mal didn't realize how lost in thought he was until he practically tripped over a tiny, grey-haired lady.

"Ma'am, I'm so sorry. Excuse me."

"Don't worry, kedvenc. I am so short that my Bela, who is about your size, tells me he's going to get one of those orange visibility flags for bikes and tie it to my head." She laughed.

Despite his foul mood, Mal couldn't help but smile.

"And I will let you make up for almost running me over by asking you if you know Kennedy Anderson and can point me in her general direction," the tiny older woman said. "Crowds are not short people's friends. I can't see anything but stomachs."

"Last time I saw her, she was towards the back of the room, but honestly, she's moving around so much she could be anywhere by now."

"Well, why don't you be my hero and play my lookout and help me find her." She patted his arm, as if she expected nothing but heroism from him.

Malcolm's mood lifted even further, and he found himself genuinely enchanted by the small stranger. "My pleasure, ma'am."

"How do you know Kennedy?" she asked as he scanned the crowd.

Now, that was a loaded question. "I've known her since she moved to Cupid Falls when we were kids. Her aunt's house is next to my grandfather's, and her flower shop is right next door to the Center, ma'am."

"Ma'am?" She snorted. "I'm no ma'am. Call me Nana Vancy. Everyone does. Even my own children. Sometimes my Bela slips and calls me Nana Vancy, too, especially when I've annoyed him. And that happens a lot."

He looked at the tiny dynamo and had no trouble believing that she frustrated *her Bela*.

"And you're connected to the Center how?" she asked.

"Technically, I own it." What was he going to do with it? Kennedy wanted it, that much was clear, and under other circumstances he would sell it to her no questions asked. But she was about to be a new mother. Plus she had the flower shop and she was mayor. He didn't see how she could take one more thing onto her very crowded list of things to do.

"If you own the business, why haven't I seen you here before? You let Paul and Kennedy do everything." There was censure in her voice.

Paul threw him for a moment, then he realized that she was referring to his grandfather. "It's a long story." He scanned the crowd and spotted Kennedy. "There she is."

The small woman's hand gripped his wrist. She was stronger than she looked. "I have time for a long story before we go see her."

Mal might find the older woman amusing, but he wasn't about to pour his troubles out to a perfect stranger. "I don't want to be rude, ma'am, but it's personal."

"Nana Vancy," she corrected, and studied him. "Oh."

There was something in that simple syllable that had him worried. "Oh, what?"

"So, you're the . . . what's the lingo for baby's father?"

"Baby's father?"

She shook her head and her grey hair rippled. "No, that's not it."

He knew the term she was thinking of, and though he dreaded using it, he said, "*Baby daddy?*"

"*Baby daddy*," she said with a whisper of an accent that said English wasn't her first language, even though she'd obviously spoken it for a very long time. She nodded. "That's it. In my day a *baby daddy* was the mother's husband. Period. But you're not that."

"Kennedy is a private person, ma'am." He didn't add that this particular *baby daddy* wanted to be the mother's husband, but she said no.

The woman's foot tapped with annoyance. "I do not like all this ma'aming. Ma'am. Ma'am. Ma'am. Please call me Nana Vancy. Everyone does. If my Bela can call me that, so can you."

She'd mentioned her Bela before, and he thought it might be a good way to sidetrack her from her baby-daddy question. So he threw out the question: "Your Bela?"

"My husband. My baby daddy . . . babies' daddy, if I want to be hip." She seemed so delighted with the terminology that he couldn't help but laugh along with her.

She glanced across the room at the very pregnant Kennedy, who was flitting from one table to another, one person to another. "So, you and Kennedy are together?"

"No, not really." The fact they weren't officially together wasn't from his lack of trying.

"Oh." She looked at Kennedy, then back at Mal, speculation in her eyes. "My friends thought it was too late for love, but they both have men in their lives now. It's never too late. You remember that."

He was afraid that it was too late before they'd even started, but he didn't say that. He simply said, "I will, ma'—" he started, but a look from the older woman made him change the word to "Nana Vancy."

She patted his hand. "Thank you. When you're ready to talk, come see me. I'll be back in a couple weeks for the Everything But a Dog adoption, then the dance. I hear they are calling it the Bow-Wow Ball?" That seemed to delight her as well.

"I've heard that, too." Suddenly he knew who Nana Vancy was. "Oh, you're *her*. Kennedy mentioned the events."

The woman—Nana Vancy—seemed pleased that Kennedy had mentioned her. "Yes. I'm her. I started Everything But a Dog to help homeless dogs find their forever homes. We've never had an event outside of Erie before, but we've had so many dogs who need homes. We thought it was time to take the search out into the county. Your Kennedy has been a wonder to work with."

He ignored her *your Kennedy* remark. Nana Vancy said it with the same sort of tone she used when she said *my Bela*. She made both sound as if the two people in question were a single unit. Vancy and Bela . . . if you were going with the current fad of mashing two names together, they'd be *Vela*.

Malcolm and Kennedy? *Maledy.*

Malady.

Yes, that about said it all.

"You sighed," Nana Vancy said with a prosecutor's sort of tone. "What are you thinking about?"

He was saved from trying to explain the hybrid name fad to the woman he'd just explained *baby daddy* to when they arrived at the woman in question. Kennedy had a hand pressed into the small of her back. He'd noticed her doing it before and wondered if her back was bothering her.

On the heels of that thought, he realized that of course it was. If he taped a bowling ball to his stomach, then stood around all day arranging flowers, his back would be killing him, too.

Kennedy narrowed her eyes as she spotted him, but she pasted a fake I'm-the-mayor-and-have-to-be-nice-to-everyone smile on her face. He could almost read her thoughts. She was thinking he had better not ask her to marry him here.

He winked, hoping she understood it meant he'd try not to ask her, but he wasn't sure she could count on his ability to control the question.

She shot him a warning look, and he was pretty sure she'd understood him just fine.

"Kennedy, kedvenc, how are you?" Nana Vancy asked.

Kennedy's gaze dropped from him to the small woman he'd brought with him. She smiled, a genuine smile this time. "Nana Vancy, it's so nice to see you."

"I came to do some shopping at your craft show and to see how the building looks when it's all set up. This is wonderful, kedvenc."

Mal wasn't sure what a *kedvenc* was, but it was obviously a good thing.

"I'm glad you think so. I ordered a rubberized flooring that's recommended for pets. I called a friend, Nikki, who runs a doggie day care, and she said they use it. It's easy on the dogs' paws, and if there are any accidents, it's easy to clean up. And—" She glanced at Mal. "I'm sorry. I need to make an introduction. Nana Vancy, this is Malcolm Carter, the owner of the Center. Malcolm, this is Vancy Salo, the driving force behind the Everything But a Dog Foundation."

"We've already met," he said.

Kennedy nodded and went back to talking to Nana Vancy as if he were invisible.

"I hardly recognized you without your Silver Bells," she said with a laugh.

He'd only just met the older lady, but he had no doubt she'd be the kind of lady who'd wear bells, silver or otherwise. There was some poem about old ladies and purple. Nana Vancy was exactly that kind of lady.

"Annabelle and Isabel have new boyfriends," Nana Vancy told Kennedy. "They didn't want to spend a day away from them."

Oh, her friends, not actual silver bells. Mal smiled. He was still sure Nana Vancy would wear bells if she were so inclined.

The older lady continued, "Since they were busy, my Bela came with me. He's walking down your Main Street, looking at the shops. He says craft shows give him hives. But the truth of the matter is, he didn't want to leave the dogs alone all day, so we brought them and he's taking them for a walk."

"Oh, the dogs are here? Can I meet them?" She turned to Mal, as if remembering he was there, and explained, "Nana Vancy's dogs, Madame Curie and Clara Barton, are the reason she started Everything But a Dog. She rescued them—"

"In order to help two people find their happily-ever-after. But don't worry, I've given up the matchmaking people hobby. Now, I only matchmake for dogs and their forever families."

Mal was glad she was out of the matchmaking business, because Nana Vancy was looking from him to Kennedy, studying them both like lab rats.

Kennedy didn't seem to notice. She nodded and added, "Her dogs have had their stories written up in the paper. They were even on the news a few times. They're famous."

"Oh, don't let the dogs hear you say that. Their fame might go to their heads. My grandson made a joke about the dogs being worried that the *puparazzi* would *hound* them. Get it? Paparazzi—*pup*arazzi?" She laughed at the rather lame play on words. "Let's go find them and I'll introduce them to you."

As if he were an afterthought, Kennedy looked at him and said, "You're welcome to join us."

She didn't have to say the words "but I wish you wouldn't" for him to know that's what she was thinking. He smiled and shot her a look that said, *if wishes were horses—or in this case dogs*, and he smiled broadly as he said, "Don't mind if I do."

Kennedy didn't look pleased at the prospect.

"How did the dogs help you start the foundation and why are they famous?" he asked as they wound through the tables of crafts.

"Now, that's a story," Nana Vancy said. She took his arm. "I probably should start at the beginning."

He glanced over at Kennedy, who was grinning. She'd obviously heard this story.

"Years ago, back in Hungary, I accidentally cursed my own family to bad weddings. Not on purpose, kedvenc. I thought I was cursing Bela's family, which wouldn't include me, since he'd left me standing by myself at the altar. But he finally made it home and married me right away. I was so happy to have him home and that he was my husband that I didn't realize for a long time that it was my own family I cursed. We moved to the United States and built a life here. That's when I learned what I'd done. And for years, I tried to undo those words I so carelessly uttered and break the curse."

She looked at Kennedy, who as if on cue, said, "Words have power."

Nana Vancy nodded, satisfied. "They do. That's the lesson. I'd said the words and cursed my family. After my grandchildren married, I managed to break the curse, then I was bored, so . . ." She looked at Kennedy again.

"She started matchmaking with her friends', the Silver Bells, help," Kennedy supplied.

"Isabel and Annabelle," he filled in.

They reached the coatrack and all three of them pulled out their coats.

Nana Vancy smiled at him as she slipped hers on. She looked as pleased as if he'd aced a spelling bee. "Yes, my friends. I adopted Clara Barton and Madame Curie to help match Annabelle's second cousin's daughter by her third marriage once removed. Bela was so mad when I came home with the dogs, but they stole his heart. There have never been two dogs so loved. And when I decided that match-making people might not be my calling . . ."

Kennedy's laughter couldn't be contained at that. "From what you told me, there were a few glitches."

Nana Vancy grinned as she nodded and admitted, "Just a few, kedvenc, but I did help bring together some very happy couples. But when I matchmaked Annabelle's second cousin's daughter by her third marriage once removed, who was a veterinarian—"

Kennedy laughed as she interrupted, "—with a man who was allergic to dogs."

Nana Vancy said, "It all worked out, didn't it? And I discovered my true calling was matching dogs to their forever homes. And with help from family and friends, I started Everything But a Dog Foundation."

That was a long story made longer, Mal thought but didn't say out loud as they walked out onto the sidewalk. He glanced to make sure that Kennedy had zipped up her parka against the cold.

She caught him at it and glared at him. He didn't need the words to know she was telling him she could look after herself.

He sighed. This time it wasn't only Kennedy who looked at him, but Nana Vancy, too. She pointed down the street at a big man with two dogs. A large black one and a much smaller white one that had a very sausage-like build.

Mal looked at the big man smile as the tiny woman approached him. He wasn't a romantic by any stretch of the imagination, but when Nana Vancy's Bela joined them with the dogs, Mal could see how much love there was between them. It reminded him of Clarence and Joan. Or his grandfather and grandmother.

Nana Vancy walked up to the big man and their bodies brushed, as if drawn together like magnets.

"Kennedy, Malcolm, this is my Bela." There was pride in her voice . . . and love.

"Bela Salo," he said, shaking their hands.

"And this is Madame Curie." At the sound of her name, the black dog sat down and offered them her paw.

Kennedy knelt down awkwardly and took the paw. "Aren't you a beautiful girl?"

The little white dog, not to be outdone, jumped up at Kennedy, anxious for some affection, too. But Kennedy's center of gravity was extremely off because of the baby. The small dog hurtling in her direction was enough to topple her, but Malcolm sprang forward and grabbed her under her arms, steadying her.

She looked up. "Thank you," she said, then turned her attention to the demanding sausage-like white dog.

Nana Vancy shot him a look that made him feel like a bug under a microscope, then she said, "And that rude dog is Clara . . . Clara Barton. She has no manners and very little brains."

Bela looked slightly insulted on the dog's behalf. "But she is all heart, that one."

As if to prove his point, Clara was busy kissing Kennedy, who hadn't asked Mal to remove his hands, so he continued to steady her as she continued to kneel by the small dog.

"I love dogs," Kennedy said, as Clara continued on her love-fest.

"Maybe I'll find your dog at the adoption day?" Nana Vancy said. "I'll find you the perfect dog."

"She's very good at it." Bela laughed and added, "Better finding dogs their match than people."

"Now, Bela," Nana Vancy scolded, "I always managed to make things work out."

"Ask the people she matched if it was easy." Bela guffawed.

"Love isn't easy," Nana Vancy said very seriously. She looked at Mal and continued, "It is not supposed to be. Because if it was, you wouldn't appreciate it half as much. Look how hard Bela made things on me, and all these years later, I still appreciate that he's mine." She turned her gaze back to the big man.

Kennedy kept petting Clara as if she thought Nana Vancy had forgotten the idea of her adopting a dog, but the older woman obviously hadn't. "I will find you the perfect dog, Kennedy."

Kennedy started to rise, with difficulty, but Malcolm gave her a tug and righted her easily.

Kennedy rested her arms on her stomach. "Nana Vancy, I'll come see you in a few years. I don't think it would be fair to a dog to bring it home and then introduce a new baby. I don't think I'd be able to give it the attention it deserved."

"Well, maybe if someone were to give you a hand?" Nana Vancy looked directly at Mal.

Kennedy obviously caught the look, because she said, "Mal's a friend and neighbor, but helping me with a dog isn't in the cards. He will be going back to Pittsburgh soon, and I'll have the baby, the flower shop, and a town to look after. In a couple years I'll get the baby a dog. I promise."

Nana Vancy didn't look convinced, but she nodded and dropped the issue.

They stayed and visited with the older couple.

Mal watched Bela as Nana Vancy spoke. Bela was a quiet man and seemed happy to let her do the talking for both of them, but he watched her every move. And it was easy to see he was enchanted by her. She'd spoken of their children and grandchildren, which meant they'd been together for a long time, and still Bela watched Nana Vancy with love in his eyes.

Mal realized he'd been watching the older man watching Nana Vancy so intently that he'd lost track of the conversation. But it was obviously over, since Nana Vancy kissed Kennedy and said, "I'll be here early on for the event. Me, Bela, our helpers, and all the dogs. And thank you for the helpers here. Oh, Angel is coming from the radio, too."

"Radio?" Mal asked, feeling as if he were playing catch-up.

"It's on the event listing on the computer," Kennedy said. "The Everything But a Dog portion of the day is being covered by WLVH in Erie."

"WLVH, *where love is more than just a song*," Nana Vancy said with a chortle. "It took me a while to learn that."

"Why would an Erie station cover something in Cupid Falls?"

"That is exactly what a man from a big city like Pittsburgh would ask," Kennedy said. "They'd cover it because Cupid Falls is part of their audience. We get all the Erie stations out here, and that means if they're covering the event, they're mentioning Cupid Falls to their Erie audience as well. That's what the town needs, more reasons for people in Erie and towns like Waterford, Union City, and Lapp Mill to come visit us. We're a picturesque small town with so many wonderful attributes. Events like this will bring us notice. WLVH partners with the Everything But a Dog Foundation in a lot of events. I remember that Angela adopted a dog with Nana Vancy's help."

"Adopted a dog and fell in love," Nana Vancy informed him.

"You are out of the matchmaking business," Bela reminded her, warning in his voice.

"Sometimes love just happens. If I give it a little nudge, well . . ." She shrugged.

He growled.

"Only a little nudge," she insisted and leaned toward him. He tucked her up under his arm as if that's where she belonged.

"The radio station won't be a problem," Kennedy said. "They'll set up their mobile unit out front."

"It's fine, Kennedy," Mal told her. She didn't need to explain. She'd done a stellar job of coordinating events.

"See you in a couple weeks," Nana Vancy said as Bela led her and the dogs down the block.

Mal wanted to say something to Kennedy. He wasn't sure precisely what, but something. He wanted to comment on Nana Vancy and her Bela. He wanted to encourage her to get a dog because he could see that she wanted one.

But in the split second it took him to think about all the things he wanted to say, Kennedy went back inside the Center and was swept away within seconds. Mal watched as she flitted from table to table. He watched her. She gave each person her undivided attention, as if they were the only person in the room.

She was in a corner of the Center talking to a group of kids he didn't recognize.

Her hands drifted to her stomach, caressing their unborn baby.

He realized he still hadn't felt the baby kick. He hadn't gone to a doctor's appointment or attended childbirth classes.

He didn't even know if she'd gone to them.

He wasn't sure exactly what they taught in those kind of classes. After all, the baby was in and it had to come out. How much was there to learn about that?

He was going to have to get a book on that and on babies. He didn't have a clue what to do with babies.

And after that, they'd have a toddler, then . . .

Suddenly he realized that the atmosphere in the room seemed to have shifted since he went outside. People seemed to be staring at him. Every time he almost caught someone at it, they instantly averted their eyes.

He felt like he was parting the sea as he walked through down the center aisle. Normally, friends would come over and talk. He didn't get home often, and there was always some news they had to share. But not today.

What was up? He scanned the room and spotted Clarence in a corner. He saw as the older man noticed he was looking at him, Clarence averted his eyes and made a move to dart in a different direction.

"Uh, uh, uh," Mal said as he grabbed Clarence. "What's going on?"

The old man shrugged. "I don't know what you mean?"

"Clarence, I might not live in Cupid Falls anymore, but I can recognize that something is up."

"Uh . . ." Clarence shifted from foot to foot.

Mal might have worried, but he had an ace in the hole. "Clarence, I could go get Joan. She'll tell me what's going on."

Clarence scoffed. "She won't. She ain't talkin' to you."

"And neither, it seems, is most of Cupid Falls. That's what I'm asking you. What did I do?" Mal couldn't think of anything he'd done. Everything seemed fine, then he went outside with Kennedy and Nana Vancy, then came back in to this communal cold shoulder.

Clarence was looking at the floor as he practically whispered, "It's about you and the mayor. I know. You said *my*, then switched it to *Kennedy's baby*. But I caught it. You don't want anyone to know."

Mal didn't know what to say to that. He realized that he didn't care if the whole world knew he was going to be a father because he was . . . excited.

This wasn't the right time, or the right way, to go about having a baby, but despite not knowing how he and Kennedy were going decide what they were going to do, he knew what he wanted to do with the baby . . . be the best father he possibly could be.

He didn't say any of that, though, knowing Kennedy wouldn't like it.

When he didn't say anything, Clarence shook his head. "No one likes you messin' with her and then walking away and letting her go through with all the baby business on her own. Not that she's on her own. She's got all of us, but that doesn't let you off the hook." Clarence looked up from the floor and glared at Mal. "We don't like it at all, Mal. Everyone's disappointed in you. You've always been someone who Cupid Falls looked up to. But not anymore. Not now. Not about this."

Mal could tell Clarence that he'd asked Kennedy to marry him and she'd said no. He could tell the older man that he'd just found out about the baby.

He could say any number of things, but any of them would be an excuse, and he wasn't about to offer excuses to the town.

This was between him and Kennedy. The town didn't fit into the equation, at least not in his mind. "Thanks for telling me."

"You gonna make it right?" Clarence asked. "I'd be happy to let them all know."

"My personal life is just that . . . personal. I won't be saying anything about Kennedy or the baby, not to you or to anyone else in this town."

Clarence looked doubtful. "If you don't mind me saying, that's a mistake."

"I do mind, and mistake or not, I'm not talking."

"Fine."

Mal walked away from Clarence, and it was as if the entire town knew what they'd said, because they didn't bother averting their eyes anymore. Their animosity was there in every look, in every word not spoken.

CHAPTER NINE

That evening, after the crafters and shoppers had all left, Kennedy looked out over the now-empty room. Well, empty except for Malcolm. He was busy turning off lights and doing a once-over before they locked up. He'd insisted she let him help. Most days she'd protest that she could manage on her own. She felt responsible for the craft show because she'd booked it. But she couldn't manage the energy to protest, much less close up on her own. She was bone-deep exhausted. Everyone kept warning her how hard it was to have a baby—how exhausting it was. She was sure they were right, but she didn't see how it could be much worse than trying to function when you were the size of a barge.

Malcolm walked down the center aisle and smiled at her. For a moment she was taken back to those long-ago high school days when she'd have given almost anything to have him smile at her that way. He'd been cute as a teen, but he'd truly come into his own as an adult. He was a *Clooney*—her own personal code for a man who only got more handsome as he aged, à la George Clooney.

On the heels of memories of her childhood crush came memories of their one night together. They'd both been so torn up over losing Val. They'd been looking for comfort, and they'd found it . . . with each other.

No, she needed to put away thoughts of their past and concentrate on the now. But then Malcolm smiled at her again as he reached her. Kennedy rose, pasted her most businessy smile on her face—one she normally reserved for dealing with May—and said, "Well, that was a good day. The show doesn't start tomorrow until noon. I'll see you before that." She zipped up her parka and turned toward the door.

It was so much easier not fantasizing about her childhood crush or the one night they'd spent together when she didn't have to look at Malcolm.

"Are you heading home?" he asked.

She really wanted to answer with her back toward him, but even though she could manage simply giving him social smiles, she couldn't quite manage being rude. So she turned back around and settled for looking at Joan's frog table, which was visible just beyond his shoulder. "Yes. I want to get something to eat before the lighting ceremony tonight."

"May I walk with you?" he asked.

She withheld a sigh, but barely. "Sure."

"Don't sound so enthused," Malcolm said with a laugh as he flipped off the light, followed her out, and locked the door behind them. "Too bad we didn't get some snow today for tonight's ceremony."

"The weatherman said there was a forty percent chance of snow, and it's definitely cold enough," she said, hugging her parka more tightly to herself. "It's been an early start to the winter this year."

He didn't say anything else as they walked to the corner. Kennedy allowed herself to hope that they'd walk in companionable silence the rest of the way home, but her luck didn't last.

"I want to say something, but I don't want you to get mad," Mal said.

She braced herself for another marriage proposal. She was getting good at saying no, but obviously not good enough for him to stop asking. "If you're worried whatever you're going to say is going to make me mad, maybe you shouldn't say it?"

"I'm worried that you're doing too much. You were on your feet all day today."

She glanced at him. Even in a thick winter coat and hat, he was hot. Darn. She immediately looked forward and assured him, "I'm fine."

"Listen, why don't you come home with me? I'll make us Thanksgiving leftovers—there's a ton. And then I'll walk over to the park with you."

The offer was tempting. "If I say yes, it would be because leftovers are my favorite part of the holiday. It's not that I want you to think we're . . ."—she waved her mittened hand between them— "well, anything more than we are."

He stopped and asked, "And what are we?"

She was forced to stop too in order to answer him. "We're soon-to-be parents. So I'll say yes to dinner, but only for the leftovers, and maybe a little because you and I are also friends. Or at least friendly. I just want to be clear."

"I accept your terms." He held out his arm, and she wasn't going to take it, but he said, "Just friends."

He was on his best behavior the rest of the walk. "You go put up your feet and I'll warm up some leftovers."

Kennedy was too exhausted to protest. She unbundled from her winter gear and sat on the couch.

Next thing she knew, Malcolm was shaking her awake. "You have to leave for the lighting ceremony in half an hour. I've got a plate heated for you on the coffee table."

He busied himself in the kitchen but came back out to the living room as she finished her dinner. "You really are a good cook," she said as she finished.

"Tonight I was simply the reheater," he joked.

~

Kennedy was thankful that she didn't really have to dress up for tonight's event. But in honor of it she'd worn her chunky red-and-green scarf and hat.

The sidewalks were clear because there hadn't been snow in days, but there was still a light coating on the grass. It was cold as they walked in silence along the winter-dark streets.

A number of the homes had been decorated for the holidays. Lights blinked on porches. Lit trees shone through front windows. She needed to put her own tree up soon.

She was thankful that Malcolm didn't feel the need to fill the quiet with a lot of talk. She simply wanted to enjoy the evening and Cupid Falls' official start of the Christmas season.

They stepped onto Main Street and found there was already a crowd waiting.

The kids all seemed to be dancing around in excitement. A lot of the adults, too. She was sympathetic because she felt that same sense of anticipation.

She walked toward the small gazebo in the center of the town's square. There'd been talk about naming the park but it never got any further than just talk. It wasn't as if people didn't know what you meant if you said the park or the square . . . there was only one in Cupid Falls. It had a gazebo in the center and a bunch of trees.

Kennedy realized so much of Cupid Falls was simply known by its purpose, rather than its name/proper noun. Town Hall, the square, the park, the Center, the creek, the falls, the flower shop, the grocery store . . .

Of course other towns had squares, shops, and parks; bigger cities had multiple ones. But Cupid Falls was so small there was no need for any more of a description. Each thing was what it was. She'd thought maybe she'd started a trend by naming the flower shop Cupid's Bowquet. But so far, no one else seemed to see the merit.

She started to say as much to Malcolm but realized that she'd lost him in the crowd. So she chatted with one group or another as she slowly made her way to the gazebo. As she approached, the crowd got quiet and Malcolm was suddenly back at her side.

Lamar was standing nearby with a group of boys she knew belonged to a local scouting group. "The microphone's on, Mayor," he said.

"Thanks, Lamar." She turned to Malcolm. "Looks like I'm good to go."

"Break a leg," he offered.

She took the first step onto the gazebo when she noticed that it was snowing. "Look. It started right on cue," Kennedy said, holding out her mittened hand. "A Hollywood production couldn't have planned it any better."

Malcolm grinned. "You ask for snow, I give you snow."

She laughed, not because what he said was really that funny, but because she felt like a little girl finding it snowed on Christmas Eve, just in time for Santa.

She climbed the rest of the stairs to the gazebo and pasted a smile on her face as she approached the microphone. "Welcome, everyone.

I hope you've all had a wonderful Thanksgiving, but more than that, I hope you spent the day with family or friends and that you took some time to count your blessings." Her hand fell to her stomach and she said a silent thanks for the baby that would be with her soon. "And if we didn't see you at the Center today, I hope we see you there tomorrow."

The crowd chuckled and she continued, "It's been years since we've had lights for the town or for our tree. The pine tree next to the gazebo supposedly came from a seed that came from a tree that came from a seed . . . well, there were more than a few seeds and trees. But way back when the first tree here was planted, it supposedly came from Maine with a certain young man who was part of General Washington's retinue when they visited neighboring Waterford. That nameless man had spent a day hiking in the area and discovered our falls, where he met a farmer's daughter. This was long before there was a town here. But the boy didn't forget the girl or this place. When his work for Washington was over, he came back to find her. He brought the seeds from his home and planted them here. Now that tree's great-something-grandchild stands in the center of our town square. Waiting. Lamar and his assistants"—she pointed to the town handyman and the scouting troop who'd helped him— "spent last week stringing lights on it, as well as down Main Street and throughout the square. And I for one want to say thank you." The audience clapped, too. She saw Jenny and her kids over to the right. Ivy was clapping hard and laughing at something Jenny had said.

"And I want to thank Lincoln Lighting for defraying the cost of the decorations. They are a new member of the Cupid Falls business community. For those who haven't heard, our new LED lights are powered by the solar panels Lincoln Lighting provided for City Hall.

So, our display isn't just red and green, it's actually very *green* as well."
Everyone laughed again.

Kennedy loved these moments—moments when she realized she *had* the audience. She wasn't some big-time politician, but even the mayor of a small town had to speak in public. The first few times, she'd been terrified. But eventually, she stopped trying to read from a script and she'd simply talked to her audience. Most of the time, she had a moment like this . . . a moment when she knew they were engaged with what she had to say.

When the laughter died down, she said, "I think that's it. I want to wish everyone a magical holiday season. And without any further ado . . ."

Kennedy put her hand on a plunger that looked like one of the old TNT plungers that Bugs Bunny used. It really didn't do anything. Lamar used it as a signal to plug in the lights. He would actually be the one lighting everything.

"Ten, nine, eight . . ." she started.

The crowd joined in. "Seven, six, five, four, three, two . . ." they all chanted with her.

". . . one . . ." She pushed the switch and Lamar did his magic. The tree lit up, and so did the rest of the lights in the park and along Main Street. The red and green LED lights cast a different glow than the old incandescent bulbs had.

The crowd made a long *awww* sound and then clapped.

"Please, everyone, help yourself to the free hot cocoa and cookies. Be sure to thank the ladies of Falls Creek Church for donating their time and the wonderful treats."

"And me," Clarence yelled.

"The ladies and Clarence," Kennedy corrected herself, and laughter rang out through the crowd.

The tree in front of her glowed.

Main Street did, too. Kennedy couldn't help but admire the banners with cupid figures dressed in Santa outfits that hung beneath each light. Tomorrow there was going to be an ad in the Erie paper with that same design that said *Come Fall in Love with Christmas in Cupid Falls.*

The crowd applauded again. Kennedy stepped down from the gazebo. She was congratulated left and right as she made her way through the crowd. She wasn't sure where Malcolm had gone. Not that it mattered. They'd walked together, not really come as a couple.

"Nice job, Mayor," Lincoln Gates said. He was a tall, good-looking man. He was new to Cupid Falls, so she had no childhood memories to compare him to, but she suspected he was a Clooney, too. He wasn't quite six foot, and though she couldn't make them out in the glow of the Christmas lights, she knew that his eyes were blue. Every woman in Cupid Falls between the ages of thirteen and ninety knew that. He had dark hair that had the slightest touch of grey at the temples. Not a grey that said, "look, I'm getting older," but rather a grey that said, "hey, notice how unbelievably good-looking I am."

But beyond his looks, which were simply a gift of good genetics, Lincoln was nice. And that, more than anything else, was what made him so appealing to the female population of Cupid Falls.

He shot her a dazzling smile and said, "Everything looks wonderful, Mayor."

Pretty much any other woman would swoon if Lincoln smiled at them like that, but though she registered his looks, they didn't affect her that way. Kennedy chalked up her nonswooning to her advanced pregnancy. "Everything does look wonderful, and a big part of that is thanks to you, Linc."

"I told you when we opened the plant I wanted Lincoln Lighting to be a part of the community." He offered her his arm.

Kennedy wasn't sure what it was that made all men think she'd lost her ability to walk simply because she was pregnant, but she took Linc's arm. "Well, you are an important part of the community. The jobs have been a godsend, but more than that, Lincoln Lighting has given us all a sense of pride. Knowing that we're instrumental in making something that's going to help save the environment."

She stopped at a cluster of people and they congratulated both Linc and Kennedy on the tree lighting. As they continued walking down Main Street, Linc said, "I wanted to talk to you about some ideas I have—ideas about how Cupid Falls can help my company, and Lincoln Lighting can help the town. I know it's a crazy time of year, but any chance you can find some time for me?"

"How about lunch on Monday?" Kennedy offered, mentally trying to juggle her day in order to make it work.

"That's perfect. I'll meet you at the restaurant at say, noon?"

"Sounds great."

He guided her farther down the street.

≈

Mal didn't think of himself as a jealous man. He'd had serious relationships in the past and he'd never minded when someone he was dating talked to another man. But watching Kennedy talk to whoever that Adonis was . . . well, he minded.

The man reached out and touched her arm and she smiled at something he said.

"Malcolm," Clarence's wife, Joan, called.

He waited, still watching Kennedy and her new guy mingle with the crowd.

"Malcolm," Joan called again.

He turned. "Yes, ma'am?"

"We know what you did, and no one's happy about it. Make it right. Kennedy deserves better." She humphed and stormed away.

Joan was the grand total of people who'd talked to him this evening. But the fact he was being shunned suddenly had an upside. As he followed Kennedy and the new guy, the crowd parted like toast under a knife.

Kennedy and Adonis were talking to May as he approached from behind Kennedy. May took one look at him, sniffed, and said, "I've got to go, Kennedy."

May glared hard enough in his direction as she left that Kennedy turned and shot him a questioning look.

Mal shrugged.

Kennedy sighed and said, "Malcolm, I don't think you've met Lincoln Gates. Linc, this is Cupid Falls' own Malcolm Carter, Esquire. He lives in Pittsburgh now and is a rising star in the legal world. He's home for a visit. A brief visit," she added, looking at him pointedly.

"Not all that brief," he said as he shook Lincoln's hand. Maybe he shook it a little too long, a little too hard, because the man gave him a quizzical look that seemed to say, *what did I do to piss you off?*

Mal glanced at Kennedy and then back at Lincoln, who had an *oh, I see* look, then gave the merest shake of his head to say he wasn't interested in Kennedy.

That very unaccustomed feeling of jealousy faded and he said, "Call me Mal," with more friendliness.

Linc nodded. "I'm Linc."

"Lincoln Lighting?" Mal asked. He remembered his grandfather and mother talking excitedly when the new company bought the long-vacant furniture plant. And Kennedy had mentioned them in her speech.

"Guilty," Linc said.

"My grandfather has nothing but nice things to say about you," Mal told the guy.

"Your grandfather is . . . ?" Lincoln asked.

It was unusual to find someone in Cupid Falls who didn't know his family. "Pap Watson at the—"

"The Center," Linc finished. "We've been in talks."

"Talks?" Mal tried to remember what, if anything, his grandfather had said about Lincoln Lighting, but other than talking about the new plant and new jobs, he drew a blank. "What kind of talks?"

"Talks he said I need to take up with you since you officially own the business, at least that's what Pap said. I have a meeting with Kennedy on Monday. Maybe you'd like to join us? I can tell you what I want to suggest for your business."

"I'm sure I can make it."

"Great," Linc said. "Kennedy and I have talked about the Center. It's aptly named. It seems to be at the heart of the community. People have celebrations there. There are events like today's craft show and the dance in a few weeks. I could use your help."

Mal couldn't help but notice that Kennedy was frowning. Maybe Linc didn't think there was anything going on between them, but maybe Kennedy did—or maybe she wished there was something between them.

Mal turned back to Linc. "When on Monday?"

"Lunch at the restaurant at noon."

"I'll be there." He noticed that Kennedy's frown deepened.

Linc looked from her to Mal, then back again. He seemed to know he was missing something, but Mal could see that Linc couldn't decide what.

"Nice meeting you, Mal. See you both on Monday," Linc said, obviously giving up trying to figure things out. He turned and melted into the crowd.

"So what was all that about?" Kennedy asked Mal when Linc moved out of earshot.

He tried to look innocent. "What?"

"There was more machismo between the two of you than there are frogs at Joan's house."

He shrugged. "I don't know what you mean."

"Fine." She started to walk down the block, so he followed. He thought about offering his arm, but he wasn't sure she'd take it, so he settled for simply walking beside her.

Mal glanced across the street. He couldn't help but notice Clarence talking to Linc, then Linc looking in his direction and scowling.

Kennedy must have noticed it as well because she asked, "And what is going on with you and . . . well, everyone?"

They walked past the Miller family, and all of them, right down to thirteen-year-old Violet, scowled at him.

"It's Cupid Falls," he said as if that explained everything. "And Clarence—"

Before he could say *guessed*, Kennedy interrupted him. "Let's go right to the horse's—or frog's, as the case may be—mouth."

She headed toward Clarence.

"What is going on?" Kennedy asked Clarence.

Clarence swept his hands wide. "A fine start to our holiday season, Mayor. That's what's going on. Everyone's talking about what a wonderful job you've done."

"You know what I mean, Clarence," Kennedy said. She didn't raise her voice. She didn't sound the least bit angry, but Mal was sure that Clarence knew she was annoyed, every bit as much as he did.

"Don't make me get Joan," Kennedy added. "What is going on with you and the entire town toward Malcolm?"

"I . . ."

"Clarence," Kennedy prompted.

Clarence looked at Mal. Other than Joan hollering at him and Linc talking to him, it was the first eye contact anyone in town had made with Mal since the craft party.

"Fine," Clarence said, glaring at Mal. "We don't like how he's treating you. We know he's the baby's father, and we all think he should step up and take responsibility." The old man turned to Mal and said, "You can't simply knock up our mayor and then abandon her. We won't put up with it."

"Clarence, it's not like that," Kennedy said.

"From where I'm sitting it is."

"He—"

Mal sensed she was about to try and save him. "Just let it go, Kennedy."

"I won't let it go," she said. "Listen, Clarence, Malcolm offered to marry me. I said no."

"Then he didn't offer right. When I asked Joan to marry me, she said no. So I sent her a frog—her first frog. It was sitting on a toad-stool and had a sign that said, 'Kiss me. I could be a handsome prince in disguise.' Then I asked again. She still said no. I sent her another frog and kept asking. Eventually I wore her down." He looked at Mal. "Sometimes women need to feel you'd go the extra mile for them."

Mal nodded, accepting advice from Cupid Falls' unlikely Romeo.

"Clarence," Kennedy said, "I'm so glad you wooed Joan. And now I know who actually started her collection. Next time you complain about it, you won't get any sympathy from me. But no amount of frogs will change my mind about Malcolm. We're both working together to give this baby two loving parents."

"He just ain't tried hard enough," Clarence insisted. "Being a father isn't about making a woman pregnant. It's being there for your kid. It's sitting up with them when they're sick or have nightmares. It's taking them to games. It's being there for their mother. I ain't seen much of you until recently."

"Malcolm didn't know—" Kennedy started again.

"Kennedy, it's fine." He didn't need her to save him from the town's ire. He understood their anger. And the truth of the matter was, they couldn't be more mad at him than he was at himself.

Kennedy shook her head at him. "Let me explain, Malcolm." She turned to Clarence. "He just found out. And since he has, he's been here. He worried I'd done too much today, so he made me take a nap, then fixed me dinner before we came here tonight."

Clarence snorted. "But he'll be going to go back to Pittsburgh. He'll be leaving you and the baby all alone here in Cupid Falls. I don't know how you can do that," he said to Mal. "We all saw the way your father neglected you after your mom divorced him. I'd have thought you'd be the last man to do something like that to your own child."

The old man turned back to Kennedy. "Mayor, don't you worry. We'll all be here to support you and the baby. You won't be alone." He shot Mal another dark look, then stomped off.

"Well, two mysteries solved. I now understand Joan's frog obsession and I understand why everyone is treating you like you have the plague. I'm sorry you're taking heat over this, Malcolm. I'll tell them all how it really is and try to get you off the hook."

He was touched that his public shunning bothered her. "It's fine, Kennedy. I'm a big boy. I can take it."

"You've never been an outsider," she said. "I'm not sure you have any inkling about what you're letting yourself in for. But I'll try to put out the truth."

"What is the truth?" he asked.

"The truth is, you've asked me to marry you and I've said no. The truth is, you've done everything you can to help me since you found out. You're still going shopping with me, right?"

"Right."

"Tuesday night?" she asked.

He wasn't sure why they were talking about shopping for baby stuff right now, but he said, "Sure."

"Well, there you go. I know I'm not an expert on men, but rumor has it they don't go shopping willingly. You obviously care and you're taking responsibility. But let's face the facts, it took two of us to make this baby. If anyone's to blame, it's me. Your father was right, I could have made an effort to tell you sooner. To be honest, I was glad you kept putting off coming home. It gave me an out. That's on me. I'll be sure to spread that little fact around. That will definitely tell everyone how hard you're trying since you found out." She smiled at him.

Despite his frustration, he laughed. "I do . . . care, that is. And I am trying."

"Well, that's enough for me," she told him with a smile.

Mal decided the whole town could shun him forever if only Kennedy would keep smiling at him like that. He extended her his arm and she took it, wrapping hers through his, and he realized how right it felt there. "I want to be a better father than my father was."

"I have no doubts that you're going to be a good father. I know I selfishly hoped you'd find out about the baby and simply leave it all to me. That would have been easiest on me. That was selfish of me, because it definitely wouldn't have been best for the baby. I'm going to have to learn to think in those terms . . . what's best for the baby."

"What's best for the baby," he said softly, "would be us being married."

"No," she said. She wasn't certain about much—well, about anything, really—but she knew that much was true. "Marrying for the sake of a baby never works."

"We're compatible. My grandfather adores you. We have a foundation for building a good working relationship."

"Maybe. And maybe I'm not quite done with my selfish streak, because I want more than a good working relationship with the man I marry." She patted his arm. "So don't listen to what Clarence said. You will be a totally different father than yours."

"How do you know?" he asked.

She looked up at him and truly smiled. "I know because I am a great judge of character. And your character has shown in everything you've done since finding out about the baby."

"Thank you."

"You're welcome." She tightened her arm a bit. "Now come walk with me down Main Street. Let's admire the lights and decorations. Rumor has it that Tavi covered up the restaurant's window in order to work on some surprise decoration."

They strolled down the street together in silence for a while. Well, he was silent, but Kennedy got pulled over by people again and again as they walked.

He was happy to sit back and watch her. She knew everyone's names and chatted easily with everyone.

As the crowd thinned, he finally asked, "So what was with the legend of the falls in your speech?"

Kennedy almost jumped with surprise as Malcolm spoke again. He'd been so quiet. She'd tried to draw him into conversations with people, but he'd been silent other than the most casual greetings. And everyone seemed pleased to pretend he was invisible.

She was going to have to do something about the situation tomorrow. What, she wasn't sure, but it wasn't fair that he was the target of everyone's ire.

When she'd first found out she was pregnant, she'd expected comments. She'd expected the town to revolt against having an unmarried, pregnant mayor. But all she'd ever received was their support.

"Kennedy?" Malcolm prompted.

"The legend? I know you've heard the stories," she said. "Everyone in town has." She remembered when she first came to live with her aunt. There'd been an article in the paper talking about the legend. She'd been enchanted by it. She remembered cutting out the piece and was sure she still had it somewhere in her desk.

Malcolm nodded. "Yes, of course I've heard the legend."

"I know that Waterford is understandably proud our first president spent time there. And I like to think that Washington indirectly had a hand in bringing our young hero here, which means Washington helped found Cupid Falls."

Malcolm laughed. "So that old story is now a legend. The word *legend* does seem to give it more authority. Did you know that Pap fell in love with my grandmother at the falls?"

"No." She'd heard a lot of family stories from Pap and Val, but not that one.

Malcolm nodded. "They were seniors in high school and had a senior skip day. Pap assured me that although it wasn't an official day off for the seniors, all the teachers and parents knew about it and didn't try to stop it. I think he was afraid I'd skip school and use that as justification."

"What, you?" she asked with mock shock. "Malcolm Carter the Fourth would never do something like skip school. I don't think you ever got in trouble in school."

"And you did?" he countered with a grin.

"Yes. I got a detention our senior year."

She could see her answer surprised him, then his eyes narrowed with suspicion. "For what?"

She dropped her voice to a stage whisper. "I've tried to keep it quiet because I don't want it to impact my political career, but I'll trust you with my secret . . . I took my shoes off in gym class. It was the first warm day of spring and we had gym class outside. Everything was so green. I think anyone who *didn't* go barefoot should have had detention."

She paused as a group of people came over to talk to her. They assured her that everything was beautiful and thanked her, and they all shot obligatory dirty looks at Malcolm.

He didn't seem to notice. When they left, he took her arm again and she didn't complain. She probably should have, but she didn't.

"You are a wild, wild, barefoot woman," he said.

"It was my wildest high school moment." She laughed at the memory. "So finish the story about how Pap met your grandmother."

"He'd been dating another girl for a while, and my grandmother had a steady beau from middle school on. But they'd both broken up with their significant others around the same time. They met by the falls for the senior skip day. He swears he looked at her as if he'd never seen her before. She said the same. And they both used to say that that was the day they really met, and after that day, they knew."

"That's lovely." Since the moment that she'd heard that story of George Washington's man, she'd loved the idea that the falls had some magical power. She liked it even more now, thinking of Pap and his wife meeting there.

"Yes, lovely." Malcolm was looking at her as he said the word.

The look he gave her was penetrating, as if he'd seen something about her he'd never seen before. It made Kennedy feel vulnerable, and she didn't like the sensation. So she tried to steer the conversation away from the falls. "Pap said he's bringing his new lady to the dance," she blurted out. "Will it bother you?"

She'd just thrown Pap under the bus, but Malcolm stopped staring at her. He looked surprised for a moment, as if weighing what she'd said, then he slowly shook his head. "No, I don't think it will bother me. He loved my grandmother and he's mourned her a long time. And he's lost my mom as well. He deserves to find whatever happiness he can."

With that, her arm still tucked under his, they walked up Main Street side by side.

People continued to stop them in order to say how much they enjoyed the lights. Even May Williams said, "I love the banners, Kennedy."

"Thanks, May." She wondered if she could convince May to adopt a dog in a few weeks. She knew what it was like to rattle around all alone in an empty house. Soon she'd have the baby. May really needed to find a dog. Not to replace June, but to be a new companion.

They walked down one end of Main Street and back up the other, ending up back in the square in front of the Christmas tree. Kennedy couldn't help but think that next year she'd have the baby with her. Despite her thick parka, her hands found her stomach, cradling this child she hadn't planned on.

"Kennedy?" Malcolm asked.

She looked at him, in his black pea coat and hat, and for a moment, that girlhood crush came sweeping back over her. He'd been so handsome, smart, and so nice . . . not that he'd ever really noticed her or was nice to her specifically. Still, she never saw him do anything out of mean-spiritedness.

"Kennedy?" he asked, for what she realized was the second time.

"Sorry. I zoned out for a minute. Chalk it up to pregnancy brain. Yes?"

"Will you marry me? Think of what a nice story that would make? I asked you in front of the Christmas tree and you said yes."

"Why?" she asked, like she had every time he'd asked.

"Because we make a good team" was his response.

She sighed and patted his arm. For one moment, that young girl who thought the boy Mal had hung the moon wanted to scream *yes*. She wanted all the times she doodled "Mrs. Malcolm Carter IV" to be true.

But Kennedy knew they never would, because she knew that even with love, marriage was hard. A marriage based on the need to provide a home for a baby didn't stand a chance.

A marriage based on being a *good team* wasn't good enough, nor was one because they were friends, or at least friendly. Maybe if he was staying in Cupid Falls they'd have time to decide if their friendliness could be anything more. But his father had given him until the new year. There was only one answer she could give. "No, but thank you for asking, Malcolm."

"I'm not giving up," he said.

"Eventually, you'll have to." She took a step back, putting a bit more distance between them. "I'm going to call it a night. I'm exhausted."

"I'll walk you home," he said, taking her arm again.

This time Kennedy did pull away.

She had to be careful not to give Malcolm any ideas that she'd ever change her mind.

She wouldn't.

She couldn't.

CHAPTER TEN

Malcolm stayed out of the way as much as possible on Sunday at the craft show. It was obvious that he was still persona non grata.

On Monday, he decided he might be a bit paranoid. It couldn't be as bad as he thought. But then he walked by May Williams on Main Street and she sniffed at him, then looked through him and he realized that it was worse.

Honestly, it was as if he were invisible.

He walked over to the restaurant and was relieved Kennedy was already at a back table. As he moved in her direction he saw that Lincoln was already there, too.

His mood got even worse, if that were possible. He tried to remind himself that he didn't think Lincoln was interested in Kennedy. At least that's what he'd thought at the lighting ceremony, but seeing him sitting across from Kennedy, the two of them so unbelievably cozy looking, he wasn't quite as sure.

Linc stood up, and for half a moment he wore the same look Mal was getting used to seeing on everyone in town. Not smiling, he shook Mal's hand. "Thank you for coming."

"I'd stand, too," Kennedy said as if she didn't notice the tension between them, "but by the time I managed it, it would be dinnertime."

Mal sat between Kennedy and Lincoln and felt better.

Tavi came over. "Oh, *you're* here," she said with a decidedly less-than-enthusiastic inflection. And in case he missed her unenthusiastic response, she shot him a look of pure malice. Then she offered Kennedy a beatific smile. "What can I get you all?"

"Coffee," Mal said.

"Hot tea," Lincoln said.

Mal had never seen a man order hot tea in a restaurant. Maybe iced tea in the summer, but not hot tea.

When Tavi came to Kennedy, she said, "You don't get a choice. A large milk."

Kennedy laughed. "Which was my choice, so ha."

"Ha yourself. We're all watching out for you." Tavi *accidentally* kicked Mal's chair. "Excuse me."

"Man, what did you do to piss off Tavi?" Linc asked, then in an instant his expression said he remembered just what Mal had done.

Mal was saved from coming up with an answer when Kennedy said, "Knocked me up. The entire town has decided I had no part in the matter whatsoever and they're blaming Malcolm. I swear, I've talked to them. No one will listen to me. If you value your life, it might be better if you shortened your stay."

"How long are you in town for?" Linc asked, diplomatically ignoring the rest of Kennedy's explanation.

"Indefinitely," Mal said. "I have a lot of things to settle here before I can go back."

"Your father must be going nuts," Kennedy said. "He can't be happy that you're taking all this time off."

She'd hit the nail on the head with that statement. Senior had called him yesterday and read him the riot act. *Any other law firm would have fired you by now*, he'd said.

Lucky for me, you're my loving, devoted father, Mal had countered. *You gave me until the new year, remember?*

He knew his father loved him in his own way, but *loving* and *devoted* had never been words he'd used to describe their relationship.

Lincoln looked from one to the other. "I feel like the third wheel. Would you like me to give you two some space?"

"No," they said in unison.

Tavi brought the drinks and kicked Mal's chair again as she left. He took a sip of his coffee and only just barely managed not to spit it out. It was not only stone cold, it was bitter.

Tavi was watching him and shot him a drop-dead look.

Mal put the coffee cup back in its saucer and resigned himself to not eating at The Cupboard for a while. He'd have to go down the road to Simple Food. Ruthy Yoder might be more forgiving.

"So tell me about your idea, Linc," Kennedy said.

He glanced from Mal to Kennedy, then back again, then nodded more to himself than either of them. "Well, you know that Lincoln Lighting not only makes LED lights, but we're starting to manufacture solar panels. I want to talk to you both about making Cupid Falls one of the greenest cities in the US. We'll offer our panels to the town's people at a special, very discounted rate. I've got a marketing idea. Your banners gave me the idea. What if the cupid was wearing green instead of red on our ads, and the slogan would be something like *Here in Cupid Falls Green's the Color of Choice*. Maybe something about *Falling in Love with Green Living. Love the Planet, Embrace Your Inner Green.* I don't know." He shrugged. "They're not very good, but we'll get our team on it. I think some kind of web ads. Video clips of the panels going in all over town. Maybe some figures on how much everyone ends up saving on their electric bills. I want to show that even in a northern climate, solar power can make sense . . ."

Lincoln went on, describing his plan, and Kennedy watched him with rapt attention.

She hung on his every word. Mal kind of agreed that Linc had a good idea, but he hated that an idea that Kennedy loved hadn't come from him.

". . . and that's where you both come in. I want to start by putting them on City Hall and then some businesses on Main Street. The Center, City Hall, and the flower shop to start. We'll put together the business owners and start the ball rolling with them. Then we'll move on to the homes in the area."

"And you'll get marketing out of it," Kennedy said.

Lincoln nodded. "But more than a marketing campaign, we'll have a real-life city showcasing what our product can do. Solar panels, LED lighting. Maybe we can come up with other green ideas."

"We'll have to run it by the town council," Kennedy said, "but I can't see any downside to this."

"I was thinking about hiring someone to document the entire project. We'll start with some meetings, maybe a section on what PV panels are, and then move on to documenting the installation. We can run them on the web. I think it could be good for all of us . . ."

Lincoln and Kennedy made plans to get the town council together, then Lincoln beat a hasty retreat.

"Well, that made him uncomfortable," Kennedy said, glaring at Mal. "I don't blame him."

"Of course you don't blame him," Mal said and was shocked at how petulant he sounded.

Kennedy frowned. "What does that mean?"

"I'm wondering if a certain man is the real reason behind your wanting me out of the picture?" Lincoln was building a life here in Cupid Falls. He was coming up with improvements for the town.

Kennedy snorted. "Linc? You think there's something between me and Lincoln Gates?" She laughed. "Seriously, Malcolm, he's not my type."

"He's handsome." The moment the words were out of his mouth, he felt emasculated.

"Then you go out with him. Appearances have never been high on my list of what to look for in a man."

"Then what is?" he asked.

"I want a man . . ." She stopped herself and Mal wondered what she'd almost said. He had a feeling that it would be telling.

She shook her head. "I don't think it matters right now. I told Nana Vancy that I wasn't able to take on a dog now. And if I can't manage that, I definitely can't manage a man. Men are a lot more work than a dog."

He should feel insulted, because he was pretty sure Kennedy had just dissed his entire gender. But she looked so serious he couldn't help but laugh.

Despite the fact the entire town of Cupid Falls had blacklisted him. Despite the fact he was about to become a father. Despite the fact the mother of his child wouldn't marry him, he found Kennedy Anderson delightful.

"It's Monday," he announced in a thank-you-Captain-Obvious sort of way. He remembered her mentioning going out with his mom on Mondays.

"Yes," she said slowly.

"Come out with me tonight. We'll have a Movie Monday in honor of my mother. I'll buy you popcorn and we'll gorge ourselves on it, then I'll take you to dinner and we'll dissect the show and complain about how full we are."

"Malcolm, that's a lovely offer, but I don't know if I'm ready to do a Movie Monday without Val. I—"

"My mother would love that we carried on the tradition," he said. "And I'll let you pick the movie."

"Your mom and I always took turns," she said.

He wanted her to go out with him. He wanted to spend time with her. If he'd met her in Pittsburgh, he'd be asking her out now. There was something about Kennedy . . . he didn't think whatever it was that attracted him to her was the fact that she carried his child, or that his mother and grandfather loved her. Or even that she was a competent, successful businesswoman. It was simply Kennedy herself.

"That's nice that you and Mom took turns choosing movies. We'll do that, too. You pick this one, and I'll pick the next."

"There won't be many. You're going to have to go back to Pittsburgh eventually. That's your home. This is mine."

As she said the words, he realized she was wrong. "I may live in Pittsburgh now, and someday I could live somewhere else, but Cupid Falls will always be home. I don't know if I realized that until now, but it is."

He glanced around the restaurant. Tavi spotted him and glared at him. A few others did as well. "Despite the fact I'm currently persona non grata, the people of Cupid Falls are as much a part of me as Pap and Mom."

Kennedy looked as if she was going to argue with him, and fighting with her was the last thing he wanted to do, so he quickly said, "Just come out to the movies with me?"

"You're already going shopping with me after work tomorrow. You don't need to spend tonight with me, too," she said.

He shot her his best courtroom smile. The one he used on cantankerous jurors. "It will be difficult, Kennedy, but somehow I'll manage to spend two entire evenings with you. We'll simply chalk it up to my amazing strength of character." He grinned and could see her fighting not to smile as well. He could see her wavering, so he added, "Please?"

"Fine." Her smile slipped through as she stood awkwardly. "If I'm going out tonight, I'd better get back to the shop. I have a few more orders to get done."

"I'll pick you up at five?" he asked.

"Five thirty?" she countered. She threw a bill on the table to cover the drinks.

She could have said midnight and he'd have agreed. "See you then."

He added his own bill to the table. Not that he thought a hefty tip would sweeten Tavi's mood.

～

"Kennedy?"

They were standing on her porch as she fumbled in her purse for the keys. Why hadn't she had them in her hand so she could simply hurry into the house? "Yes?"

"I wouldn't have pegged you as a blood-and-guts movie fan. You watched most of those scenes through your fingers."

"That was for your mom. She said she went to action films with you when you were growing up and she got addicted. I picked it because I thought you'd like it more than the rom-com I thought about."

"If we'd sat through a romantic comedy, maybe you'd be inclined to say yes if I asked, Kennedy, will you marry me?"

"Tell me why you think we should get married. Give me a good reason. Good reasons."

This time instead of giving her some lame reason, Malcolm asked, "Why ask *why*? I'd think the answer was obvious. We're going to be parents."

"Not good enough."

"We're compatible. We could make a go of it. And it would be best for our child to have two loving parents."

"Malcolm, I grew up with two loving parents . . . they loved me, and they loved each other. They couldn't walk by each other without touching. Something as small as just their hands brushing as they passed each other. I know we'll both love our baby, but we won't have what they had. Marrying me would be like . . . well, it would be like when Aunt Betty took me in. She did love me . . . in her own way. But when I left for school, she didn't miss me. I'd been an obligation that she'd met. Someone she grew to love, but never like my parents. I deserve more than that. So do you. So does our child. That's why I keep saying no."

"What if I said I thought we could find what your parents had?"

She shook her head. "They grew up together. They knew everything about each other. You don't know me that well."

She didn't say she didn't know *him* that well, because she did. Val had shared everything. She knew that he volunteered his legal services to small start-up companies. She knew he worked hard. She knew he loved his mother and grandfather unconditionally. She knew he liked action movies as much as his mother did. Every time they'd see one, Val would be anxious to tell Malcolm all about it.

But of all the things she knew, she remembered the boy in school who'd seen her, a new girl in the cafeteria, and invited her to sit at his table. Not next to him, not because he was interested in her, but because he was fundamentally a kind boy . . . who'd grown up to be a kind man. The type of honorable man who'd asked her to marry him.

Those were all reasons for her to be sure he'd be a good father. She wasn't sure how she'd ever believed that he would walk away from his child. She'd been selfish. Something Mal wasn't.

Oh, he was busy and distracted sometimes, but he wasn't selfish.

"I'm going to change the subject now," he informed her.

She sighed. "So we're not done talking? Do you want to come in where it's warm to change the subject?"

"No. I want to point out that this was our first date, and as such . . ." He didn't finish the sentence. He didn't ask her permission. He simply leaned in and kissed her.

It was a gentle kiss. His body pressed to hers. His lips pressed to hers.

And for one moment, Kennedy felt as if every girlhood fantasy had come true. She almost wrapped her arms around his neck and deepened the kiss herself, but the baby kicked. She remembered this was no fantasy, and she was no girl.

Malcolm pulled back. "Was that the baby?"

"Yes."

"May I . . ." He paused. "Never mind."

Kennedy knew he had been about to ask to feel the baby kick. The baby's movements had become so much a part of her life that she'd never stopped to consider that Malcolm had never felt him kick. He didn't know that the baby got hiccups. The other night they'd been so severe she couldn't sleep.

She unzipped her parka, reached out, took his hand, and placed it on her stomach with her hand on top of his. "He likes to kick me right . . ." As if on cue, the baby obliged and kicked.

"Wow" was all Malcolm said, his voice little more than a whisper, as if he didn't want to startle the baby.

"That was my reaction when the baby first started moving, but when he kept me up the other night hiccupping, I thought I was pretty much over it."

He looked surprised. "They do that? Hiccup?"

"Oh, yeah. I think he's practicing for football or some other sport, the way he kicks."

She could tell he was reluctant as he drew his hand back, but he finally did and very formally said, "Thank you for sharing it with me."

She turned to go in the house, then stopped. "Malcolm, when you came into my flower shop a couple weeks ago, I thought I knew what I wanted. I wanted you to know about the baby. And after you found out, I wanted you to turn around and head back to Pittsburgh. I wanted you to leave me with him because it would be easier for me. I was selfish, because everything I know about you tells me you'll be a wonderful father."

"What do you want now, Kennedy?"

"I don't know what I want." That was as honest an answer as she could give.

"Maybe that's a start," he said slowly. "I do think we should marry, but I don't know how we'd make that work. You'll be here and I . . . won't."

"Well, then maybe that's a start, too."

"As long as we're starting, let me try this one more time." He pulled her back into his arms and kissed her again. This time, it was no gentle introduction. This was the kiss she remembered from almost nine months ago. And for the first time since Malcolm had come home, she let her guard down completely and kissed him back.

When they finally broke apart, he smiled and said, "Yes, maybe this was a start. And maybe it's okay if neither of us is sure exactly what we're starting. See you tomorrow, Kennedy."

CHAPTER ELEVEN

The next morning Kennedy realized she was excited that she'd be seeing Malcolm again tonight to shop for baby furniture. She tried to tamp down the feeling, but it kept bubbling back to the surface. Except last night's kiss—kisses—couldn't happen again. Kissing Malcolm would complicate their relationship, which was already complicated enough.

Working on six arrangements for a funeral helped dampen her enthusiasm for the evening. She hadn't personally known Steve Stevenson. He was an older farmer who had lived on the outskirts of the county. His son was taking over the farm. He'd called and ordered the family's arrangements. She loved that his son, Jonah, was taking over the family farm. He'd mentioned he'd be the fourth generation to farm that land.

What would that be like? She couldn't imagine having that deep connection to a place. She longed to have roots like that. That's what she was trying to build for her baby here in Cupid Falls. She wanted her child to walk down the streets and know everyone, not grow up in some impersonal city where no one even made eye contact.

She wanted them to look at a divot in the floor and know they put it there when they dropped something. To see the tree in the backyard and remember climbing it, or swinging on it when they were young.

She wanted to tell them the legend of the falls and someday maybe they'd take someone they loved there. Or maybe, like Pap, they'd simply meet someone there and know—heart and soul—that was the person they'd spend their life with.

She wanted her child to go out in the world and spread their wings but to always come back to Cupid Falls and have it feel like coming home.

The bell rang, and like Pavlov's dogs, Kennedy automatically put her clippers down and put her fantasies for her child away as she walked out front.

"Hi, Mayor," Jenny Murray said with none of her normal bubbliness.

There was something in her tone, in her eyes, that made Kennedy ask, "Jenny, what's wrong?"

"I came in to order some flowers from everyone at The Cupboard for Mr. Stevenson's funeral."

"Were you close to him?" she asked, thinking that might be why Jenny seemed so upset.

Jenny shook her head. "He used to come into the restaurant. I've waited on him. He was a very nice man."

"So I repeat, what's wrong?"

Jenny teared up. "I downloaded some do-it-yourself divorce papers and sent them to Wade. He's working in Ohio. Only an hour away, but he hasn't seen the kids, or even talked to them on the phone. He called me, furious, and said if I get a divorce, he's filing for sole custody of the kids."

"I don't understand," Kennedy said. "If he's left you, why wouldn't he want a divorce?"

"He thinks if we stay married, things can go on like they've been. He doesn't have to send any money for the kids. And he said I'm the best dating tool he's ever had. Women can't get too serious about a married man. But I think mainly he's afraid if we're divorced, I'll take him to court. He'd have to pay child support and he doesn't want to do that."

Tears welled up in Jenny's eyes. "I should never have married him. I was only eighteen when I got pregnant with Timmy, and my family insisted. Wade was working at Dad's garage. It was a twenty-first-century shotgun wedding. The next year we had Lenny, then Ivy. I felt stuck. I think the best thing Wade Murray ever did was leave me. But I'll stay married to him if that's what it takes to keep my kids."

"What can I do?" Kennedy asked.

"Nothing, Mayor. Really. I don't think I'll ever want to date another man, much less marry one. Marrying someone is a leap of faith. You're saying you trust them to catch you when you take that jump. Wade never caught me."

Kennedy didn't want to see that lowlife Wade Murray take advantage of Jenny's love for her kids. "You should talk to Malcolm. He could help."

"If I had money for a lawyer, it wouldn't be for some slimy deadbeat like Mal."

Seeing sweet, sunny Jenny come into the shop so upset had been a shock, but hearing her talk about anyone like that was an even bigger shock. "Jenny, what on earth did Malcolm ever do to you?"

"It's not me, it's you. Everyone in town knows, Kennedy," she said with unexpected ferocity. "And we all think it's perfectly rotten of him to get you pregnant and leave you to deal with things on your own. Tavi said she kicked him *accidentally*"—she air quoted the word—"the other day. I told her I would have dropped his coffee on him." She paused a moment and added, "*Hot* coffee," just to make her intentions known.

Of all the scenarios Kennedy had imagined with her whole situation, the town's anger toward Malcolm hadn't even made the list. She didn't know what to do about it. "Jenny, first off, you, more than anyone, should know that marrying for a baby's sake never works."

Rather than softening Jenny, the reminder of her soon-to-be ex made her look more fierce. "I'm not talking about marrying, I'm simply talking about supporting you. You've gone through your whole pregnancy on your own. Helping out Pap with Mal's business and dealing with your own, plus being mayor. Where was he? In Pittsburgh, that's where. That's how it is with men. They have no problem dumping everything on women."

Kennedy shook her head. "There was no dumping between me and Malcolm. I didn't tell him until he came home two weeks ago. Actually a bit less than that. And ever since, he's tried to help me, whether it was cooking Thanksgiving dinner for me, feeding me leftovers, offering to shop for the baby and set up the nursery for me . . ."

It wasn't simply that he asked her to marry him; he'd stepped up and tried to help where he could. And it wasn't even tangible things like cooking. There was the house. Every time she went home and saw it reflecting more her style than Aunt Betty's, it was because of him. Because of his suggestion to make it more her, to start making it look like *her* home, rather than someone else's.

He'd made her feel more at home at the house than she'd ever felt.

"Listen, I'm going to ask Malcolm to talk this over with you because he's the best lawyer I know. He graduated top of his class and he's won every case he's worked on so far." She held up a hand.

"And before you say something about him bragging, I heard that all from Val and Pap, not Malcolm. He's not only good, he's the best."

She switched topics. "And I'm going to ask you to do something for me in return."

"Anything, Kennedy. I hope you know that."

"I need your help putting out this particular fire. I'd appreciate it if you'd spread the word that Mal didn't know anything about my pregnancy until he got home for Thanksgiving. Seriously, he didn't even know I was pregnant, much less pregnant with his baby. He's offered to marry me and I said no, but he's staying in town for a while to help me get ready for junior here." She patted her ginormous stomach, hoping the reminder of the baby would soften Jenny's feelings toward his father. "We're going shopping for baby furniture tonight. Does that sound like something a deadbeat dad would do?"

"No," Jenny said slowly.

"Malcolm has been nothing but honorable. If you could spread the word, I'd appreciate it."

Jenny seemed to consider what Kennedy had said for a moment, then slowly nodded. "I will."

"And if Malcolm agrees, will you go see him for advice?" Kennedy knew she didn't need to worry about him agreeing. He would say yes because she asked. She knew that as sure as she knew her own name.

"Yes, I'll talk to him." Jenny reached out and hugged Kennedy. "Thank you, Kennedy. For everything."

Kennedy patted Jenny's back.

Jenny pulled back and Kennedy said, "In the meantime, why don't we call Jon and let him know what's going on with Wade? As a cop, he'll know what to do if Wade shows up." Kennedy didn't say it, but she was worried. She'd never liked Wade Murray. He'd flirted with her more than once while he was married to Jenny and she had no respect for the man. She wouldn't put it past him to show up and simply take the kids. And since he was still married to Jenny, Kennedy didn't think there was any legal reason he couldn't. But Wade struck her as a coward, so if Jon was around, he probably wouldn't do anything. And she was sure Malcolm could do something so that he didn't have the right to.

"I'm seeing Malcolm tonight and I'll ask him. If he can't, I'm sure he'll know someone who can."

"I can't afford much, Kennedy," Jenny admitted.

She brushed Jenny's concerns about money aside. "That is the least of your worries. We'll figure that out. Right now, you go call Jon, and I'll talk to Malcolm and get back to you tomorrow morning."

"Thank you." Jenny started toward the door and then turned around. "I'll tell everyone about Mal, like you asked, but know if it comes down to him or you, I'm on your side. And if you need anything at all, you just holler."

"Thanks."

"I'd like to think we've always been friends," Jenny said slowly.

Kennedy nodded. "That's how I think of you."

"Well, they say the difference between a friend and a good friend is when you tell a friend a man's done you wrong, they commiserate. When you tell a good friend, they ask where you want to bury the body." She offered Kennedy a small smile. "If you need me to help bury the body, you simply have to say so."

Jenny was as sweet as the day was long, but looking at her expression, Kennedy felt as if Malcolm had better really watch his step, because burying the body might be something Jenny took care of on her own.

~

Mal glanced at Kennedy as they drove into Erie again for the second night in a row.

Mal thought that was the wonderful thing about Cupid Falls . . . the city was practically on their doorstep. Cupid Falls' residents had access to Erie's Millcreek Mall and the Great Lake, the bayfront, the Broadway theater series . . . and if Erie's amenities being a half hour away weren't enough, there were three major cities within a couple of hours' drive—Pittsburgh, Buffalo, and Cleveland.

There was a huge baby store on upper Peach Street, a shopping mecca up from the mall. The entire shopping district was Christmased up to the hilt. Lights. Garlands. Santas. Peach Street and the mall had it all going on.

Mal couldn't help but notice that for someone who was making do with a cradle next to her bed, Kennedy definitely got into the fun of things.

She oohed and aahed over the seasonal displays, and she explored the baby gadgets with a great deal of enthusiasm.

Two hours later, they had a crib that later converted into a youth bed. They had a changing table that converted into a plain dresser. There was a car seat that mounted onto a base in the car and mounted on a stroller as well.

"Can you think of anything else you need?" he asked, thinking he was glad he had an SUV. The furniture would be delivered, but the rest of the baby stuff they'd take now.

"I think that's it."

"What about a rocking chair?" he asked, pointing to a collection in the back corner of the store.

"There's one in the basement. It was my mom's and before that, her mom's. I was going to bring it up. I like the idea of the baby being rocked in the same chair that family had been. My mother will never know the baby, so it's a nice connection." She paused, then reached out and took his hand, whispering, "Sorry. I didn't mean to remind you."

Mal realized she was apologizing for reminding him that his mom would never know this baby, either. For a moment he was almost floored with the pain of that knowledge. His mom would have loved the baby. And the baby would have loved her.

He'd mourned for her, but he realized since he'd come home he'd been so focused on the baby and Kennedy the pain had receded a little. Maybe it was simply having someone who understood his loss. "I have a small table that my grandmother gave Mom. She brought it with her to Pittsburgh, then brought it back when we moved home. If you'd like, I'll bring it over and you can put it next to your rocker. That way, every time you rock the baby, they'll both be a part of it."

Kennedy teared up. "Thank you."

"As for the rocker, you won't bring it up. I will. When they deliver the furniture, I'll help you move things around."

She sniffed and wiped at her eyes, then smiled. "You're bossy. Is it an attorney thing?"

"I think it's a genetic thing. You've met Senior, right?" He clarified, "But I meant it as a genuine offer, not a command."

"Then I'll accept your offer of the table and your offer of the assistance. Thank you."

"And I'd like to pay for the nursery items."

That moment of connection was gone as quickly as it arrived. She visibly bristled. "I don't need you to pay."

"I didn't think you did. But I'd like to. I'm going to be the baby's father. You're going to have to let me help."

She considered what he said for a moment. Mal wondered just what she was thinking. She didn't vocalize her thought process. But finally she nodded. "Fifty-fifty?"

He'd have preferred to simply pay for all of it, but it was a compromise. "Fine."

They carried the slips for the furniture and a cart of extras toward the register. Mal stopped at a rack of books before they got there. He scanned the titles and put three in the cart.

"What did you get?" she asked.

"Just some basics for me. A book on pregnancy, one on the baby's first year, and one on breastfeeding."

He was surprised when Kennedy actually blushed. "Why on earth do you need a book on breastfeeding? I'll be the one doing it."

"I don't know anything about it, other than it exists. I want to understand the process and see if there's any way I can help you."

"I don't mean this rudely, but that is one area where I'm sure I won't need your help."

He shrugged and didn't remove the books.

They split the bill, and after the car was packed, he said, "I don't suppose you would let me treat you to dinner?"

"No. I don't suppose I will. But I could probably manage to eat," she said.

Malcolm thought tonight was progress. "Fine. Then dutch treat it is."

∼

On the drive back to Cupid Falls, Kennedy broached the Jenny question.

"Malcolm, I need to ask you a favor—"

She didn't get any further than that when he interrupted and said, "Anything."

She couldn't help but smile. She'd told Jenny she was sure he'd help, and she had been, but his quick response without knowing what favor she was going to ask was more than she'd expected.

"No, it's not for me or the baby. It's for Jenny Murray." She filled him in on everything Jenny had said. "She can't afford much. Heck, she can't afford anything. Wade hasn't paid her a penny since he left right after Ivy was born. She's got her family's house, but Wade took out a mortgage on it and the Cupid Falls rumor mill says he didn't give Jenny a dime of it."

His eyes stayed forward, on the road, but he nodded. "Pro bono then."

Kennedy was not an expert, but she was sure that an offer of free legal services would be an insult to Jenny. "No, you can't do that. She'd never agree. But maybe you could make some kind of reduced fee?"

He nodded as he drove. "I'll work it out with Jenny then."

"Thank you," she said formally.

"You're welcome," he said.

They rode in silence for a while. Approaching Waterford was a sign they were almost home, and Kennedy knew there was one more thing she had to say. "Malcolm, I want to say that I was wrong. I should have told you sooner. You've been nothing but a gentleman about the entire situation. And I want to thank you. I look at what Jenny's going through, and I know—what I should have known from the beginning—you would never walk away from your child like Wade did. You are in so many ways your mother's son. And I know that things are crazy now, but we'll work it all out together."

She paused a moment and made what she knew was a promise: "I swear, we'll make it work."

"We could work it out right now if you'd marry me."

"What if you asked and I said yes? What then, Malcolm? So I say yes, we get married, and . . ."

He glanced at her, then back at the snowy road. "I don't know what you mean."

"Oh, come on. You're an attorney. You're smart. You've got to figure that the fact I live in Cupid Falls and you live in Pittsburgh would make some huge logistical issues."

"One of us would have to move. Maybe we could split the distance?"

"You'd want me driving an hour down I-79 every day with a newborn?" They'd had snow off and on this year, but it was nothing to what they'd get later in the season.

"Earlier I know I said I'd be the one to move back to Pittsburgh and you'd stay here with the baby. But you could always sell the flower shop and move to Pittsburgh," Malcolm suggested.

"I'm the mayor of Cupid Falls. I can't do that and live in Pittsburgh. And I have some good ideas for the town . . . ideas that will help it maintain everything that's wonderful about it but keep it financially viable in the future. Things like our partnership with Linc and . . ." She thought about her dream for their child. Roots. She wanted to give her baby that sense of home—a sense of permanence. She shook her head. "I'm not moving."

"But—"

She interrupted him. "If you're honest, you're not ready to walk away from your practice in Pittsburgh. You're your father's heir apparent. Your career is guaranteed if you stay there. There's no way we can split the difference, and neither of us can move."

"Well, we *could* move, but we *won't*. Neither of us is willing to give up our lives for the other."

"Maybe if things were different, one of us would, but . . ." Kennedy didn't finish the sentence. She didn't say if they were in love, they'd figure it out. She was sure he had to know it.

He didn't say anything.

Neither did she, because they both knew there was nothing left to say.

They didn't kiss good night, and Kennedy tried to tell herself that was a good thing.

~

The next day at lunch, Jenny Murray came into the Center's office. "Mal, I want you to know, I wouldn't be here if Kennedy hadn't convinced me that my kids were more important than my . . . well, if you'd asked me yesterday, I'd have said my dislike, but Kennedy stood up for you. She said you didn't know about the baby. She said you'd been supportive since you found out. But I still don't trust you. With most guys I'd say, it's not you, it's me. But I've already proven my judgment is skewed by marrying Wade, so I'm not sure if it's you or me, but I plan to be wary."

"Well, when I became an attorney, I knew that being liked by everyone wasn't in the cards. Doesn't the saying go, 'first, kill all the lawyers'? If I'd worried about popularity, I'd have been a firefighter."

"Firefighter?" Jenny asked with a smile playing behind her frown.

"They rush into burning buildings and rescue people. What's not to like?"

Jenny couldn't hide her smile any longer, though Mal watched her try.

"I'm smiling on the outside," she told him, "but still standoffish on the inside."

"Have a seat, Jenny, and tell me about Wade."

She did. Her words tumbled, one over another, in a rush to get the whole story out. He could see her fear. Here was a mother who'd do anything for her kids. She was willing to stay married to her jerk of an ex rather than risk losing the boys and Ivy. She was willing to let Wade walk away from his parental duties, as well as his financial responsibilities, in order to keep her kids with her.

When she was done, Mal said, "You've made it clear that you don't trust me, at least not with Kennedy. But do you trust me as a lawyer?"

"Pap, your mom, and Kennedy are always going on about cases you've won, and what a great lawyer you are," she said slowly.

"Kennedy talks about me?"

"Don't get all conceited. She was your mom's best friend. The two of them came in to lunch at The Cupboard a few days a week. Dinner sometimes, too. You should have seen them. They were always talking as if they hadn't seen each other in years. And laughing. Mal, your mom loved Kennedy. Loved her like a daughter. And your mom was so proud of you. Of course she shared that with Kennedy, and maybe Kennedy mentioned your successes on occasion."

He felt lighter than he had in a long time. Kennedy had mentioned him, which meant even back then, back when his mom was alive, she had thought about him. They might be no closer to reaching any resolution, but he knew she'd thought about him from time to time. Maybe that meant something. If she'd thought about him in the past, maybe that would bode well for their future.

"You can't take it back," he said, jokingly. "And you don't have to like me in order to let me help you with Wade. I can see to it that he doesn't take your kids and gives you your divorce."

"You're sure? The kids are the most important thing. More important than me being free of him."

"Trust me at least about your divorce. You're not going to lose custody of your kids."

She nodded. "About money. I can't pay your whole fee at once, but I can make a payment on it." She pulled out her checkbook.

"How about this? Let me see how quickly I can wrap this up. I think it's only fair if Wade pays you child support, and when that happens, we'll work out some payment plan out of that."

He thought she was going to argue, but she tucked her checkbook back in her purse. "The money doesn't matter as much as the kids . . . they're my everything."

"Noted."

She got up to leave and said, "You know, there's a chance Kennedy's right and you're not such a bad guy."

"Thanks . . . I think," he said.

"Do you want some unsolicited advice?" she asked.

Mal smiled, sure that the advice had to do with Kennedy. "Could I stop you if I said no?"

"Okay, here goes for you. Kennedy is a catch, Mal. Don't let her slip through your fingers, because . . . well, I don't carry tales, but I hear things at the restaurant, and if you let her slip through your fingers, someone else will be happy to catch her."

She was probably talking about Linc. No matter what the guy indicated, how could he not want Kennedy? Jenny was right. She was a catch.

"Hey, wait, before you go. Kennedy is having some back pain. I know you've had three kids. I wondered if you had any suggestions."

Jenny turned back and studied him a moment, then asked, "Did she tell you that?"

He shook his head. "I noticed. She's always shoving a hand in the small of her back."

This time Jenny shot him a smile that he recognized. He'd seen it on opponents. Other lawyers who knew something he didn't. The smile got even bigger as she answered, "I got these belly bands that were for back support. They're miracle workers."

"Where?"

"There's a maternity store in the mall in Erie. Call them. I'd think they'd have them."

Jenny paused, studied him for longer than was comfortable, and finally chuckled at whatever she'd seen. "I take everything back. I do like you, Mal. And I believe you'll get this all figured out."

CHAPTER TWELVE

Mal couldn't help but think about Jenny's warning that there might be someone waiting in the wings if he let Kennedy slip through his fingers.

He could ask her to marry him again, but nothing had changed. And even if she had changed her mind, what would they do?

Kennedy's life was here in Cupid Falls. She owned a store. She might be able to find someone to manage that, but she was also the mayor of Cupid Falls. She couldn't do that long-distance, and she couldn't hire someone to handle that for her.

And he couldn't see her resigning her position as mayor. It was a small town, but she was passionate about her job. She was actively working to ensure the town's future. Just look at her tentative plans with Lincoln Lighting. And her work to bring more tourism their way.

So what would they do if she said yes, she'd marry him?

He couldn't ask her to leave Cupid Falls.

And how on earth would they make a long-distance marriage work?

A better question—how would he make long-distance fatherhood work?

Mal stared out the window, his thoughts chasing one another. He wasn't getting anywhere.

He'd forgotten how much he loved it here. He'd grown up looking out of this very window at this very view. Not much had changed. The trees were more mature now. But otherwise, it was the same.

It was a warm day for December. He'd only worn a light jacket on his walk over today. Well, *warm* was a relative term. Pittsburgh might only be a couple of hours south of Cupid Falls, but that hundred-plus miles made a huge difference in the winter weather. Pittsburgh didn't get nearly the snow that the towns near the lake did. Here in Cupid Falls along with neighboring Erie, Waterford, and other lake cities and towns, the term *lake-effect snow* was bandied about all winter as cold Canadian air swept over the open lake and deposited huge quantities of snow on the shores.

But despite the early snow this year and the fact that it felt like winter, it was technically still autumn, and today was one of those rare December days when winter had backed off and warmer weather got to make a brief reappearance.

It had to be at least fifty out, Malcolm mused as he looked out the office window. He had all the Center's business under control. His mom and Kennedy had done a great job of streamlining their system.

He'd made some calls for the upcoming Everything But a Dog benefit. He'd also made some calls on Jenny's behalf. It turned out that Wade didn't have a lawyer. He'd thought his threats would be enough to get his way with Jenny.

Malcolm let him know in no uncertain terms that was not the case. Jenny had said she didn't need child support, but he didn't tell Wade that. He warned Wade that they would be suing for . . . he spouted a long list of charges, most of which bordered on the absurd, but Wade didn't seem to realize that. As he sputtered, Mal threw out a figure that had Wade whining on the other end of the line.

Then Mal laid out a simple alternative. Sign the divorce papers. Give Jenny sole custody of the kids. And start paying reasonable child support. Otherwise, he was taking Wade to court, and when he got done with him, Wade would have nothing left.

Mal hung up the phone feeling pretty certain Wade was going to comply. He felt as if he'd made a difference. This was how he'd imagined having a law practice would be. Helping people—people who were at a low point in their lives. Making a difference.

The only difference he felt he'd made at his father's firm was lining the pockets of their corporate clients as well as lining the firm's pockets. He couldn't remember the last time he'd felt as if his law degree had made a positive impact on anyone in a personal way.

Well, he'd made a difference for Jenny. He had decided to go over to the restaurant and give her the good news when a movement outside caught his attention.

It was Kennedy. She was walking on the path down toward the woods.

Mal had grown up walking that path down to the creek and the falls. In the summer they'd gone swimming at the hole at the base of the falls. In the winter they rode sleds down the steep hill.

It was a steep enough hill no pregnant woman should try to go it down alone.

He got up and sprinted out the back door.

He realized he hadn't locked the building but didn't stop to go back and do so. This was Cupid Falls. Pap never locked the door. It wouldn't have occurred to him to do so.

Mal thought about shouting for Kennedy to wait, but he was afraid she'd simply walk faster, so he kept jogging along after her.

The path snaked its way down, first to the right, then to the left, never straight down. It wove in between the ash, maple, and hickory trees that made up the woods.

He reached the bottom and slowed. Kennedy was standing at the edge of the swimming hole, staring at the falls. They weren't much when compared to Niagara Falls, but the five-foot drop had seemed huge when he was a kid. The sound of the water was enough to cover the sound of his movements. He didn't want to startle Kennedy, so he quietly said her name.

"Kennedy." She turned and he saw that she was crying. "What's wrong?"

"Nothing. I'm just being pregnant," she said, as if to make light of her tears.

He wasn't buying it. "Really, what's wrong?"

"I did some funeral arrangements the other day for Steve Stevenson. He's a local farmer. I'm sure I saw him in passing around town, but I don't know him. I talked to his son, Jonah. He stopped in today to tell me how beautiful the arrangements were, and then he talked about the farm and his dad. His father was born Amish. Did you know that?"

"No. I don't think I knew the family, although his name sounds familiar."

"He was a few years behind us in school. I don't know. After he left, well, I needed a break. This is my favorite place in Cupid Falls, but it's been snowy, and given my barge-like form, I don't come down often. But today was so warm, I wanted one more visit before the baby comes."

They stood next to each other, watching the falls. Out of the corner of his eye, he could see Kennedy occasionally brush away a tear.

"I'm sorry for the family's loss," he finally said.

"According to Jonah, his father had time to say good-bye and put his affairs in order. He died at home, surrounded by family. He knew Jonah was going to take over the farm. They'd worked side by side for years. It was a good way to go. It's good he got to say good-bye."

In hindsight, he knew how important that was. "Did you get to say good-bye to your parents?"

She shook her head. "In a way, but not really."

Mal realized that he knew she'd lost both her parents, but he'd never asked how. He'd never asked anything.

She'd been there for him when he'd lost his mother, and knowing her aunt, he suspected no one had really been there for her when she'd lost her parents. If there were do-overs, that's one he'd want—being able to be there for her back then.

"What happened?" he asked, not sure if she'd answer.

"Mom and Dad had plans to go away for a weekend—an anniversary celebration. So I was spending the weekend at a friend's—Lori Ann's. I'd felt sick the night before, but I got up to go to school with my bag packed for the weekend. Mom said if I didn't feel better to call and they'd cancel their weekend. I told her I'd be fine . . ."

She stared at the creek and Mal thought she was done, but then she whispered, "I said good-bye to them both when I left for school. I said I'd see them on Sunday. Dad kissed my head and Mom hugged me, then asked if I had my homework . . ."

Mal could see she was lost in the past, and he could see that even after all these years, she felt the pain. He reached out and wrapped an arm around her. "I'm so sorry."

She shook her head. "It was a long time ago. And I guess I did say good-bye, I just didn't know I was saying good-bye forever. For years I wondered what would have happened if I hadn't spent the night at Lori Ann's. What if I'd called and said I still felt sick? What if I'd come home?"

"What happened?"

"I found them in bed on Sunday. It was carbon monoxide. They went to sleep in their room and never woke up. The doctor said I'd probably been sick because I'd been exposed to the carbon monoxide, too. He said I was lucky I left. I didn't feel lucky."

He couldn't imagine what that would be like. A sixteen-year-old girl finding her parents like that. More than anything he wished he'd known her then. He'd wished he'd been with her.

He wanted to say something to ease the pain of the woman in his arms, something that would ease the horror that sixteen-year-old had found. She'd walked in and not only found her parents dead, she'd found her entire world upended.

But because he couldn't find the magic words, he held her close and whispered the only words he could find. "Oh, Kennedy, I'm sorry."

"Thanks," she whispered.

～

Kennedy sat, wrapped in Malcolm's arms.

She couldn't believe she'd just told him all that.

She hadn't expected to feel like this over a stranger's death. When Jonah Stevenson talked about his father leaving his family and the Amish way of life behind, she'd felt this huge hole she hadn't known existed open up and threaten to swallow her. Jonah talked about how out of place his father had felt as he'd tried to build a new life for himself in a new community. The Amish called non-Amish people English. And Jonah talked about his father's difficulties in the English community.

She wished she'd met his father, because she knew exactly how he'd felt. She remembered when her parents died. Lost. Alone. Adrift. She'd lost her family, her home in Cleveland, and her friends.

Aunt Betty had taken her in out of a sense of obligation. For the first few years Kennedy couldn't find any footing. She was a stranger in Cupid Falls. An outsider. At school, the kids had all known each other from kindergarten on. They had circles of friends and cliques. She didn't feel as if she fit in any of them.

And her aunt didn't know what to do with a confused, angry teenage girl. She sheltered her and fed her, but Kennedy wasn't sure Aunt Betty had ever loved her.

She'd worked hard to build a place for herself here in Cupid Falls, but despite the fact she had the store and was the town's mayor, there were still times she felt like that sixteen-year-old girl—lost and alone. A girl whose whole world was taken away from her in the course of a weekend.

Listening to Jonah Stevenson speak, she knew she still felt every bit as much an outsider as his father had been.

Malcolm didn't say anything. He simply held her and waited.

Well, she'd had enough baring of her soul for the day, so she sat up, pulling away from his embrace, and said, "Jonah mentioned that Gideon had been at the funeral. If you sell me the Center, I'd like to hire him to do some of the renovations."

She felt a kinship with Gideon, as well as Jonah's father. People who were displaced—who didn't quite fit in.

She put her hand on the baby, who kicked as if to remind her that she wasn't alone anymore. She'd never be truly alone again.

"Is the baby kicking?" Malcolm asked. "I saw your hand jump."

She nodded.

"May I feel him again?"

There was no way to say no to such an earnest request, so she nodded. She reached out and took his hand and placed it on the spot where the baby had just kicked. She felt him kick again, as if he knew his father wanted to feel him.

"Wow. He's strong."

"Tell me about it. He likes to kick about three in the morning. I live in terror that his night owl tendencies will continue when he's born. I'm not sure how I'll manage being up all night and work."

"If you married me, you could qui—"

"Quit?" she finished for him. She tried to tamp down her annoyance at his suggestion. "You think I'd give up everything I worked for because it was hard? You think I'd let down the town who elected me and resign being mayor? I know Cupid Falls is a small town— that it's the kind of town you'd be hard-pressed to find on a map— but it's my responsibility. I come here to the falls and remember that story about a man and woman meeting here and falling in love. And all the other couples after them. They all gave this town its name. And while it will never be a big city, it's got a big heart. I like to think that its heart is a reflection of that first couple."

"Maybe some of it, but I think any heart the community has is a reflection of its mayor."

She shook her head. She didn't know what to make of him. First he suggested she give up everything she'd worked for, then he offered her a sweet compliment. "I've got to get back to work. Thank you for the proposal, but no."

"Before you go," Malcolm said. "I got a hold of Wade Murray."

"And?"

"It will be fine. He'll not only sign the divorce papers, he's going to start sending Jenny child support, so hopefully things will get a little easier for her."

"I know Wade, and that doesn't seem like something he'd just up and offer to do. And I know Jenny wasn't worried about support, she simply wanted him to leave the kids with her."

"I know. But it seemed unfair to me that he expected her to raise their kids on her own. And I might have implied I was ready to help Jenny sue him for five years of back child support. Even a nominal amount for each kid multiplied by five years with interest would be a lot." He smiled a devilishly pleased smile. "And my ballpark figure seemed to put the fear of God in him. He's going to sign the papers immediately and start making payments this month. In return, Jenny will generously agree not to pursue back payments."

She laughed. "Does Jenny know about her generous offer?"

"I was about to go find her at the restaurant when I saw you."

Kennedy gave a delighted squeal and hugged him. It was an awkward hug, but she couldn't help but think that the baby liked being sandwiched between its parents. "Thank you, Malcolm. Thank you so much. You've made a huge difference in her life."

She realized that she was still hugging Malcolm and pulled back. "Sorry."

"No apologies required. Just think, if you agreed to marry me, you could hug me as often as you liked." He said it as if they were joking, but he watched her with more intensity than was required.

Kennedy shook her head. "And while hugging you is very nice, it's not enough of a reason to marry someone. But seriously, thank you. You've changed somebody's life today."

∾

Malcolm's talk with Jenny had been satisfying. He'd made a difference for her.

183

She'd started crying and hugged him. Tavi and the rest of the customers in the restaurant were still giving him the stink eye, but he noticed Tavi didn't kick or step on him. That was progress.

And this morning with Kennedy at the falls . . . that was progress, too. She'd shared with him. Trusted him with her past. It might not be a marriage, but they were . . . closer.

He walked down the holiday-decorated street and felt lighter. His life was still a mess, but he felt a sense of optimism. Things would work out.

He'd see to it.

He stopped outside the Center and stared at the building. The building Kennedy wanted to buy. Maybe he . . .

His phone rang. He checked the caller ID and almost groaned when he saw his father's number. When his father called before lunch, nothing good could come of it.

Mal wanted to send the call to voice mail, but instead, he hit Talk. "Sir?"

"Do you have those files on the Thompson case?" his father barked with no preamble or salutation.

"Yes. I was going to—"

"You're off the case, so you don't need to do anything other than bring them in to the office ASAP."

Mal felt a stab of regret. The Thompson case was a big one. But on the heels of that regret came annoyance. "You know, you could start a conversation like a regular human being. Something like 'Hi, Mal, how are things? I've missed you,'" he said sarcastically.

"I'm glad you find this amusing," his father harrumphed. "I need those files."

"I could e-mail you the information."

"I prefer the hard copies."

"I'll bring them tomorrow."

184

"Fine." His father disconnected.

"Good-bye, son. Can't wait to see you," Mal said to no one but himself.

He went inside, scribbled on a Post-it note, put it on the front door, then headed over to Kennedy's.

He walked into her shop. It smelled sweet with an undercurrent of something spicy.

Kennedy came out of the back room, an apron over her stomach. It had an arrow pointing at her huge stomach that said "Mama's Little Bud" with a picture of a rosebud.

She saw what he was looking at and smiled. "Jenny and Joan were talking at the restaurant. Joan found a site that would make you whatever kitchen item you wanted. So, Joan got me this one." She pulled a second apron out from under the counter, and it had a frog on it and said, "Mama's Little Tadpole."

"Those are awful." He grinned as he said the words because they were awful in a wonderful way.

"Yeah, they're pretty bad," she said, laughing.

Mal knew that bad or not, she'd wear them. "I brought you a present, too. It's for the baby, so you can't say no." He handed her the small bag.

Slowly, she took the bag and opened it. She looked at the wrapper.

"It's a band you wear that's supposed to help support your stomach," he said.

When she didn't say anything, he added, "It's supposed to help with back pain."

She looked up at him. "How did you know my back hurts?"

"I pay attention," he said.

Kennedy looked from the bag to the man who'd given it to her. "Malcolm, I don't know what to say."

"Well, I'm hoping you'll say you'll keep an eye on things at the Center tomorrow. I've got to go to Pittsburgh and take some papers to my father. That was the second reason I came over. There's nothing much going on other than a book club meeting. Saturday there's the Comstock family's annual pre-Christmas party."

Kennedy laughed. "That isn't simply a family . . . they're a clan. Vivienne's got four siblings and her dad was one of eight."

Mal nodded. "Pap always said as long as the Comstocks kept having babies, the Center will have financial security. They can't fit in any one person's house. I can't imagine they'll need anything, they've done parties with us so often, but in case . . ."

She nodded. "I'm on it."

"I was going to set up the tree at the Center tonight. It was something Pap, Mom, and I always did together. I wondered if you'd come over and help."

Kennedy paused, and for a moment he thought she was going to say no, but she nodded. "Okay. I helped them the last few years."

"Because I didn't come home." He regretted all the times he didn't find time to come home. All the trees he didn't decorate. All the moments he missed. He thought of Jenny. Of her warning that he'd regret the moments he missed with his child, and he knew with absolute certainty that she was right.

"Malcolm, that's not what I meant. It wasn't some slam."

Kennedy looked contrite, and he hurriedly assured her, "I know that's not how you meant it. But I blame myself for not coming home. For not making my family a priority. I felt as if I had to put my career first. And you know my father. He's not big on time off for holidays. I had cases . . ." He shrugged. "Those are only excuses, my way of trying to make myself feel better, because you and I both know I should have been home."

"If you thought your mom was sick, that she needed you, you'd have been here. I know it. She knew it." Kennedy rested her hands on the silly apron over the baby. "You had no reason to believe you wouldn't have years of holidays to spend with her."

"But I didn't have those years of holidays." And that was something he'd have to find a way to live with, but he'd always regret missing those moments with his mom.

"No you didn't," Kennedy said. "But you can't live your life expecting the worst. You didn't know."

He didn't want to rehash his guilt over not being here more for his mom, so he changed the subject. "I better get back to work on those papers for my father. I'll let you get back to your work. When you're done here, why don't you come over? We need to go pick up a tree and then decorate. I'll bring the boxes up this afternoon so we'll be ready."

"Sounds good," Kennedy said.

~

After Malcolm left, Kennedy tried on the belly band, and it did ease the nagging ache in her back.

She wished she could do something to ease Malcolm's ache over the times he'd missed with his mom. She knew that Val had always known he loved her.

She also knew that she could tell him that and she could reassure him, but he wasn't going to believe her, even if he knew she was right.

Knowing and feeling were two very different things.

She suddenly realized she did have something that might help Malcolm.

She went on her computer, dug up the file, and burned it to disc.

She closed the shop early and ran home to take care of the second part of her reminder for Malcolm and was practically skipping by the time she walked into the Center. *Practically skipping* because she was the size of a small house, and houses don't skip.

"Is that you?" Malcolm called.

"No, it's someone else entirely," she called back. She was almost giddy with excitement.

He peeked out of the office and eyed her suspiciously. "What are you up to?"

"Why would you think I'm up to something?" she asked as she hung up her coat and had a moment of thankfulness that she hadn't needed boots. It was impossible to see her feet anymore and next to impossible to tie shoes.

"You have a look about you." Malcolm spotted the plate in her hand. "What do you have there?"

"Come into the office before we start the tree. I have something for you."

She walked in, and because she spent so much time working on the computer, she felt at home dropping the disc into the drive.

"I made this last year and hadn't thought about it until you mentioned the tree tonight. I'd bought myself an iPad for Christmas and set it up on the shelf to film us. And then never gave it another thought."

She hit Play.

Mal sank into the chair and watched the scene play across the computer screen.

"Deck the halls with . . ." Val sang merrily. The merriment was the only thing that kept her off-key rendition bearable.

"Daughter, when the good Lord was handing out pitch, you were at the back of the line."

Val pooh-poohed her father. "It's Christmas. Carols sound good no matter how off-key you are."

"You couldn't hit a note if it were the side of a barn."

She pooh-poohed him again.

Kennedy ignored the banter and put the ornaments up, one by one. She fingered each, wondering what the story was behind them. She knew that Val would tell her soon enough. And as if on cue, Val cried, "That's one of my favorites. Mal's scouting troop had their Christmas party here one year, and all the kids made us an ornament as a thank-you. That's Mal's." She fingered the star made out of sticks. It had a red-and-black-checked ribbon on it and a small gift tag marked Mal. "Look, all the boys have one. Here's Jon's and . . ." She pulled each stick star and read the name.

"I'm sorry he's not here to put them up with you," Kennedy said, knowing she was a poor replacement.

Val laughed. "Oh, he's here. Every ornament is a memory, and he's part of all of them. I know it sounds like a greeting card commercial, but he's always with me. He's out proving himself, and if I know him, he's loving every minute of it. He's never lost a case, you know." Her voice was brimming with motherly pride. "He loves me, he knows he's loved, and he's living a life that he loves. That's all any mother could ask for."

"He'll find his way back to Cupid Falls. It's in his blood," Pap added.

"I know he'll be back because I never taught him how to make my oatmeal cookies. The only way he gets them is if he comes home to visit. I'm that diabolical," Val said with a mock-villain laugh.

"Yeah, the world lives in fear of my daughter," Pap said.

"Speaking of fear, Kennedy, I have a gift for you."

"It's not Christmas for a couple weeks."

"I know, but I want you to come to Christmas dinner, and I'm volunteering you for the pumpkin pies. This might help." She pulled out a cookbook. "I've written all my recipes in it. I always thought I'd give it to *a daughter, and for a long time, I didn't think I'd be able to, then I realized that you don't necessarily have to give birth to your daughter."*

~

Kennedy watched herself burst into tears as she hugged Val and the video blacked out.

"I killed the battery on my iPad. I wish I could have caught the rest for you, but I thought you needed to hear what she said. She loved you and she knew you loved her. She never doubted that. She never resented that you weren't with her."

"That's how you got the recipe for her cookies?"

Kennedy nodded and unwrapped the plate of cookies. "I thought this was an occasion that called for them."

For a moment, Malcolm didn't say anything. He reached out and touched the computer screen, as if that movie had left some imprint on it. He turned to Kennedy. "Thank you."

"You're welcome."

"I don't know how I'll ever repay you for this . . . gift." His voice was laced with emotion.

Kennedy reached out and put her hand on his shoulder. He reached up and covered it with his as he looked at the now-blank computer screen. "It does help. I still hate all the opportunities I blew, but . . ." He stopped, as if trying to get his emotions under control. "It helps knowing that Mom understood. I wanted to prove myself. I thought if I worked harder than anyone else my father would realize what an asset I was. Maybe I thought I could buy his approval . . ."

"And his love?" Kennedy filled in.

He shrugged. "It sounds silly to hear it out loud."

"No. It sounds human. I like you more when you're real."

"What am I when I'm not real?" Malcolm asked.

Kennedy wished she hadn't said that. "I don't know. You're Malcolm Carter the Fourth. Cupid Falls' golden boy. You aced every class in high school and were captain of the football team. You went to an Ivy League school and made a success of yourself. You're a local legend."

He snorted. "The only legend in Cupid Falls is about the waterfall. I'm just me. I've messed up plenty."

"No you haven't," she said staunchly, maybe a hint of that teenage-girl crush creeping into her voice.

"I've messed up you and the baby."

"I want to be real clear about something: this baby is a blessing. I know it wasn't planned, but Malcolm, that night that you and I . . ." She didn't finish the explanation because he was there. He knew what they'd done.

Her voice was little more than a whisper. "I hurt so bad. Val was my best friend. For so long I felt as if I didn't belong anywhere, but that night, when she gave me that cookbook and hugged me . . . it was the first time since my parents died that I felt like I belonged, if that makes sense. And when I lost her, I was adrift again. But that night, you held me and you grieved with me. You . . . well, that night was special, and this baby came from that. I didn't plan to be a single mother, but I'm beyond excited about the baby. And I love knowing that a part of your mom will live on in our child."

He didn't say anything.

"And if you hadn't worked so hard, you couldn't have changed someone's life today."

"I didn't—"

"Jenny would disagree. You changed her life for the better. Remember that, Malcolm." She leaned over and kissed his cheek.

It was just a small gesture of comfort for a friend, she told herself.

Problem was, she wasn't sure she believed it.

CHAPTER THIRTEEN

You've changed somebody's life . . .

Kennedy's words kept replaying in Mal's head on Friday as he drove south on I-79 to Pittsburgh. He drove over overpasses and under underpasses until he reached the heart of the city. He parked his car in the underground parking ramp, but rather than taking the elevator from the garage directly to the law firm's floor, he went out onto the sidewalk. He stared at the huge office building that had been a big part of his life since he finished law school. No one seemed to notice him as they walked around him on their way to their destinations.

In Cupid Falls, someone would have stopped. They'd ask what he was doing, or ask if he needed something, or simply stop to shoot the breeze. Well, they would have done that before; now, they'd walk by him and glare because they all felt that he'd treated Kennedy poorly. But things were beginning to soften there.

When he'd been at the falls with Kennedy, he'd mentioned she was the heart of the community. She'd laughed at the notion. She talked about losing her parents and being her aunt's obligation. She'd felt alone. He didn't think she had any clue how much the town looked to her and counted on her—he wasn't sure she realized how much a part of the community she was.

He'd watched the flower shop since he'd been home, and he couldn't help but notice how frequently people went inside to see her. And while she did a steady business, he suspected that a lot of the visits had nothing to do with flowers.

As he thought about Kennedy and Cupid Falls, he stared at his father's office building. He waited to feel some sense of happiness to be coming home.

All he felt was a need to get back to Cupid Falls—to get back to Kennedy. He'd worried the whole way up here that Kennedy would go into labor, or that she'd need him for something and he wouldn't be there.

He continued to stare at the building, waiting to feel something. But the only thing he felt was the need to go back to Cupid Falls.

Finally, Mal went inside and took the elevator to the firm's floor.

He nodded at people in the halls as he walked back to Senior's office. It wasn't like being at home in Cupid Falls. When he visited there, people would call out his name. They'd smack his back and ask how things were going.

He'd been gone for two weeks . . . had it only been two weeks? It felt like he'd been back in Cupid Falls much longer. But he'd been out of the office for two weeks and no one seemed to notice.

He smiled at his father's assistant. "Is he in?"

"He's expecting you." She shot him a look of warning.

"Bad mood?"

"I wouldn't know what you're talking about," she said, even as she nodded and winked at him.

"Wish me luck," he said.

"You'll need it," she said in a quiet voice.

He knocked on the door and then opened it.

His father looked up and glared. "So the prodigal son has returned."

"I'm simply here to drop off these." He set the files on his father's desk.

"You've been gone for two weeks. When I said you had until the holidays, I didn't think you'd take it. You need to wrap things up there and come home."

"I'm needed at home." As he said the words, he realized his father had used the word *home* to refer to Pittsburgh and he'd used the word *home* when referring to Cupid Falls. "Most of my work is being handled by others right now, but they can call if they need me."

His father didn't say a word. He simply stared at Mal.

Mal waited. He knew this was one of his father's famous attorney tricks. Say nothing. Force the opponent to fill in the empty space. Most people couldn't stand the silence, and as they raced to fill it, they frequently gave his father ammunition.

The question that occurred to him was, when had he become his father's opponent? On the heels of that he asked himself, what kind of father looked for ammunition against his son?

He folded his arms and waited, as silent as his father, not breaking eye contact. It was a battle—a battle of wills. Mal wasn't sure what he was trying to prove, but still he waited.

Finally his father said, "I'd fire anyone else for walking away from their duties."

"There's a flaw in your argument. I'm not walking away from my duties, I'm attending to them. I have a child on its way."

"And you have your duty to the firm."

"One's a child. One's a job. The child wins." Suddenly he realized that his father had faced this same decision and had made the other choice. He looked at his father. He'd never remarried. Mal wasn't even sure he'd ever dated anyone other than his mother seriously. His father was married to the firm.

That struck Mal as a sad thing. Like Pap had said, no one ever looked back and wished for more time at work, but that's all his father would have to look back at.

Mal knew with complete and utter surety that he didn't want an extended leave. "I'm resigning." The words felt right as he said them. "Thank you for the opportunity, sir. I learned a lot working here."

"So you're quitting? You're walking away from this? Do you realize what an opportunity I've given you? You're going to throw it away for what?"

"For a child," Mal said. "For *my* child."

His father shook his head. "You're a fool."

"Maybe. But I can practice anywhere." Half-formed ideas chased after each other in his mind. Helping Jenny Murray. A practice in Cupid Falls? There was an office at the Center. He was close to Erie. "I need to be in Cupid Falls for my child."

"That child will have its mother in Cupid Falls."

"Speaking from experience, I can tell you that having a mother there is important. I'm sure Kennedy is going to be a wonderful mother. But that baby will need me . . . they'll need their father."

His father was still silent, and Mal couldn't think of anything else to say, so he simply said, "I'll be going. I'll type up my formal resignation before I leave, and I'll clear my office out." He started toward the door.

"It's her, isn't it?" Senior asked.

Mal turned around. "Pardon?"

"That woman got what she wanted. She's trapped you. You're giving up your future to move to that Podunk town to do what? Waste yourself. You've got a great legal mind, and working with me you can make the most of it. What will you do with it there?"

"Cupid Falls is right outside Erie, sir. I can open my own practice." And he could hang out a shingle in Cupid Falls. Malcolm

Carter IV, Esquire. "I can take cases that interest me. I can work for people who need me."

"Your clients here need you," his father said stubbornly.

Mal realized what his father didn't say—what he would never say—that *he* needed Mal. That he wanted his son with him.

"My clients here are predominately corporations. And while I know that area of law is a valid one, it's not the kind of law I want to practice. I took on a client who was terrified and didn't know what to do. I'm helping her with a divorce. I made a difference in her life. In her children's lives. And I thought back to all my other clients, and I can't remember anyone who needed me like she did. It meant something. I want to take cases like that. I want to make an actual difference."

"What is it about that town?" His father wore a rare expression for him—total perplexity. "You leave here a young, talented attorney who without any nepotism would someday be a partner in the firm, and you're throwing it all away to open up a solo practice taking on divorce cases and tractor parking violations."

"I didn't come to argue," Mal told his father. "Frankly, I didn't know I was quitting until I got here. I think I figured out that I couldn't work here again as I looked at the building, but as we talked, I knew for sure."

"It's that town. Your mother could have had everything with me. Money, a place in society. She threw that all away for the town."

"She never had you, Father." Mal purposefully called him Father, not Senior or sir. The word felt foreign on his lips. "You never loved her. You felt she trapped you."

"She did," his father said stubbornly.

Mal shook his head. "You're wrong about that, just as you've been wrong about so many things. She loved you. She thought she could change you, that she could help you see that there was more to life than a corner office. She thought she could make us a family, but she couldn't. That's why she left you. And I'm thankful she took me with her."

"Go. Just go."

It would be easy to simply turn around and leave, but Mal felt he had to try to reach his father for his mother's sake. "I know you're angry. But I'm all you have, sir. And Pap said something to me when I first got to town. It's stuck with me. He said it isn't work, but the people in your life who count. Well, I'm all you have. I'd like to think I count for something. I want you to know that just because I'm leaving the firm doesn't mean I'm leaving you. I'd really like it if you came up to Cupid Falls for the holidays. I'd like to have you around when the baby arrives. He'll have Pap as a great-grandfather, but you'll be his only grandfather. I want you to be part of his life." He paused a moment and added, "I want you to be part of my life."

His father didn't say anything, so Malcolm turned to leave a second time.

"Are you going to marry her?" his father called out.

Mal turned back to his father. "I've asked; she keeps saying no."

"Carters don't know the meaning of the word *no*," his father scoffed.

Mal took that to mean his father was offering him his support. "I do hope you'll come down for Christmas, sir."

~

Mal wrote up his letter of resignation. Turned over all his files and notes to the colleagues who'd taken over his cases, and packed up his office. Then he headed home.

Home to Cupid Falls.

He planned for his new solo practice on the two-hour drive.

A practice built on making a difference.

There were vacant storefronts on Main Street . . . no, no. He owned a building on Main Street. He could cut his overhead by working from the Center, which would mean he could take more pro bono cases. And . . .

The miles flew by. It started to snow as he parked the car in front of the Center under a streetlight that had a cupid dressed as Santa Claus banner flapping on it. He looked down Main Street to the identical lights and banners.

He looked at the flower shop's window, which was illuminated with a small tree and huge poinsettias.

He sighed.

He was home.

He went to find Kennedy because he knew it wasn't Cupid Falls that was home.

It was Kennedy. It was the baby they'd made together.

∼

Saturday morning Kennedy stumbled into the kitchen wearing some knee-length maternity yoga pants and a giant T-shirt. She wished she could start the coffeemaker. Wanting a cup of coffee more than she'd ever wanted anything. She settled for starting the teakettle for a rousing cup of herbal tea.

The baby kicked, as if thanking her.

"As soon as you're here, I'm going to mainline a giant cup of coffee," she told him.

He began a staccato burst of kicking. She sang to him as she started making breakfast. She'd found music seemed to soothe him, and the kicking quieted. He was particularly fond of Lady

Antebellum's "Golden." She couldn't argue with his musical taste because she loved that entire album.

She gently massaged her stomach with her left hand as she poured granola in a bowl. She added some raisins and vanilla yogurt. The teapot whistled and she went with lemon tea this morning.

The song done, she sat down to her breakfast. One bite in, there was a knock on the back door.

Who on earth was at her door before seven in the morning? And at the back door no less. The curtain blocked her view, so she shifted it to one side and . . .

Of course. Malcolm. Who else would knock at her door before she'd even dressed? She felt . . . pleased. More than that, she felt happy. Happy to see him. Happy that these early morning visits had become a common occurrence.

She opened the door and he held out a bag. "Happy St. Nicholas Day," he said.

It was December sixth. She'd totally forgotten. She hadn't known about St. Nicholas Day until she became friends with Val. Her parents and Aunt Betty had never celebrated it. But it didn't surprise her that Val did. Val looked for any excuse to celebrate.

Thinking of her friend didn't bring the same degree of pain that it had at first. Now there was more a sense of wistfulness at the happy memory.

"So are you going to invite me in? Turns out St. Nick didn't have a key to your house, so he left your booty at my house."

She laughed. "Come in. And you really shouldn't have," she said as he set the bag down on her table.

"I think Mom would like to know we're carrying on the tradition. I'm hoping that we can do the same for our baby." He reached in the bag and pulled out two oranges. "One's for you and one's for the baby. I thought since you were eating for two, you could eat the second one for him."

She smiled. And he reached back in the bag. "And this is for the baby."

He pulled out a tiny red-and-white romper, then added a tiny cotton Santa-looking hat. "It's for a newborn, so it should fit. I thought it was in keeping with the season."

She picked it up. It was a thick, soft cotton. "It's wonderful. We can put him in it on Christmas Day . . . if he's here by Christmas Day. Frankly, if he's not here by Christmas Day, I might explode."

"I was afraid you'd go into labor while I was Pittsburgh yesterday. We haven't really talked about it, but I'd like you to call me. I want to take you to the hospital. I want to be with you for as long as you want me . . . I mean, I know some parts may be uncomfortable for you to have me there . . . I just . . ."

Kennedy was touched. Malcolm had asked her to marry him, but they hadn't talked about the birth. She wouldn't have known if she should call or not. "I'd like to have you take me to the hospital. And as for staying with me . . . let's leave it at, you can stay until one of us feels uncomfortable."

He nodded. "That's more than I hoped for."

He sighed and reached in the bag one last time. "Well, St. Nick brought you something as well." He pulled out a large leather book. "Baby's First Year" was embossed on the cover.

"Oh, Malcolm, it's beautiful."

"I thought you might accept a present that was baby related. My mom had one for me. She wrote all these notes in it. I pulled it out the other night and was looking through it. I thought you might enjoy doing the same for our baby."

"Thank you, Malcolm."

"You're sure about marrying me?" he asked with a grin.

"Yes. But I will treat you to breakfast."

"What's on the menu? Eggs? Bacon?"

"Granola and yogurt."

He looked like a little boy whose balloon had floated away. "Really? I'd take you out for eggs, or waffles. I mean, everyone loves waffles."

"Your baby needs nutrients, not syrup." She sighed a bit because her craving for coffee was now replaced by a craving for syrup. And it turned out it was easier to ignore the craving for something she *couldn't* have than it was to ignore the craving for something she *shouldn't* have, but could.

"Hey, it's St. Nick's Day. I think waffles are going to be our new addition to the tradition. And if we want to introduce it to the baby as our tradition, we need to start on it."

Kennedy couldn't help herself. "Your logic is impeccable. I mean, how can I say no when our family's future tradition is at stake?"

"You can't. I'll wait while you get dressed, then we'll go see Tavi."

She started for her room, laughing at Malcolm's logic. She sobered up as she realized that their talk of their own tradition simply emphasized the fact that they were not together. She'd referred to it as their *family's tradition*.

Like it or not, he was part of her life now.

She waited to feel trapped or scared he'd try and take the baby from her.

All she felt was a sense of rightness . . . and hungry for those waffles.

Something changed after St. Nicholas Day. Mal wasn't sure if it was the waffles or the presents or some other factor he couldn't put his finger on. But Kennedy seemed far more at ease with him.

She didn't protest when they spent time together.

They'd worked together on the annual Comstock pre-Christmas party.

They ate most meals together and had coffee together every morning—decaf coffee.

They set up the baby's nursery together. They watched a movie from Kennedy's doctor's office titled *Giving Birth—The Unvarnished Truth*.

He'd stoically watched it with her. Every gritty, agonizing moment of it. When it finished, she said, "I could have used a bit of varnishing."

He hadn't been able to agree fast enough.

She didn't mention him moving back to Pittsburgh.

He wasn't sure why he hadn't told her he wasn't going back.

No, he took that back. He was sure why. He wasn't sure how Kennedy was going to take it. After all, she wanted to buy the Center. But part of his plan involved keeping it.

Not that he had much of a plan. He was working to nail it all down so when Kennedy asked, or he simply told her, he could give her specifics.

He'd talked to a few law firms in Erie.

He'd put his condo in Pittsburgh on the market.

He hoped to have things up and running soon. He had enough in savings to allow him to take some time and set things up the way he wanted them . . . but first he needed to decide how he wanted them.

He wasn't sure of much, but he was sure that what he wanted was to be here in Cupid Falls with Kennedy and the baby.

CHAPTER FOURTEEN

That Saturday, Kennedy walked into the Center and looked around. Malcolm had taken over the Everything But a Dog event and everything looked perfect. The new mats they'd bought for the floor were in place, along with small makeshift pens to hold the dogs.

A brunette walked up on the small platform just to the left of the door. Wires ran from it out to the radio station's van in front of the building. There was already a good turnout at the event. Kennedy was hoping the crowd grew as the day went on.

"Hi, everyone," the DJ cried out. "For my listeners, I'm here in Cupid Falls, Pennsylvania, at a very special event. And for those in the audience, I'd like to thank everyone for coming out today. I'm Angela Hart. That's Hart—"

"H. A. R. T.," a few voices in the crowd yelled.

"I see we have a few WLVH listeners out there." Angela smiled at them. "And that's right, I'm a disc jockey with WLVH radio, *where love is more than just a song*. And my last name is Hart. Yes, I do get some ribbing about it.

"WLVH has been partners with the Everything But a Dog Foundation for a couple years now. I adopted my own Sera at a Valentine's event. I think you all will agree she's a very special little dog." She nodded at the little dog that was strapped into a dog wheelchair.

"Today there are a lot of dogs like Sera. Dogs who are looking for someone to love them. Dogs who are looking for their forever home. We're hoping our listeners will come out to Cupid Falls today. It's about a half hour drive from Erie, and Mother Nature has cooperated. It's beautiful out. Just enough snow to remind us it's almost Christmas, but not so much to make driving a pain. Come meet some of the dogs that are here today. Maybe you'll find the one that's meant to be yours. And to that end, let me introduce the woman behind Everything But a Dog, Nana Vancy Salo."

Kennedy was standing at the right of the makeshift stage on the fringes of the crowd. She sensed Malcolm was behind her before he said a word.

She turned and he smiled at her. "You look beautiful today."

She snorted. "I look like a water balloon that's been filled to the max. And that's how I feel. As if at any moment, if I'm jostled wrong, I'll burst."

Nana Vancy reached the mic and Angela helped her adjust it down . . . way down. "Thank you, Angel—"

"Angela," the disc jockey said with a smile that told Kennedy this was an old argument.

"You'll always be a Christmas Angel to me, and to your Sera. I'm Vancy Salo, but everyone calls me Nana Vancy. My friends and I are here today to help you find a pet. According to the Humane Society, more than two million animals are euthanized every year because they can't find a home. That's where you come in. Come visit us at the Cupid Falls Community Center and we'll help you find your perfect match."

"You can tell she's done radio with Angela before," Kennedy said to Malcolm.

"They're like a vaudeville routine up there," he said as the two continued their banter.

"Kennedy, do you have a minute?" Jenny asked.

"Sure." She turned to Mal. "Pardon me."

She walked over to Jenny's kids. Ivy thrust a wrapped tube at her. "Here, Miss Mayor. I made this for the baby." It felt like a cardboard tube that Christmas wrapping paper came in. "Mom helped with the words, but I did all the pictures and it was my idea."

". . . my own dogs, Clara and Curie . . ." Nana Vancy said.

"Mom said your baby ain't got no daddy, just like me and the boys don't," Ivy said. "And you don't got no mom or dad, so it ain't got a grandma or grandpa, too. My friend Alice is adopted, and she got a bunch of aunts and uncles, and so we're adoptin' it."

Kennedy wasn't sure what *it* was.

Jenny must have seen her confusion because she said, "Unwrap the paper."

Kennedy did and found it was a cardboard tube. Inside there was a piece of paper. She took it out and read aloud, "This document certifies that . . ."

"See, it's blank so you can fill in its name. Ivy's a good name," Ivy said helpfully.

"Ivy is your name, so that might get confusing," Jenny told her youngest.

Ivy considered her mother's point, then said, "Yeah, so not Ivy, Miss Mayor."

". . . Blank," Kennedy read, "is hereby adopted by the Murray family. Jenny Murray will be known as Aunt Jenny, and Ivy, Lenny, and Timmy will be its cousins. They'll teach it to do all kinds of fun things—"

"Lenny wants to teach the baby to spit, but Mom says they do that all on their own. He said *gross*," Ivy said.

". . . and they'll help babysit when it's older and won't break."

"I wrote that part," Ivy said.

"And Aunt Jenny will babysit and kiss boo-boos—"

"She's a very good boo-boo kisser," Ivy said. "Even though the boys are too big to want her to, sometimes she does it anyway."

"And the whole Murray clan will love *blank* forever and ever."

"See, I drew all kinds of fun stuff so's the baby knows what we're talking about. There's bubbles and balloons, and cookies and ice cream, and that's a bike, but Lenny said it don't look so much like one, but it is."

Kennedy frantically wiped at her eyes, trying not to cry, but knowing there was no way she was going to succeed. Awkwardly, she knelt and held out her arms to Ivy. "If your mom is my baby's aunt, then does that make me your aunt? Because I'd really, really like to adopt you all, too."

Ivy threw herself at Kennedy, who almost toppled, but a firm hand caught her back. She didn't need to turn around to know it was Malcolm. He seemed to be making a habit of catching her before she fell.

Ivy hugged her. "Yeah, I always wanted an aunt. You know, aunts buy kids presents for Christmas, right?"

"Ivy," Jenny said, obviously shocked by Ivy's blatant hint.

But Kennedy would willingly buy this little girl the entire toy department if she had the money. She nodded seriously. "Oh, they do. And aunts need to know everyone's birthdays because they buy presents then, too. And I'm pretty sure that in the summer, aunts sometimes take kids into the Erie Zoo, or back to the swimming hole by the falls."

Malcolm took Kennedy's hand and helped her to her feet, unasked.

"You are going to be the best aunt ever," Ivy said. "Come on, guys. Let's go put together a Christmas list for Aunt Kennedy. She ain't never had to shop for us before, so she'll need help."

"Ivy," Jenny started, but Kennedy stopped her. "Please don't. I can't tell you how much that meant to me. Let them have their fun."

"They're demons, but they've got good hearts," Jenny said with more than a touch of motherly pride. "You'd think with the boys being older they'd run the show, but truly, it's Ivy who came up with this, and they were only too happy to follow her lead."

"She's going to be a handful as she gets older. She'll need both of them, and a certain Aunt Kennedy, helping you rein her in."

"You're telling me," Jenny said. "I'd better go find them, otherwise you might find them giving you the entire toy store catalog." She chased after the kids.

Kennedy watched them go, holding the "adoption" papers. She was going to frame them and hang them somewhere.

She sniffed and wished she had a tissue.

"You okay?" Malcolm asked.

"Yeah, I'm fine. Thanks for saving me from toppling on my butt."

"I didn't mean the fall." He reached out and gently brushed the edges of her eyes. It was a light, feathery touch. Kennedy knew he only meant it to be helpful. Just like she knew his marriage proposals were for the baby's benefit, nothing more, but sometimes she forgot.

Now, she could almost imagine his touch was something more. That he had feelings for her that extended beyond the fact she was the mother of his child, and she'd been a friend of his mother's.

"There's Pap." Malcolm pointed at the door, where Pap stood with a small older lady. They were holding hands.

Pap leaned down and said something to her and she blushed.

Malcolm studied the two of them. "That's Pap's mystery woman."

"There's no mystery there," Kennedy said. "That's Annabelle. She's one of Nana Vancy's friends." Another taller, thinner woman came in behind them. "And that's Isabel. The Salos call them the Silver Bells. They helped Nana Vancy with all her matchmaking couples, and now they help with Everything But a Dog."

Pap spotted them and steered Annabelle their way. "Just the people I was looking for. Annabelle Conner, this is my grandson, Malcolm. And you know Kennedy."

Annabelle gave Pap a small nudge with her elbow. "Of course I know Kennedy. She's the reason we met, after all. Kennedy, sweetheart, you look . . ." She paused as if looking for the proper word to describe her.

"Huge," Kennedy filled in. "And I am."

Annabelle laughed. "How soon?"

"At my last visit the doctor said anytime, though he warned me not to get too concerned with whens . . . first babies take their time."

"He sounds very wise. Is he married?"

"No—" Kennedy paused. "Oh, no you don't. You all just match dogs to homes, not people. No more matchmaking people."

Annabelle laughed. "Well, you could say Vancy helped match me and Paul here, so maybe we're not totally out of the people matchmaking business yet." She turned to Malcolm. "I'm so glad to finally meet you. Your grandfather has done nothing but brag about you since we met. I want to thank you for coming home and taking care of the Center. He was worried it was too much for Kennedy, along with her flower shop, being mayor, and having a baby. Have you made a decision about what you're doing with it yet?"

For a split second, Malcolm had an expression that looked a bit like guilt to Kennedy, then it was gone and he said, "I'm weighing my options."

"I hope you're seriously considering my proposal," Kennedy said.

"I hope you're seriously considering mine," he countered.

She shot him her *not in front of your grandfather and Annabelle* look.

He countered with his *whatever it takes to get my own way* look.

She glared at him.

He grinned.

Pap and Annabelle watched them both, saying nothing.

Kennedy decided that sometimes retreat was the better part of valor. "Why don't I let the three of you catch up and I'll go see if Nana Vancy and Isabel need a hand."

Kennedy hurried toward Nana Vancy, who was surrounded by the Murray kids.

∿

Mal watched as Kennedy made her way to the other side of the room. "What was that about?" Pap asked. And before he could answer, Pap added, "And how are you still here?"

"You and I both know there's more to it than the Center."

Annabelle said, "I'm sorry. This is obviously none of my business. Why don't I go help the girls out while you two talk."

She kissed Pap's cheek, then surprised Mal by kissing his as well. "You and I will have plenty of time to get to know one another, but I already feel as if I know you through your grandfather. I know things are messy right now, and you don't like messy, but it will all come out right in the end." She started to walk away, then turned back. "Vancy always says that words have power. If the words you're using fail you, then maybe you need to think about some better words."

She smiled, gave a tiny wave, and walked toward her friends at the other side of the Center.

"She seems very nice," Mal said.

"She is," Pap assured him. "And I think she's right, words have power, so I'll say out loud right now, I am going to marry that woman."

"Pap," Mal said as he tried to wrap his brain around the idea of his grandfather remarrying. He settled for saying, "Does she know it?"

"Not yet. I'm planning to ease her into the notion." His tone got serious. "But when I do marry her, I'll be moving to Erie. She lives at this nice little retirement center on Erie's bayfront. Right now, her and Isabel live together, but Isabel's got her own beau, and him and me, we've talked. We're hoping we can break up the dynamic duo. It won't be tomorrow, but I'm not getting any younger and I don't have time to waste, so it won't be too long, either. When the time comes, I'll be giving up the house here. You'll have to go through it and pick out what you want, if anything. It'll add an extra half hour or so on to your drive when you come see me, but son, we both know you don't make the drive that often. It won't be too much of a hardship."

Mal felt off balance. He'd come into town four weeks ago expecting a normal visit with his grandfather, and he'd discovered he was going to be a father, and now, that his grandfather was moving out of his childhood home.

There was a certain sense of comfort knowing that even after his mother died, his grandfather was here. Mal had a place to go to. A place he belonged. But if his grandfather left, he'd lose his tie to the town.

No. He'd have the baby and Kennedy.

"Congratulations, Pap" was all he said.

"Thanks. You want to talk about you and our Kennedy yet?"

"There's nothing to say yet."

"Well, even if I move to Erie permanently, you know I'm always here to listen."

"I do know that, Pap. Now, let's go see some dogs. And then, afterward, a bunch of the local kids are coming over to help pull up this flooring and get ready for tonight's dance."

"Quick turnovers like this are tricky, but you'll do fine." Pap slapped his back.

Mal realized that his grandfather and his mother had always believed that he could do anything he set his mind to. On the heels of that realization, he thought about what Annabelle, then Pap had said—words have power.

"Pap?" he asked.

"Yes, boyo?"

"When things settle down, I'd like to talk to you about buying the house when you're ready."

Pap's eyes narrowed. "Now why would you do that?"

He said the words, hoping Nana Vancy was right. "Because I'm staying in Cupid Falls. I'm going to live next door to Kennedy and my child, and I'm going to continue to ask her to marry me. If words have power, maybe one day I'll wear her down and she'll say yes."

"Why do you want to marry her?" Pap's question echoed the one Kennedy had asked so many times.

Mal realized he'd given her all kinds of answers. Because they were going to be parents. Because they made a good team. Because they were friends.

If words had power, those were all lackluster words at best. And suddenly he knew the most powerful words there were. And he knew if he had any hope of Kennedy saying yes, he'd have to use them.

"Are you coming to the dance?" he asked his grandfather, ignoring his question.

Pap was an insightful man. He didn't press for an answer. "Yes. I'll be at the dance. Annabelle and her friends need to take any unadopted dogs home to Erie, but then they're coming back for tonight's fun."

"Good," Mal said distractedly. His mind was on how he was going to use those most powerful words and convince Kennedy to say yes.

～

Every week Kennedy thought, *this is it. The baby can't possibly get any bigger before it's born because there's simply no way it will fit.* And every week—heck, every day—her girth had expanded at an alarming rate. She noticed how much as she knelt down in order to look at a small dog inside the baby-gated area. The rest of his cage-mates had been adopted and he was the only one left in this enclosure.

The dog looked like a gremlin. Small, dark—he couldn't possibly top five pounds. And his tail was disconcertingly long. But he looked at her with doggie hope in his eyes. As if he were saying, *I know you'll help.*

Kennedy had promised herself as soon as the baby was potty trained, she'd get a dog for him. "Sorry," she whispered to the small dog as she held the side of the enclosure in order to hoist herself back into an upright position.

She walked farther down the aisle. May had been helping at the refreshment table, but now she was standing next to an enclosure that held three dogs. "May, do you see a dog that you like?"

"Oh, no. I've thought about it. Really I have, but I still miss my June." She dabbed at her eyes. "I was talking to Nana Vancy—it seems absurd to call a woman who is my age Nana anything, but she insisted, and you know me, I try to oblige people and not make waves."

Kennedy was proud that she didn't laugh. She didn't even crack a smile at that statement.

"But Nana Vancy is wandering around like a whirling dervish. She said that scruffy one right there"—May pointed at a scruffy medium-size dog—"is Rico. That one"—she pointed at a minpin—"has a mouthful of a name. Walburga. They call her Wallie. And that one"—she pointed at a medium-size white Jack Russell terrier mix. "His name is August."

Kennedy knew immediately that May wanted the Jack Russell. She could see it in her expression. May's longing was almost palpable.

Malcolm came up behind her. "How's it going?" he asked.

"May was telling me about the dogs in the pen," Kennedy answered. "She told me that the Jack Russell over there? He's named August."

She saw that Malcolm understood exactly what she wanted. He turned to May. "You know, I'm an attorney. I don't believe in fate. But May, this one time, I might be willing to admit, this might be fate."

"Kismet, even," Kennedy said.

"That Nana Vancy woman says he's older. Nine, they think. I wouldn't want a puppy. I don't have the energy to train it. But she says August is housebroken. She said he likes to sleep, but when one of the staff puts him on a lead to go for a walk, it's like he's a puppy all over again," May said.

Kennedy and Malcolm were silent as May stared at the dog. "I do like to walk," she murmured, her eyes never leaving August.

"I think you should seriously consider adopting him," Kennedy said. And knowing that sometimes saying less was more, she said, "If you'll excuse me a moment, I need to talk to Malcolm, but I'll check back with you." She took his hand and pulled him toward the office.

"Are you okay?" Malcolm asked. "Is it the baby?"

Kennedy glanced over her shoulder and saw that May was still standing, staring at August. "No. I wanted to give May some space to think about it. Since June passed, she's been difficult. I think she's been lonely."

"I—"

Whatever Malcolm was going to say was lost under the deafening sound of "Aunt Kennedy." Ivy raced down the aisle, her brothers following, and Jenny behind them. "We did it," the little girl said excitedly.

"Did what?" she asked the little girl.

"Lenny and Timmy and me, we did it. We know what we want for Christmas. We don't need to make no list, though. Come on, I'll show you." She took Kennedy by the hand and led her back to the enclosure where the small gremlin-like dog sat.

Lenny walked into the enclosure and the dog ran over to him and jumped into his arms. "We all petted him and he loves us."

She looked down at the dog that Lenny was currently holding, and then up at Jenny, who said, "I've told the kids that it would be really hard to have a dog. They're at school all day and I'm at work. No one could let a dog out."

"Maybe he could go help Aunt Kennedy at her shop? He'd be a real good flower dog. I bet if you said 'hey, dog, go get me a dandelion,' he would. He's smart," Ivy said with perfect confidence.

"We'd really like a dog," said Lenny, who hitherto had allowed his sister to do the talking for him. "I mean we'd really, *really* like one, Aunt Kennedy."

"Yeah, really," Timmy said. "Mom said she won't get it for us, but if you did, she'd have to let us have it 'cause it would be a gift.

And she says even if you don't like a gift, you gotta say 'thank you' and suck it up."

Kennedy looked at Jenny again. She rolled her eyes and gave the slightest nod, giving her silent permission.

"Well, I can see that the three of you have given this some thought," Kennedy said, looking at her new nephews and niece.

"He's a very little dog, so he can't be too much trouble," Ivy wheedled.

"If I, as your new aunt, were to buy you the dog for a Christmas present, I'd need some assurances."

"Like what?" Lenny asked, his eyes narrowing.

"For instance, I'd need you all to promise you'd let him in and out when he needs to go. And on garbage day, you'd have to take a shovel and clean up all his poop—"

Ivy giggled. "She said *poop*," she stage-whispered to her brothers.

The boys laughed too. And Kennedy could see Malcolm was trying valiantly not to laugh at this blatant manipulation by a five-year-old charmer.

As the three kids snickered, Kennedy realized she'd moved up a decided notch in the cool new aunt department. "You'd have to play with him and—"

Ivy couldn't contain herself. She squealed with delight. "That means yes, right? If you're giving us rules, it means yes. You're buying us our dog for Christmas." She threw herself at Kennedy, who was standing, so she didn't topple, but she noticed that Malcolm's hand came instinctually to her back to steady her anyway.

She leaned down awkwardly and hugged Ivy. "It means yes."

"You are the best aunt ever. Maisey's got an aunt and she buys her candy, but a dog is better than candy."

"Why don't you all take your dog and see Nana Vancy. I'll be right there to help with the paperwork," Kennedy said.

"And pay," Ivy said. "A dog this good might be expensive."

The way she said it told Kennedy that Ivy had been told in the past that something was too expensive for her mom to afford. She could see that the little girl was worried.

"He's a very little dog, so he won't be too expensive," Kennedy assured her. "I promise."

A look of relief swept over Ivy.

"Sorry," Kennedy told Jenny. "I guess that being an honorary aunt means that I get to be a bit of a pain in your butt on occasion. But I will offer to help with the puppy. You don't live all that far from the shop. I can go let him out on your long days."

"We'll work it out," Jenny said. "Look at them. Even if the dog ends up being extra work, it's worth it to see them that happy." She turned and followed the kids.

"So how's the adoption working out for you?" Malcolm asked with laughter.

"I think it helped that Christmas is around the corner. I mean, having someone else to buy you a gift can never be a bad thing when you're five."

Malcolm shook his head. "I don't think that's it at all, Kennedy. You're special, and even a five-year-old can recognize that. If you love someone, it's forever. There would be no halves about it. Anyone you love is lucky. *Our* baby is going to be so lucky."

The way he said *our baby* and looked at her made Kennedy feel flustered, because for a moment, just a moment, as he was talking, she could almost imagine that someday he'd talk about her like that. *My Kennedy.*

As if she were a part of him.

She shook her head and pushed that fantasy away. "I'd better go buy my present."

She followed the Murray family over to the table by the door. She would be willing to place a bet that Malcolm was watching her, but she didn't turn around.

Nana Vancy and Angela, the disc jockey, were talking to Jenny.

"I wanted to check and make sure it's okay for the kids to go on air at my next broadcast?" Angela asked.

"Sure," Jenny said.

Nana Vancy motioned Kennedy over. "You did a good job picking the *gyermekek's* dog. Have you ever thought about being a matchmaker?"

Kennedy smiled. "The kids picked him out themselves."

"But you knew it was the right dog for them. That's a talent. Are you sure we can't find a dog for your baby?"

"Next year. I'll let him come pick out one with me."

"Her," Nana Vancy said with absolute conviction. "The baby's a girl."

Kennedy placed her hands on her stomach and the baby kicked, as if to confirm Nana Vancy's proclamation.

"Time will tell," she said.

Nana Vancy grinned. "Yes, it will. And here comes your love."

"He's not my—" she started to protest.

Nana Vancy interrupted her. "Kennedy, kedvenc, you can lie to him and you can lie to yourself even, but you can't lie to me. Words have power. I learned that the hard way. You'll know when it's the right time to say the words. The true words, not the lies you've been telling."

Kennedy thought about protesting that she didn't lie and that she didn't know what Nana Vancy was talking about, but instead, she simply ignored the older lady and busied herself making out a check for the minimal fee to the Everything But a Dog Foundation.

Malcolm came up behind her as she put her wallet back in her purse. "The kids got the dog then?"

She smiled. "It was my first present as their official adopted aunt."

He whistled. "That was a very good present."

"And you?" Nana Vancy asked Malcolm. "You found your dog?"

"I'm not looking for a dog," he assured her.

"He's going home to Pittsburgh soon," Kennedy added. "It would be hard to have a dog in the city."

Nana Vancy laughed. "You both are so wrong about so many things." Then she muttered something in another language and chuckled again as she walked away.

"She's . . ." Malcolm said, letting the sentence hang as if he couldn't adequately describe Nana Vancy Salo.

Kennedy nodded. "Yes, she is."

They fell into an easy step and walked around the room. There were half a dozen people milling around the makeshift enclosures, which were old-fashioned wood play yards for kids. There were less than half a dozen dogs left.

Kennedy walked over to Gideon and Annie Byler. "Miss Annie, how are you?"

"I'm fine, Kennedy. And how's the *boppli*?" she asked, reaching out to touch Kennedy's stomach.

Normally, Kennedy shied away from people who tried to touch her stomach, but it was impossible to take offense when it was Miss Annie. "The baby's fine, Miss Annie."

"And you?" Miss Annie pressed.

"Just fine. Ready to not be pregnant." What she wouldn't give to see her feet, or simply get off a couch without looking like some gag reel of *I Love Lucy*.

Annie took a step back and studied Kennedy a moment. "It won't be long. No, not long at all."

First Nana Vancy and now Miss Annie. She was surrounded by mystics today. Kennedy didn't say as much; she simply nodded. "I hope you're right. Are you getting a dog?"

"I am. My nephew built me a wonderful good small house behind the shop, and with a door right off the back, I can let a dog in and out, which I couldn't in the apartment upstairs. So, I'm here to find my dog."

"Hi, Gideon," Kennedy said. "I'm not sure if you two remember each other. Mal's lived in Pittsburgh a long time and you . . ." She started to say *didn't mingle with the English*, but she switched to "are younger than we are."

"Not so much younger. Nice to see you again, Mal."

Kennedy wished Annie luck with her dog search and then left her and Gideon to it.

"I've seen a lot of faces I'm not familiar with today."

"I know. That's why I thought today was such a great idea for both Everything But a Dog and for Cupid Falls. It's a way to bring some people in from surrounding communities. Tom at Books and Stuff put together a whole new-dog package. It comes with food from Elmer's Market and dog dishes, a lead and collar, and some toys. Everything a new pet owner needs."

They stopped at an enclosure that only held one dog. Or maybe a horse.

"That is a big dog," Malcolm said.

Kennedy looked at him closely. There seemed to be a bit of wistfulness in his voice.

"You want him?" she asked, but she didn't really need to question it. She could see in his expression that he wanted the dog.

Kennedy stared at the big dog, who stared back at her with mild curiosity in his eyes. She smiled at the dog, whose big tail swished across the floor.

She held out a hand and he got up and slowly came over. He sat and lifted one of his giant paws. She shook it with delight.

"He likes you," Malcolm said.

At the sound of his voice, the dog turned and offered Malcolm a paw.

They shook and Malcolm patted the large dog's head. "You are smart, aren't you?"

The dog tilted his head as if to say, *of course.*

"Ah, you found him," Nana Vancy said from behind them. "We've been calling him Jethro. He reminds me of that boy in the old *Beverly Hillbillies* show. We think he's part lab and part Great Dane. He's so big that a lot of people pass him by, but he's a real gentleman."

Jethro turned toward Nana Vancy's voice and his giant tail swished again.

Nana Vancy wasn't much bigger than the dog, but she didn't seem unnerved by that fact. She opened the gate and stood next to him. "He's a good dog. I brought him today because I had a feeling his real home was here in Cupid Falls. And it is. With one of you. This is the first time I'm not sure who he belongs to."

Kennedy wanted to pet Jethro but she was afraid that if she did, she'd say yes. And sensibly, she knew she couldn't cope with a dog the size of a small moose, a new baby, the town, and her business.

Jethro looked at her and there was a sad knowing in his eyes. As if he understood why she couldn't take him. She reached out, despite herself, and patted his huge head. His tail wagged, sweeping the floor as it went. He reached out and daintily licked her arm.

"I'll take him," Malcolm blurted out. "He can live with me."

"Malcolm, a dog this big won't do well in a city apartment."

"About that—"

Everything in Mal wanted to tell Kennedy now. He wanted to tell her he wasn't leaving. He wanted to tell her he was opening a law practice here in Cupid Falls in the Center.

But more than any of that, he wanted to tell her that he loved her.

When he'd asked her to marry him before, none of the reasons he'd given her were enough to make a marriage work. She'd been right about that.

But he wanted to ask for the right reason now . . . he knew the words.

Yet as he looked at Kennedy, clutching the adoption papers from Jenny's kids, he knew that despite the fact she was a vital part of Cupid Falls, part of her was still the sixteen-year-old orphan whose aunt took her in out of a sense of duty.

Then he'd offered her an obligatory marriage proposal.

He was going to say the words, and he was going to ask her to marry him again. She might say no, but he'd keep asking.

But more than anything, he was going to see to it she knew what an important part of Cupid Falls she was. Even if she wouldn't marry him, he was going to see to it she knew she had a home.

"Kennedy, I need to talk to you about so many things, but right now, I've got a few things I have to see to. Do you think you could finish up here and get the kids started with setting up for the dance?"

She looked confused but nodded. "Sure."

"Nana Vancy, let me go sign the papers for Jethro." He took the older lady toward the front and left Kennedy standing with her adoption papers and his dog—their dog. She didn't know it yet, but Jethro was their dog as much as the baby was theirs.

As soon as they were out of earshot, he said, "Nana Vancy, I need your help. To be honest, I'm going to need everyone in Cupid Falls' help."

Mal had never believed in magic, but when Nana Vancy nodded and said, "Yes, she does deserve the most special proposal ever," he knew he'd never doubt again.

And if he believed in the Hungarian grandmother's magic, logically he had to believe in Cupid Falls' magic, too.

All his half-formed ideas solidified. He looked at Nana Vancy and said, "So here's what I need . . ."

CHAPTER FIFTEEN

Malcolm insisted on picking Kennedy up for the dance, though she had protested that she was perfectly capable of walking on her own. He was acting odd. She wasn't sure what was up, but he kept . . . well, looking at her. And she knew how kindergartenish that sounded, but there it was. Malcolm Carter was *looking* at her, and it was making her uneasy.

The boys she'd hired to help change from a dog show to a dance venue had pulled up the dogs' matting, and the old hardwood floors shone in the light. There was a DJ in the far corner. Red and green streamers joined holly and poinsettia decorations. The room was perfect. It practically screamed Christmas.

She'd thought this Christmas dance was a nice way to give the community a chance to get together for the holiday while at the same time earning money for the Everything But a Dog Foundation. Hence Clarence's nickname, the Bow-Wow Ball. Tonight the nickname made her smile.

She stood in the doorway and admired the room. "It's beautiful."

"You planned everything down to a T," Mal said. "I simply followed your list."

They were the first ones to arrive other than the DJ, who was still setting up his equipment in the corner. Malcolm gave him a nod as Taylor Swift's "You Belong With Me" started to spill from the speakers. Mal looked entirely too pleased with the song choice.

"Dance with me?"

"I—" She didn't get to finish her answer. He already had her in his arms, slow dancing, despite the fact the DJ was just testing the system.

"You know, we haven't really kissed since that first date," he said almost conversationally.

"It's for the best," she said. More of a warning to herself than to answer Malcolm's statement. Because if she kissed him now, she might find herself head over heels, and that wouldn't do at all.

He might be the father of her baby, but he had a life in Pittsburgh and she had a life here. They'd share a baby. They didn't need any more complications . . . and a one-sided love would be nothing but complicated.

Malcolm didn't respond to her comment but switched topics. "You know, I've given you a few reasons you should marry me, but here's one more . . . I'd let you share my dog."

There was no pressure, just a grin that said he was teasing. She realized that he'd finally accepted that she'd never agree to a marriage born out of obligation.

"Jethro is a great dog, but no. Thank you for asking, though."

She felt relieved when he smiled. "That's what I thought you'd say, but I'm going to ask again. I've been assured that words have power . . . I just need to find better words," he said, and there was something different in his expression.

Kennedy wished he'd stop. So as they turned in small circles in the middle of the dance floor, she tried to explain, to really make him understand. "Malcolm, I've spent my entire life trying to carve out a niche for myself here in Cupid Falls. Trying to fit in. You wouldn't understand how it feels to always be the odd man out. You've always been the town's golden boy."

All the boys in school had wanted to be Malcolm. All the girls had been halfway in love with him. He'd had Pap and Val.

She wasn't sure he'd ever understand, but she said, "I've always been Betty's orphaned niece. You were born with a place in town, but I've carved mine out bit by bit. And now my baby will belong here. I don't need you to make things easier. I don't need to marry someone who is a friend, or who's a good partner. I guess what I'm saying is, I don't need you. I don't need to marry you at all. And while it's nice of you to offer—to keep offering—I don't need to settle."

Mal nodded. "No, you don't. You shouldn't settle. Ever. You deserve more than that."

And that was the last Kennedy had seen of him. The night had become a blur. It seemed as if everyone in Cupid Falls wanted to talk to her. She was whisked from one person to the next.

But thankfully, people had started to leave. Soon the DJ would play the last song and Kennedy could go home. She was tired, but in a job-well-done sort of way.

Jenny was saying, "The baby will come, and soon we'll be sitting in the house watching your baby and my kids run around with their dog. Speaking of dogs, the kids said you're the best aunt ever."

Jenny glanced at the front door for the umpteenth time.

"Are you looking for someone?"

Jenny seemed flustered by the question. "No. It's just a mother's instinct. Even if they're not here, if I mention the kids, I check . . . a sort of reflex."

"They're good kids."

"Good, but always into something. Now they've added a dog to the mix?" She shook her head.

Kennedy laughed. "I am never going to be able to live up to this first present."

"You being there for the kids, that's enough. And I want you to know I intend to return the favor." Jenny glanced at the door again and grinned as Malcolm came through the Center's front doors and walked toward them.

"Kennedy, come outside with me, please," he said. "I have a surprise."

"I don't think I'm up to any surprises, Malcolm." She was exhausted. She just wanted to go home and crawl in bed.

"Please?" He looked like one of Jenny's kids earlier as they'd asked for a dog. "Just put on your coat and come out front."

Jenny stood next to him, grinning. And Kennedy knew that she was in on whatever Malcolm's surprise was.

Given that grin, she knew she wouldn't have an ally in Jenny, so Kennedy followed Malcolm, bundled up, and opened the front door to see Jenny's kids in a sleigh. An honest-to-goodness Currier and Ives sleigh with lanterns hanging from hooks on the front. She recognized the driver. "Gideon, what are you doing?"

"I'm only the driver, Kennedy. You'll have to talk to Mal." He turned around and said something to the kids, who climbed out of the sleigh and retrieved their dog from where they'd tied his lead to the Center's front railing.

"Your carriage awaits . . . literally," Malcolm said.

Kennedy looked at the step it would require to get herself up on the sleigh and she wasn't sure she could manage it.

"Malcolm, it's freezing out," she tried.

"That's why we've got the sleigh."

And before she could think of any other protests, he scooped her up and deposited her in the sleigh, then covered her with a thick blanket. "Guess I'm going for a sleigh ride," she muttered, which made Gideon laugh.

"Just down to the falls," Malcolm said. "I have something you have to see."

He looked happy. Too happy. Suspiciously happy.

"What are you up to?" she asked.

"We'll see you soon," Jenny called as she and the kids took off up the block.

"Malcolm?" Kennedy said as he climbed in after her and sat beside her. He sat too close, to be honest. She edged as far over as she could get.

"I don't bite," he said softly.

"I'm big as a house. I need the extra space," she grumbled.

They rode in silence. The sleigh glided along the side of the Center and into the back.

Gideon turned it onto the path that led to the falls. As they turned the bend, Jenny and the kids were standing there with the dog. Lenny and Timmy held lanterns and Ivy held a wooden sign. Kennedy could read it in the lamplight: "The Demis."

"Hi, guys," Kennedy called, but they didn't answer. They simply fell in step behind the sleigh.

Malcolm grinned. And Gideon sat on the front seat, laughing and muttering something to himself in Pennsylvania Dutch.

"What is going on?" she demanded.

"You'll see," Malcolm said, all mysterious.

Clarence and Joan were a little farther up the path. Clarence held a lantern, and now that the lights from town and the Center were around the bend, the lantern light seemed brighter as it illuminated the night-dark woods. Joan held a small wooden sign with a frog dressed in a cupid outfit in each corner. It read "Leto's Frogs."

"That one's a stretch," Malcolm said before she could ask. "Joan was bound and determined to find something, and she found a Greek myth about Leto. She turned some rude people who wouldn't let her drink from her well into frogs. Joan says Clarence is going to build her a pond this spring. She's going to mount the sign in front of it."

Joan and Clarence joined Jenny and the kids and walked behind the sleigh. "Malcolm, seriously, this is ridiculous. I don't understand what is going on."

They pulled up to the creek, just down from the falls.

The first thing that struck Kennedy was the light.

There were lanterns hanging from trees. It was a different light than a flashlight might have cast. Softer, warmer, and glowing. There was enough of a breeze that the trees shifted, making it flicker shadows against the snow-covered ground.

On the heels of that came the realization that the clearing was full of townspeople. And there was Angela Hart, from WLVH radio. "Welcome, Mayor Kennedy Anderson. I'm here with WLVH, *where love is more than just a song*, covering what I think is going to be a very special event for the community. Sometimes it's fun to give our nighttime listeners a treat . . . and this is definitely going to be that."

The crowd started clapping wildly and Kennedy was even more confused.

Angela waved at her and continued talking into her mic. "Let me describe the scene to my listeners. Lanterns hanging from branches. They flicker, casting their light down on snow-covered ground, the creek, and the waterfall. The very *special* waterfall. Everyone at WLVH knows that magic is real and this . . ."

Kennedy looked around as Angela spoke. She noticed a lot of the business owners held wooden signs. With small cupids somewhere on them. Elmer from the grocery store and his wife, Marge, held a small wooden sign that read "Ceres's Market." Gus and Tavi had one that read "The Ambrosia Restaurant." "Hestia's Antiques," "The Muse's Museum," "The Siren's Call Bookstore". . .

Mal pulled out a large wooden sign with the cupids on it. It read "Olympus." "The center of everything," he explained.

"I don't understand," Kennedy said again.

"Clarence?" Malcolm called.

Gideon got out of the sleigh and moved into the crowd as the old man shuffled up to the microphone. "Mayor, I know I was the worst at picking on you 'cause you changed the name to the flower shop to Cupid's Bowquet, but we had a town meeting at the dog show today—"

"Wait. You had a town meeting at the dog show?" she asked. "Where was I?"

"Mal here pulled us into the office a few at a time. Pretty much all of the town was there."

"Why wasn't I invited?" Kennedy asked.

"It was about you, that's why. And we decided that you were right. Your Everything But a Dog Foundation adoption day and then the Bow-Wow Ball brought a bunch of people into town. All the stores said they had more business than usual over the weekend. So we thought we'd put up signs on all the businesses. Not really change their names, mind you, but put up signs that fit in with the Cupid Falls theme. Even some of the houses are going to do it, too. Like me and Joan. We think you can bring a lot more people into town. So, it's our Christmas present to you."

"Everyone who could went to Gideon's this afternoon and made them," Tavi said. "I helped them come up with names that fit the different stores."

Everyone started to talk. It was a quiet murmur at first, and then got louder and louder.

Linc was holding a sign that read "Apollo's Lights." He saw her look in his direction and waved.

Kennedy felt choked up and blinked desperately, trying to keep the tears from falling. "Thank you, everyone."

Tavi stepped closer. "Mayor, we want you to know that we appreciate all you have done and are doing for the town. We'll get behind you. Not only because you're the mayor, or because you've got some good marketing ideas, but because you're ours."

"Yours?" she asked.

"Yes," Tavi said. "Why do you think Mal was in so much trouble? We didn't like how he was treating you. You're ours. You're an important part of Cupid Falls. We all trust you. That's why we elected you mayor."

"Thank you all for the lovely gift." She felt a small cramp. She'd had a few after the dog show. This one felt like it might be more than a Braxton Hicks contraction. She didn't say anything but took a long, deep breath.

Malcolm jumped out of the sleigh and walked around to where she sat. He looked up at her.

"Thank you, Malcolm," she said.

"You're welcome," he said softly. "But there's one more thing. I want to ask, here in front of the entire town. Kennedy Anderson, will you marry me?"

"I don't want to do this here," she said. She looked out at the community, all armed with the new wooden signs, and felt . . . like she was truly home. For the first time since she'd moved here, she felt as if she belonged. She didn't want to tell Malcolm no in front of everyone and ruin the moment. "Please, don't," she whispered.

"Sorry. I want some witnesses. More than that, I want some people who are on my side. So, I'll ask again, will you marry me?"

Kennedy couldn't believe he was putting her in this position so publicly. "No."

He frowned. "You're messing up my script. You're supposed to ask me *why*. You've asked me *why* every other time I've asked you. Ask me why, Kennedy. Kennedy, will you marry me?"

She sighed. There was no way out of this. "Why?"

"Because you're having his baby," Jenny called from the crowd, "though I can tell you from experience, that's not enough of a reason to marry someone."

"Because he's a good friend." Joan reached out and took Clarence's hand. "And while that's very important, it's not enough of a reason to marry someone."

Pap called out, "Because you two are a good team. Like me and Annabelle are now, and like I was with Mal's grandma. But that's not enough of a reason."

"Because it would make everything easier," said Malcolm's father, who stepped out from the crowd. "But I know more than most that that's not a good enough reason. But let me add a reason of my own. Because I'd be proud to call you daughter, but even that's not a good enough reason."

"Because he'll share his dog with you." Nana Vancy and her Bela came forward as well. "But that's not enough of a reason, is it, Mal?"

"No, those are all good reasons for you to say yes. I could add more. Reasons like I won't sell you the Center, but if you'd marry me, you'd be half owner. Like if we got married, I'd have a constant stream of Mom's cookies, but I guess that's more for me than for you. How about if you married me, we could start every morning together sharing coffee and breakfast? I can't think of a nicer way to start every day for the rest of my life. Or how happy my mom would be to know we were married. But none of those are the right words, are they, Nana Vancy?"

"Say the words, Mal. Say the right words. The only words that matter," Nana Vancy said. "Because everyone knows that words have power."

"The crowd is waiting to hear what words Nana Vancy is referring to," Angela said into the microphone.

Mal got down on one knee in the snow, illuminated by the glow of the lantern light. He pulled a small velvet box out of his pocket. "Marry me, Kennedy Anderson, for all those reasons, and one more very important one. Marry me because I love you."

Nana Vancy was right, those were the only words that mattered, but only if he meant them. "Mal, don't . . ."

"I love you. You said that we didn't really know each other well. But you're wrong. Whenever I talked to my mom, her conversation was full of Kennedy news. Things you'd done for the town and things you did for her. She didn't tell me specifically about Movie Mondays, but she told me about teaching you to bake and about joining the book club with you, and she told me about all the things you did for the town and everyone in it. I think I was halfway in love with you when I came home for her funeral. That night, I found someone who'd suffered her loss as much as I did. I found comfort in your arms. And at the time, I might have thought I could have found that in anyone's arms, but now I realize, I found comfort in your arms because I loved you even then. I loved you before I knew it."

"You don't have to—"

"It's not something I have to do. It's not even something I can control. It's simply part of me. I love you. When I adopted Jethro today, you protested he wouldn't like an apartment. You're right—he wouldn't. And it turns out, neither do I. I'm moving back home and opening my own practice here. If you say no today, I'll still ask you tomorrow and every day after that. But from now on when you ask me *why*, my answer will always be the same. *Why?* Because I love you."

Kennedy was silent. Tears rolled down her cheeks, and her hands held on to the baby in her stomach as if it were a lifeline.

"When I ask you to marry me, I'll tell you that wherever you go, I'll follow," Mal continued, "but I don't see you leaving Cupid Falls. You're part of it and it's part of you. But if you ever did leave, I'd follow."

Clarence called out, "Mayor, we want you to know that even though we're helping Mal out, if you say no, we're behind you. Me and Joan already talked about it, and we'd like to help with the baby when you need it."

"And I'm gonna be its cousin," Ivy called out, "so me and the boys will help."

The crowd all murmured their agreement.

"Whatever you decide," Clarence said, "we're on your side." ·

Kennedy looked at the town, holding their signs and pledging their help. They were waiting for her response. Nana Vancy stood with the Silver Bells, her Bela, Isabel's Leo, and Pap. May was holding her new dog August's lead.

"Words have power," Nana said, and smiled, as if she knew Kennedy's answer.

The fact of the matter was, Nana Vancy probably did know her answer. There was only one answer Kennedy could give. But first she checked, needing to be sure. "You love me?"

"Absolutely. Completely. Baby or not, I'd be asking you to marry me, Kennedy, because I love you."

She took a deep breath and felt an even stronger cramp. This went beyond a cramp to straight-up pain. She waited a moment for it to ebb, then said her powerful word. "Yes."

Malcolm moved in and hugged her, even though her girth made it awkward.

"I should add, I love you, too," she told him.

"Yeah, I know," he said with a teasing grin. "I mean, what's not to love?"

Kennedy scoffed.

"Will you marry me before the baby comes?" he asked. "I'd like to be your husband when he arrives."

"I'd like to say yes to that, but I think that I've had a couple contractions."

His expression changed from triumph to panic. "If you're in labor, why are we still in the woods?"

"Shh," she said. "First babies take time. But I do want to marry you before the baby. The official papers can come later, but we're here at the falls and we're surrounded by friends and family. Will you marry me now? Here. Surrounded by friends and family."

"I'm not going to ask why," he told her. Then loudly said, "Does anyone feel like having a wedding here and now, before Kennedy has my baby?"

The crowd went wild. Angela said into her mic, "I think this might be a record. Mal and Kennedy are going to say their vows right here and now, if I understand it correctly."

Mal helped Kennedy to the edge of the falls. Standing there, in the lamplight, with the slivered moon peeking through the clouds, in front of their friends and family, he held Kennedy's hand and said, "The Quakers don't use ministers when they get married. The two people in question stand together and make their promises before God, their family, and friends. I have a friend who had a Quaker wedding and it was beautiful. It seems appropriate to say my vows to Kennedy by the falls, which, if legend is to be believed, is the reason our town sits here—because countless men and women have fallen in love here. This is where I'll pledge to love you for the rest of my life. To be your friend. To be your partner. To be the father to your children. But mostly to love you with all my heart."

Kennedy stood in the midst of her . . . family. She'd always felt as if she didn't quite belong, but she only had to look at the signs that people still held to not only know she had a place here, but to feel it.

And she only had to look into Malcolm's eyes to know she had a place with him. Next to him. For the rest of her life.

"Malcolm, I didn't plan to be here today saying these words to you, but I love you. I have loved you in so many ways. I first loved you as a teenage crush. Soft and fragile. Later, I loved you for how kind you were to your mother and grandfather. I envied you having them. Then, I loved the part of you that was growing inside me. But all of those versions of love pale next to how I feel about you now. I love you heart and soul. I love your kindness, how you . . ."

She grabbed her stomach and froze. Trying to remember what they'd said about breathing. Keeping oxygen flowing. Trying to ride out the contraction, not fight against it. As it ebbed, she looked in Mal's concerned face and said, "I think we'd better head to the hospital, but I love you and I'm proud to be your wife and have you as my husband."

She knew that this wedding was anything but legal, but she also knew that no other words or legal documents could make her feel more married than she did right now to this man who was rushing her to the carriage.

Words have power. She was convinced that Nana Vancy was right about that. So for good measure she said, "You are my husband and I love you."

He grinned as he climbed up next to her in the sleigh and Gideon took his place at the reins.

"I love you," Malcolm whispered back.

EPILOGUE

On Christmas Day, Kennedy cradled her daughter close as Malcolm hung up the phone. Jethro was on the couch next to her. He'd adopted little Evie as his own. It was amazing to see how gentle the big dog was with the tiny baby. Wherever Kennedy carried Evie, Jethro followed.

Pap and Malcolm's father were whispering in the corner as if they were afraid they'd disturb the baby, but so far Evie showed no signs of being disturbed by anything. She basically ate, slept, and looked out at the world with happy interest.

The fire was going and the smell of turkey filled the room.

Malcolm came back to the couch and Kennedy felt a sense of complete and utter happiness.

"That was Nana Vancy," Malcolm said. "She said to tell you that she was right, it was a girl. And that she was right about you getting a dog. She added that that's a lot of *right* for one little old lady."

Kennedy laughed as Malcolm sat on the side of the couch that Jethro didn't occupy. "She's going to be unbearable," Kennedy said.

"She also said that if the Murray kids could adopt you as an aunt, then she's officially adopting Evie and the two of us as well. I heard Annabelle in the background saying since she was Pap's girlfriend, *she* should do the adopting."

Pap slapped his knee. "That woman is a pip," he said, and at the sight of him, Kennedy suspected there would be another wedding in Cupid Falls soon.

Malcolm nodded and continued, "And Isabel said, well, she wasn't going to be left out. Let's just say that it looks like Evie's got a number of surrogate grandmothers."

Kennedy wiped away tears.

"Hey, no crying," Malcolm said.

"For the longest time, I felt alone, and now I'm surrounded by family. Having you all here, and having all of us connected through Elisabeth Valerie Carter." She loved that they'd honored her aunt and Malcolm's mother. They'd tried out the initials. EVC. And liked EV so much, that's what they'd ended up calling her. Evie Carter.

Malcolm hugged her. Which only added to her feeling overwhelmed. She had Malcolm and Evie. She had Pap and Senior. She had the entire town of Cupid Falls.

She was a rich woman. A lucky woman.

She was a happy woman. "I love you, Malcolm Carter."

"And I love you."

Pap cleared his throat.

"I told you that sharing a holiday with a couple still on their honeymoon might not be a good idea," Pap said to Senior.

"How long do you think they'll be like this?" Senior asked.

Pap looked at them both and said, "According to Nana Vancy, they'll be obnoxiously mushy like this for the rest of their lives. Their very happy lives," he added.

Kennedy looked at Malcolm, Evie, and even Jethro and knew that Hungarian magic or not, Nana Vancy was absolutely right.

FROM THE AUTHOR

Dear reader,

I hope you enjoyed the first Cupid Falls book! And for all you Nana Vancy fans who wrote to tell me that you miss her, I hope you enjoyed her visit to neighboring Cupid Falls. I'll confess, I was happy to see her again. And of course, I was thrilled to include more dog adoption stories. For those who don't know, the dogs on the cover of *Everything But a Dog* are mine, and the bigger dog, Ethel Merman, was a rescue. We got the smaller one, Ella Fitzgerald, to help ease Ethel's separation anxieties. Yes, I bought my dog a dog. They were the models for the dogs in the book, and they've so enjoyed their fame . . . no, the *puparazzi* hasn't *hounded* them yet, but they did make the local paper. They're thrilled they got a cameo on this new book, too.

I'm including Mal's mother's oatmeal cookie recipe, which is actually mine. It took a lot of experimentation to find one that suited my taste. I love that although it's a treat, it's actually very healthy as treats go. Mal reminisced about his mother's cookies, saying that she taught him to cook, but he'd never asked to learn this recipe because it was *hers*. For Mal, coming home meant a big plate of his mom's cookies waiting for him. It was a sign of his mother's love. It was a tangible signal that he was home. For me, as a writer, the first indication of Kennedy's true feelings for him was when she made that plate of cookies for him.

Food is a big part of our daily lives. I love how a dish (or a cookie) can bring back a memory or remind us of someone. When my own grandmother (who was just plain Nana to us) was alive, she made this green Jell-O salad. Jell-O (always green, though I'm sure other colors would work), pineapples, cottage cheese . . . and horseradish. It sounds awful, but we had it every holiday growing up. After she passed, I tried making it, but it wasn't like hers and I haven't tried to make it again since. I think each cook adds something unique to their special dishes. I might be able to add the right ingredients, but I can't add my grandmother's love. Maybe that's why Mal loved Kennedy's cookies as much as his mother's. It wasn't just the recipe . . . it was that she added her own love to the mix.

I want to wish you all a very Merry Christmas!

Holly

Valerie Watson Carter's Oatmeal Cookies

2 sticks of softened butter
1 cup lightly packed dark brown sugar
½ cup sugar
2 eggs
1 tsp. vanilla

Cream these ingredients, then add:

1½ cups of whole wheat flour
2 tsp. cinnamon
1 tsp. baking soda
½ tsp. salt
3 cups old-fashioned oatmeal
1 cup raisins
1 cup walnuts (nuts are optional—I've used pecans, too, and love them)

Bake about 10–12 minutes at 350°.

ACKNOWLEDGMENTS

A special thanks to Ellen and her inspirational frogs, and to all the Nana Vancy fans who were disappointed to see the Everything But . . . series end. All I can say is thank you for loving her as much as I do and . . . she's baaaaaack!

I'd really like to thank Kelli Martin and Helen Cattaneo. Working with new editors is like going on a blind date: you never know how you're going to mesh. Well, I lucked out! Working with you both has been nothing but a joy! Thank you for working with me to make my stories as strong as they can be!

ABOUT THE AUTHOR

 Award-winning author Holly Jacobs has sold over two and a half million books worldwide. The first novel in her Everything But . . . series, *Everything But a Groom*, was named one of 2008's best romances by *Booklist*, and her books have been honored with many other accolades.

Holly has a wide range of interests, from her love for writing to gardening and even basket weaving. She has delivered more than sixty author workshops and keynote speeches across the country. She lives in Erie, Pennsylvania, with her family and her dogs. She frequently sets stories in and around her hometown.